Betrayed By Your Kiss

ALSO BY LAURA LANDON

Intimate Deception

The Most to Lose

Intimate Surrender

A Risk Worth Taking

Silent Revenge

Betrayed By Your Kiss

LAURA LANDON

Montlake
Romance

Text copyright © 2015 Laura Landon

Published by Montlake Romance, Seattle
www.apub.com

Amazon, the Amazon logo, and Montlake Romance are trademarks of Amazon.com, Inc., or its affiliates.

ISBN-13: 9781477827444
ISBN-10: 1477827447

Cover design by Anne Cain

Library of Congress Control Number: 2014954304

Printed in the United States of America

To my editor, Hai-Yen Mura, who didn't give up on me, and made this book a reality. Thank you, Hai-Yen!

And to Montlake's Author Relations Manager, Jessica Poore—I couldn't ask for anyone better to work with. You're the best!

Hugs to you both!

Betrayed By Your Kiss

Chapter 1

Lady Olivia Sheridan knew without a doubt that she was the luckiest person on earth as she stood in the receiving line with her beaming father, the Marquess of Pellingsworth, on one side and her fiancé, Damien Bedford, Earl of Iversley, on the other. Damien's mother, Lady Iversley, stood blissfully beside her son.

"Are you happy, Liv?" Damien smiled down at her and his midnight-blue eyes sparkled with affection.

Olivia's heart flipped in her breast. "Oh, yes. It's not possible for me to be happier."

Damien reached for her hand and held it, then gave her fingers an affectionate squeeze.

Olivia felt a searing heat spread through her body. It was this way every time she was near him. She knew it must be sinful to feel this way, but she couldn't help it. Oh, how she wished she and Damien could go somewhere private. Oh, how she wished he'd kiss her like he had the last time they were together.

As if he'd read her thoughts, he smiled and the two creases that dented either side of his mouth deepened. His full lips parted just enough to expose a set of beautiful white teeth, and she felt an even more intense stab of desire. He leaned down and whispered in her ear.

"I love you, Liv."

A shiver ran the length of her body, warming her in the most surprising places. She gasped. How could he say something so intimate when there was no chance of escaping the nearly five hundred people who'd come for their betrothal celebration? When all she wanted to do was throw her arms around his neck and kiss him?

As if he knew what she was thinking, he tipped back his head and laughed—a deep, rich, caressing sound that wrapped around her heart and held it. The gleam in his eyes made his rugged good looks even more breathtaking.

There wasn't another man in all of London who was nearly as handsome. There wasn't another female in all of London who was as blessed as she to be the woman he'd picked to be his bride. Just a few more months and she'd be the Countess of Iversley. A few more months and she'd be Damien's wife.

Olivia's father's voice interrupted her thoughts and forced her to turn her attention back to her guests. She tried to control her exuberance as she accepted the Countess of Pottingjay's greeting.

"Lady Olivia," the countess said, reaching for Olivia's hand and squeezing it tightly. "You look absolutely radiant tonight. The picture of happiness."

Olivia couldn't help but blush. "Thank you, my lady."

The countess turned to Damien. "I assume you are responsible for the glow on Lady Olivia's face, my lord."

Damien bowed then looked at Olivia with an expression of extreme satisfaction. "I would like to think so, Lady Pottingjay. Nothing would make me happier."

The countess smiled. "It's lovely to see true love in a couple just starting their lives together. It happens so seldom among those of our acquaintance, you know."

"That's most unfortunate," Damien answered, twining his fingers with hers. "I dare say, they don't know what they are missing." He lowered his gaze to catch Olivia's and held it.

Olivia noticed a flash of regret in the countess's eyes when she glanced at her husband. Olivia wondered if Lady Pottingjay had once had dreams of a love-filled marriage. She wondered if Lady Pottingjay had been as happy as she was tonight, then watched that joy dim until the light died. She wondered how many ladies here tonight lived in loveless marriages and envied her for the love she and Damien shared.

The elegant woman recovered quickly, however, giving them another of her most regal smiles before walking into the crowd with her husband following absently behind her.

"I think it's time the two of you joined our guests on the dance floor before you can't find room," Olivia's father said, motioning to the crowded ballroom with a proud look on his face. "I don't think there was an invitation turned down for tonight. The two of you are considered quite the match. Your mother would have been elated, Olivia."

"I know." Olivia gave her father a loving kiss on the cheek followed by a quick hug, then went with Damien as his arm wrapped around her waist. He led her onto the crowded dance floor and turned her toward him.

Olivia came to a halt when the music started. "They're playing a waltz," she said in surprise.

Damien pulled her into his arms and held her close. "I know."

"But a quadrille usually follows . . ."

Damien arched his brows in a look of feigned innocence.

Olivia laughed. "It's not acceptable to bribe the orchestra, Lord Iversley."

"It would have been infinitely more intolerable to suffer through a quadrille when that particular dance wouldn't allow me to hold you in my arms."

"Has anyone ever told you you're incorrigible?"

"Often, my lady love. I take great pride in such compliments."

Olivia couldn't stop her laughter as she twirled with Damien around the room. He held her closer than was probably acceptable, but Olivia didn't care. Not tonight. Nothing could mar this perfect evening.

The two of them glided across the room in dizzying circles. When they reached the other side of the room, Damien stepped with her out the open French doors and into the cool night air. He didn't stop until he reached the far side of the terrace.

"Damien—"

Her words were cut off when his mouth came down on hers. Olivia was so desperate for the feel of him against her she didn't even think to protest. She wrapped her arms around his neck and gave in to his kisses.

His lips were warm and firm. The feel of him pressed against her stoked the fire burning deep in her belly until she thought she might burst into flames. He opened his mouth atop hers and she followed suit, waiting with anxious expectancy for his tongue to mate with hers.

Carnal thoughts clouded her thinking, driving her to a fevered frenzy. She pressed her fingers firmly against his back and gave in to his pleas. He kissed her again, thoroughly, exquisitely, desperately. She teetered on the brink of uncontrollable desire, and he took her closer to the edge.

He deepened his kisses even more. Olivia moaned as she swept her hands over Damien's broad shoulders. The feel of him beneath his expensive jacket was hard and muscular. Another wave of passion pulsed through her, one she couldn't rebuff.

"We have to stop, Liv," he rasped, lifting his mouth from hers.

Olivia moaned in disappointment. When Damien pulled her against him, she clung tight to him and struggled to catch her breath.

In the silent darkness, his heavy breathing matched her own. Her lips trembled into a smile. "I don't think I'm going to survive for three more months if you continue to kiss me like this, Damien."

"Neither am I. But I can't make myself stop."

With that, he brought his mouth down to hers and kissed her again. When he broke off their kiss, he wrapped his arm around her shoulder and moved with her to a small stone bench angled in the corner of the flagstone terrace.

"Did you ever once think we would end up like this?" he said, his voice soft and thoughtful as if his mind were a thousand miles away.

Olivia smiled. "Of course. I knew it the moment Father brought you to live with us after your father died. I think I fell in love with you that first night at dinner when you announced in such a grownup manner that you appreciated my father's kindness, but you were old enough to live on your own. You were, after all, nearly grown and were now the Earl of Iversley."

"I was a terrible brat, wasn't I?"

"No. You were fifteen years old and trying to cope with your father's death, and the fact that your mother had given you over for Father to mentor."

"Do you remember how your father answered me?"

Olivia laughed. "Yes. He laid his fork down and looked at you as if seriously studying your proposal. Then, he nodded his head as if your suggestion had merit and said, 'Quite admirable, Lord Iversley. A suggestion worth pondering. Would you be willing to wait to discuss it in a few more months, when you turn sixteen?'"

Olivia lifted her head from where it rested against Damien's shoulder. "Did you? Did you discuss leaving when you turned sixteen?"

"Yes."

"What did Father say?"

"He convinced me to postpone leaving until my seventeenth birthday. But by then, I felt so at home, I had no desire to leave."

"Not until you turned twenty."

Damien smiled. "It seemed time then."

"Father said you needed to sow your oats. He may have believed a delicate lady of seventeen would be fooled by such terminology and think you'd gone to your country estates to oversee the planting of the fields. I knew what you were up to, however."

"You did?" Damien said, tipping her chin upward with a lift of his finger. "How did you know?"

"You were all the talk during my coming-out that season. You and your scandalous behavior. Especially when you took up with that actress with the flowery name."

Damien looked shocked, which pleased Olivia to no end.

"However did you hear about her?"

"I made it my business to know everything about you, Lord Iversley. I loved you even then, you see. I just had to be patient and wait until you realized you loved me too."

Damien leaned down and kissed the tip of her nose. "Perhaps if you would have enlightened me to your little secret earlier, I wouldn't have waited until I was twenty-four years old to ask for your hand."

Olivia shook her head. "You needed the time." She paused. "Time to make sure you weren't in love with Cassandra Morley."

Damien stiffened beside her. When she looked up at him, her heart skipped a beat. The dark look in his eyes gave her reason to pause. For just a second, Olivia glimpsed a part of Damien she was sure he intended to keep hidden. Although she had promised herself she'd never think of what Cassandra Morley may have meant to Damien, she couldn't help but feel a twinge of wariness.

She brushed her misgivings away, but not quickly enough. Not before Damien saw them.

"I never loved her, Liv."

"But the two of you were an item for a time. Everyone thought you would ask for her hand. I just needed you to be sure it was me you wanted."

"It was, Liv. Never doubt that it was." His expression softened and he held her closer. "How did I ever deserve you?"

"We were meant for each other, Damien. Nothing can change that." Olivia lifted her head to give him a quick kiss, then pushed away from him. "But if we don't go back inside soon, we'll cause a scandal, and Father will be forced to move the wedding up to tomorrow."

Damien laughed, rose to his feet, and pulled her next to him. "Suddenly, that thought is most appealing."

Olivia knew he'd kiss her again if given the chance, so she took his hand and led him across the terrace. This was her engagement ball, after all. She'd waited a lifetime for this night.

They stepped back across the threshold and the crushing crowd parted to give her a clear view of her father who stood with his lifelong friend, Captain Phineas Durham. With a gleam of wetness in his eyes, her father lifted a glass in a toast.

Every person in the room also held a glass of champagne, which they lifted with her father. Olivia looked to her side as a servant held out a tray with two glasses. Damien took them and handed one to Olivia. She was caught for a moment in the depth of emotion in his eyes. In the honest, open sincerity of his feelings. It was truly the most perfect night of her life.

"My friends," her father said, pulling her attention away from the man she loved.

"You have been invited here tonight for a very special celebration. Other than the night Olivia's mother placed my daughter in my arms for the first time, tonight is truly a most joyous occasion."

Olivia found it hard to stop tears from filling her eyes. Damien's arm slid around her waist as her father continued.

"It is only once in a father's lifetime that he has the privilege of making this announcement. And I make it with overwhelming happiness and joy. I proudly announce the betrothal of my daughter, Lady Olivia Sheridan, to Damien Bedford, Earl of Iversley."

A thunderous vote of approval echoed around the ballroom as guests drank to her and Damien.

Her father silenced them by raising his hands. "I make this announcement with mixed emotions. First, one of elation because of the man standing beside her. The man with whom my daughter has chosen to spend her life."

All eyes turned to Damien.

"I couldn't have picked a better man to have as a son if the choice had been mine to make. And sorrow, because another man will now take my place in my daughter's life. Every father knows the sorrow of losing a daughter, and the joy of gaining a son."

There was another loud cheer of approval.

"And so, I want you to celebrate with me. This is truly a momentous occasion and—"

At that moment, Olivia heard a commotion in the hallway beyond the ballroom doors. Something was far from right, and she realized Damien felt the same. He stepped in front of her to act as a shield, but not before she saw the concern on her father and Captain Durham's faces.

A loud, angry voice boomed over the murmurs of the crowd. "Where is he? Where is the bloody murderer!"

The crowd came to a deafening hush. Two men stood at the top of the stairs, one raging uncontrollably, his voice bellowing through the room. Recognition dawned, and she realized who they were. Cassandra Morley's father, the Earl of Strathern, and her brother, Nathan Morley Viscount Poore. Their taut, demented features were a frightening sight, and the haunted look in their eyes caused her to step even closer to Damien.

Strathern led the way, and his son followed. As the earl staggered down the stairs and into the room, Olivia tried to make sense of what the earl was saying. Tried to understand his garbled words and angry accusations. He was distraught to the point of madness. And from the slurring of his words, more than a little drunk.

"Where is he, Pellingsworth? Where's the murderer you're harboring under your roof?"

Olivia's father rushed to Strathern's side.

"You're obviously upset, Strathern. Why don't you come with me?" Olivia's father said. "I'm sure we can straighten out this problem."

Strathern threw her father off as if he were a small man. "Leave me the hell alone! I just want the man who killed my daughter."

There was a loud gasp from the crowd, then a hushed murmur as everyone strained to see and hear what would take place next.

"Come now, Strathern. You're obviously distraught. Why don't you—"

"Where is he?" Strathern searched the crowd, his eyes wild. He stopped when he landed on Damien. Before her father or Captain Durham could stop him, Strathern pushed his way forward like a drunken madman. "You! Murderer!"

In the blink of an eye, Strathern pulled a gun from his pocket and stumbled closer. Loud screams echoed in the ballroom as Damien reached out his hand and pushed Olivia further behind him. "You lying, deceiving bastard! You killed her!" Strathern aimed the gun at the center of Damien's chest, but Olivia's father shoved Strathern's arm upward as he fired. A loud explosion echoed in the ballroom, followed by the guests' frantic screams as the bullet struck the ceiling. Pandemonium followed as Olivia's father and Captain Durham subdued the Earl of Strathern.

"He killed her! He killed Cassandra!"

"Let's go someplace where we can discuss this," her father said.

Her father and Captain Durham escorted Strathern and his son out, and she and Damien followed. Olivia felt the tension in Damien's grasp. The muscles in his arms bunched beneath her fingers as they walked from the room. "Damien?"

She wanted him to look at her. That's all she needed, just a look and then she'd know that everything was going to be all right. But he didn't. He placed one foot in front of the other as he walked through the crowd with his gaze fixed straight ahead.

Olivia had no choice but to hold her head high and walk as bravely as he did. Her heart thundered in her chest as they followed her father up the ballroom stairs and out into the foyer. The murmuring of the crowd echoed in her ears, engulfing her with a sense of foreboding. Olivia glanced up, searching for any expression on Damien's face that would reassure her. She saw none. His features were hooded and unrevealing. The healthy bronze of his skin now seemed washed, devoid of color.

They walked in silence to her father's study where they could be assured of privacy.

A gnawing fear ate at the pit of her stomach with each step. When the door closed behind them, Olivia blanched. The sound indicated an end to the bliss she'd enjoyed minutes before.

Olivia slipped her hand in Damien's as her father and the captain settled Strathern. Strathern's son stepped into the shadows. But the calm was short-lived. The minute they stepped away from him, Strathern bolted from the chair. Damien stepped in front of her to protect her.

When both the captain and Pellingsworth reached to subdue Strathern again, Damien held up his hand to stop them. He stepped forward and faced his accuser squarely.

"I realize you've suffered a terrible loss, Lord Strathern, but I assure you, I had nothing to do with your daughter's death. I'd appreciate a reason for your impossible accusations."

Strathern stepped closer to Damien, his icy glare one of intense loathing. "You know damn well what you've done, you heartless bastard. You killed my Cassandra."

Her heart skipped a beat. Why would he accuse Damien of being responsible for Cassandra's death? Any connection between them was over before he began courting Olivia.

"I assure you, Strathern. I had nothing to do with Cassandra's death."

"Liar! You are as responsible for her death as if you'd stabbed a knife through her heart yourself. She died trying to rid herself of the babe you planted in her."

It took Olivia a moment for Strathern's words to sink in. When they did, a lump formed in the pit of her stomach.

Her gaze lifted to Damien, but his expression remained blank, unreadable.

Strathern took a menacing step closer. "Did you think she would take your name to her grave? Did you think you would escape unscathed after what you'd done to her? That I wouldn't force her to tell me the name of the bastard who'd caused her death? Your name came from her lips, Iversley. She screamed your name with her dying breath."

"No!" Damien roared. "The babe was not mine!"

"You bastard!" Strathern bellowed. "But you won't get away with it. I'll have my revenge," he said through clenched teeth. "You're going to receive the same sentence as my Cassandra. You're going to pay with your life."

Olivia couldn't stop the gasp that escaped her. She looked at Damien, but only her father spoke.

"Strathern, listen. Surely you can't believe Lord Iversley would—"

"I not only believe it, I am certain of it. My daughter's dying words confirmed it. She said when she found out she was carrying a child, she begged him to marry her, but he refused."

A painful grip tightened inside her chest. "Damien?"

Damien took a threatening step toward Strathern. "The babe your daughter died trying to rid herself of was not mine, Strathern."

"You bastard. I should have known you wouldn't own up to what you'd done." Strathern stepped closer to Damien, his fists clenched at his sides, his face red with fury. "You used her, and when you were finished, you abandoned her for Pellingsworth's daughter."

Olivia stepped back from the hatred she saw in Strathern's eyes.

"Everyone knows the only reason you're marrying her is for her father's ships."

Olivia's heart shifted inside her breast. She knew Damien loved her. But suddenly she needed him to deny Strathern's accusation. She wanted to hear Damien say the ships meant nothing to him.

But he didn't.

For the first time since Damien had asked her to marry him, she felt alone, abandoned. Before she could erase the disappointment from her eyes, the doubt, Damien turned his head. His gaze locked with hers. The blackness of his eyes hardened, and Olivia felt the earth fall away from her. "Tell him that isn't true, Damien." She waited. "Tell him the ships mean nothing to you."

"My saying the words mean that much to you?"

She wanted to deny that they did. But she couldn't. And in that moment, she knew he thought she'd failed him.

He turned away from her.

"Damien?"

Olivia reached out to touch him, but the tensing of his muscles beneath her fingers made her draw her hand back. Strathern's words stopped the breath in her throat.

"You will meet me at dawn tomorrow morning in Miller's field, Iversley, and only one of us will walk away."

Damien nodded. "As you wish, Strathern."

"No. Damien, no!" Olivia didn't realize the cry had come from her until Damien turned his head and silenced her with a look.

He turned from her as if she'd wedged a barrier between them that could never be breached.

"At dawn, Iversley. I'll be waiting."

Olivia watched as the Earl of Strathern and his son left the room. Not until the door closed behind him did she take a breath. Damien turned to her father with a stoic look on his face and an emptiness in his eyes that frightened her.

"Lord Pellingsworth, I will need a second in the morning."

"Iversley, I'm not sure—"

Damien held up his hand to stop him, and Olivia's father cut his sentence short as if he understood Damien had no choice.

"Perhaps you can make my excuses to the guests," Damien said to her father. "I have a number of personal details to see to before morning."

Without looking at her again, he left the room, the door shutting behind him.

"It'll be all right, Olivia," her father whispered, staring at the closed door.

But she knew it wouldn't be all right. She knew nothing would ever be right again.

Chapter 2

It was an unheard of hour as a large circle of men gathered. The earth was still eerily quiet. It would be a long time before the sun burned off the heavy mist that filled the darkness. Before even the birds awoke to proclaim the arrival of a new day.

Olivia drew her cloak tighter around her shoulders to ward off the pre-dawn chill. A shiver wracked her body, and she buried herself deeper against the squabs of the carriage. It took every ounce of strength to breathe through her terror.

She couldn't believe this was happening. Couldn't believe that her whole world had fallen apart. And the worst could yet come. Before the sun had risen above the horizon, she could be holding Damien's lifeless body in her arms.

She'd done nothing but pace the floor all night. There had to be a way out of this for Damien. There had to be a way to convince Strathern that Damien wasn't responsible for Cassandra's death.

A picture of Cassandra's beautiful face appeared in Olivia's mind's eye. She'd always been the belle of the ball, always the most sought after debutante. Damien's name had been linked to Cassandra's before he'd asked Olivia to marry him, but that was no reason to believe he'd fathered her babe. And yet, she remembered the look on Damien's face when she'd mentioned Cassandra in the garden last night. And there was still the nagging question that refused to go away. One question to which she couldn't find an answer.

What possible reason could Cassandra have had for telling her father the babe was Damien's?

She swept away another tear with trembling fingers and closed her eyes. Her head ached and her eyes were red and swollen.

"We're almost there, Lady Olivia," Johns, the driver, said from atop. "Are you sure you don't want me to turn around and take you home?"

"No, Johns. Keep going."

"But you shouldn't be here, my lady. Your father isn't going to like it one bit."

No, her father wouldn't like it. And neither would Damien. But she really had no choice. She had to come. Not to stop what was going to happen. When had any female had the power to stop men's foolishness? But to tell Damien she loved him. To tell him she believed him.

"Just hurry, Johns. Please."

The carriage rumbled toward the outskirts of the city then slowed to turn down a path that seemed little more than a country lane. They were almost there. The terror churning in the pit of her stomach told her so. She forced herself to look out the window.

Several men stood in a circle across the meadow, their number growing by the second. Olivia couldn't find Damien and her father, but she knew they were there. She knew Strathern was there, too.

A thick blanket of fog hovered over the low-lying area, wrapping around the somberly dressed men and swirling at their feet like gnarled fingers of dread. Someone would die today. Death was standing at the ready, prepared to snatch its unsuspecting prey. God help her. She didn't want the victim to be Damien. She couldn't survive if it were.

As her carriage approached, Olivia searched the area and prayed she was in time. When her eyes finally rested on him, she nearly cried out in relief.

Olivia opened the door and her feet touched the ground. She pushed against the dark-clad figures until, one by one, the men parted to let her through. Their brows arched in surprise and disapproval, but no one said a word about her being there.

For the most part, they stood in silence. The only sounds, other than the gay chirping of waking birds, were the ominous whispers of a few onlookers wagering on the outcome of the duel. Some thought Strathern had an advantage. Hatred was powerful motivation. Others were convinced Damien would be victorious. He was known as a crack shot, and there was his youth.

A huddle of men blocked her path, and before she could make her way past them, their words stopped her.

"It doesn't matter which of them is the better shot. Not if what I heard is true."

"What did you hear?"

"The insurance Strathern put on today's outcome. The price Strathern put on Iversley's head in case Iversley survives."

"What insurance?"

"Ten thousand pounds. To whoever kills Iversley. Even if he survives today, he's a dead man."

Olivia's heart thundered in her breast and she shoved past the men in a greater hurry to get to Damien. She had to warn him. Had to tell him what Strathern had done. Had to tell him she loved him.

Damien tried to keep his breathing steady. Tried not to dwell on the fact that he might kill a man today. Or that today he might die.

He shifted his gaze to Strathern, whose loathing was a living, breathing monster that wouldn't be satisfied until Cassandra's death was avenged.

Damien recalled the look on Olivia's face when Strathern had made his accusations. He saw how the bliss had died in her eyes. But it wasn't the claim that Damien had fathered the child Cassandra was carrying that did the irrepairable damage. Their love would have weathered that storm.

It was what came after that was more devastating.

How could she think that he was marrying her for her father's ships? How could she doubt that he loved her? How could she not know that she was his world?

A movement to his right caught his attention. His heart froze in his chest.

Olivia was racing across the meadow and didn't stop until she stood directly in front of him.

"Get the hell away from here, Olivia! Now!"

She shook her head. Her face was lined with worry, her eyes filled with a terror she couldn't hide. "Don't do this, Damien."

"Go away from here, Olivia. Now!" Damien reached for her arm, but she shrugged him off.

"You don't have to fight him. You know I don't believe you fathered Cassandra's babe."

"And the ships? Do you think I'm only marrying you for your father's ships?"

"Of course I don't."

"That's not what the look on your face said last night."

She shook her head. "I didn't mean it. I couldn't think. I didn't know what to say."

He wanted to believe her. But how could he? He'd seen the look. He'd seen her doubts.

She clasped him harder, her fingers clutching his forearms. "We'll run away, Damien. Go to France. America. Anywhere. Nothing matters as long as we're together."

"Do you hear what you're saying?"

"I love you, Damien. I don't want to lose you."

He looked at her. He wanted to believe her. Deep down in his heart he did, but—

"Go home, Olivia. You don't belong here."

"No, Damien. I love you!"

"Go home. We'll decide what to do when this is over."

She opened her mouth to plead once more, but he quelled her words with a look. Then his expression changed.

"Olivia—" he began, but didn't finish his sentence.

He closed his eyes, took a steadying breath, then looked at her father. "Get her out of here, Pellingsworth."

"No! Damien!" she pleaded.

Her father rushed forward and placed his hand at her back. But before he led her away, he turned back to Damien with a final warning.

"I know your sense of honor dictates you allow Strathern the first shot. You think if you somehow survive, he'll be satisfied that he has avenged his daughter's death, and this whole business will be finished. There's a very good reason why you're wrong. Strathern won't miss. He's an expert shot and he's killed before. The only way you can escape his revenge is to kill him."

Damien nodded. Everything Pellingsworth said was true. And he didn't want Olivia to see the outcome.

Tears streamed down Olivia's face, and he couldn't stand to see the heartache he'd caused her. He turned and walked to Strathern and his son Nathan.

Damien stood in front of Strathern and spoke in low, whispered tones she couldn't hear. Strathern shook his head violently, then replied with an obscene oath. Damien walked away from Strathern and took his place in the center of the two long lines of men that had formed on either side of them.

Olivia stared at Damien, unable to convince herself this travesty was really happening. Unable to convince herself that two grown men intended to kill each other in cold blood. Her knees gave out, and her father wrapped his arm around her shoulders to steady her.

"Papa," she whispered, her voice a desperate plea. Her father's answer was to pull her closer and hold her tight. It was all he could do. All anyone could do.

Olivia focused on Damien. He'd removed his jacket and waistcoat and rolled up his shirtsleeves to just below his elbows. His tanned, muscular arms hung at his side, and he clutched a pistol in his right hand.

"Papa, do something," she pleaded again through the tears that streamed down her cheeks.

"I wish I could, Olivia. But it's too late. Strathern's left Damien no choice."

Olivia wanted to argue further, but stopped when Strathern's loud voice echoed in the still morning.

"May you rot in hell for what you did to my Cassandra."

"Enough, Strathern! Let's have this done," came Damien's reply.

"It will never be done. Not until you are dead."

Strathern's taunting was cut short when Lord Chastain stepped to the center between the two long lines of observers and held up his hand. In a most austere voice, he laid down the rules: the correct number of steps each man would take away from the other; the forbiddance of either duelist to fire before the white flag hit the ground; the requirement that each duelist be allowed only one shot; the option for either man to default by firing into the air.

Olivia wanted to laugh. The pompous idiot made it sound as if he were listing the rules to a lawn game instead of a duel where someone would die. When he called for Strathern and Damien to take their places, Olivia couldn't breathe. Chastain cleared his throat and held up his hands for complete silence.

"Lord Strathern, since you were the instigating party in this situation, you will be given one last chance to bring it to a peaceful conclusion here and now. Do you wish to do so?"

"I do not!"

"Very well. On the count of three, you will begin your ten paces. One. Two. Three."

Damien and Strathern stood back to back, then stepped at the same time. First one step, then a second, then a third.

Olivia stood close to her father. She needed his strength. His support.

Four, five, six, seven.

She kept her eyes focused on Damien. On his ruggedly handsome features, on the strong, powerful arms that had held her with such tenderness. On his full, warm mouth that had kissed her with such passion. And she knew she could never survive without him.

Eight, nine.

A thin film of perspiration covered her forehead and her whole body trembled uncontrollably. In her mind, she screamed the word "No!" over and over until she thought she'd go mad. But still they did not stop.

Before they took their last step, Olivia pushed forward, not knowing what she intended to do. Perhaps come between Damien and the bullet Strathern intended to fire (surely Strathern wouldn't fire if she stepped in the way). Perhaps to just hold Damien one last time while his flesh was still warm and vibrant with life. Whatever her reason, it didn't matter.

Her father's arms tightened around her and held her firm.

Ten.

Strathern and Damien turned at the same moment and Chastain dropped the silly white flag he held in his hand. They both raised their pistols, but Damien didn't fire.

"Fire, Damien," her father whispered.

"Fire the bloody gun," Captain Durham echoed from beside him. "Now."

For one infinitesimal second, Olivia thought Strathern wouldn't fire. She thought he'd realized his error. But when she looked into Strathern's face, she saw eyes so filled with hatred it sent ice water racing through her veins, and she knew how wrong she was.

Strathern waited as if he knew Damien would not fire first, toying with him, prolonging his agony.

"Rot in hell, Iversley."

Then, with a bitter laugh, Strathern squeezed the trigger.

The bullet hit the right side of Damien's chest and Olivia muffled a scream.

Please, God. Don't let him die.

Damien staggered from the impact of the bullet, but his face showed no emotion. He took an uncertain step to the left, then steadied himself enough to bend his right arm at the elbow and fire into the air.

Olivia felt an unimaginable lightness as one wave of relief after another surged through her. The duel was over and Damien was alive!

A large, dark circle grew with alarming quickness on the front of his shirt and she pulled against her father's arms to go to him.

"Stay, Olivia," he warned, and Olivia stilled herself until Chastain stepped forward.

"It's completed," he issued. "Seconds, remove the weapons."

Strathern's bellow stopped them. "No!"

From that moment on, everything moved in slow motion. Strathern turned toward Damien with his gun in his hand. He lifted his arm and prepared to fire.

Two men stepped forward to grab Strathern's arms while Chastain wrested the pistol from his hand. No one, however, was close enough to reach Cassandra's brother. Before anyone knew what was happening, Nathan, Lord Poore, raised his arm and fired.

"No!"

Damien spun to the side when Olivia screamed but not fast enough to avoid being hit. He fell to his knees, his startled expression filled with pain. He collapsed to the ground and fired one shot, hitting Nathan in the leg.

"Foul! Foul on Strathern! Foul on Poore!"

The crowd of onlookers reacted violently, every one of them appalled by Strathern's son's lack of gentlemanly conduct.

"Damien!" Olivia cried out as she raced toward him. His shirt was now covered in blood and his face devoid of color. "Lie still. Don't move."

Ignoring her pleas, Damien struggled to his feet. Four men had Strathern subdued on the other side of the field, but that didn't stop him from issuing more threats.

"You won't escape, Iversley. It's only a matter of time until you pay for what you did."

"Let's get Damien out of here," her father ordered, and he and Captain Durham helped Damien.

"I can walk," Damien said, moving awkwardly. Blood seeped from the two wounds on his torso, as he leaned against her father and Durham for support. Olivia followed behind.

Two carriages raced forward, the one her father had come in, and her carriage, with Johns on top. Her father issued the order for Johns to go ahead for a doctor, then led Damien to the other. Olivia opened the door and stepped up. She reached for Damien, who accepted her help and sat down on the cushion. Her father and Captain Durham climbed in after him.

Damien's face seemed pale, his breathing labored. Olivia sat down beside him as the carriage took off.

"Here," her father said, stripping his cravat from around his neck. "Press this against the wound on his shoulder."

Olivia opened the neck of Damien's shirt and pressed the cloth against the wound. Damien flinched, but other than a small movement, made no indication of the pain.

"Take me . . . to my . . . home."

"There's no one there to take care of you," her father interrupted. "You'll come with us."

Damien started to argue but her father stopped him. "You need a doctor to tend to you. If you want to go home afterward, that's up to you."

Her father's words seemed to appease him, and Damien nodded, then closed his eyes.

His lips were taut with pain and the grimace on his face tightened with each bump of the carriage. By the time they reached the Pellingsworth townhouse, huge beads of perspiration covered his forehead and his skin had taken on a gray pallor that caused Olivia to ache with worry.

"The doctor's on his way," Chivers, the family butler, said as they dismounted. "There's a room ready with hot water and bandages and anything else the doctor might need."

"Good," Olivia's father said as they helped Damien up the stairs. Olivia rushed ahead of them. She wanted to be with him. But her father's voice stopped her.

"Olivia, stay down here and wait for the doctor."

"But I—"

"Stay here. I'll come down as soon as I know something."

Olivia felt desolation unlike any she'd ever experienced before. A few hours ago, her worst fear had been that Damien would die and she'd lose him forever.

Now, her greatest fear was that even if he survived, she'd still lose him.

Strathern wouldn't give up until Damien was dead.

Chapter 3

Olivia sat in her father's study, waiting for the doctor to finish. Damien was going to live, she knew he was. She only needed her father to come down to tell her.

She was about to pace the room for the hundredth time when her father entered with Captain Durham.

Olivia shot to her feet. "Is he all right?"

Her father walked across the room and pulled her into his arms. "He's bad, Olivia. But he should survive."

Olivia sank against her father's broad chest and breathed a heavy sigh. She wanted to cry with relief, but she'd shed enough tears since Strathern had entered their lives to last a lifetime. Now, she was just numb. "I want to go to him. But first I need to talk to you." She looked at Captain Durham. "Both of you."

Her father and Captain Durham sat, and she sat opposite them.

"Strathern put a price on Damien's head," Olivia said. "Ten thousand pounds."

Her father's eyes opened wide, and the captain uttered a vile curse word. "Where did you hear that?" her father asked.

"I overheard some men in the crowd say it. That large an amount will bring out every lowlife in London. Even if Damien survives his wounds, he won't survive the first minute once he walks out of this house. For that amount of money, Strathern can sit back and wait for Damien to die by a bullet in the back, or a knife blade through the heart from an unknown assailant. Damien will never be safe."

"That blackguard," Captain Durham hissed.

"I can't lose him, Father," she said in a voice barely above a whisper. "I'm not sure I can survive without him."

"I know how much you love Damien, but there's nothing you can do. This is something only Damien can take care of."

"Strathern won't give up. Damien doesn't stand a chance." Olivia took a deep breath. "He can't stay in London. He has to leave."

Her father's eyebrows pulled together in a startled frown. "What do you mean he has to leave London?"

"The *Princess Anne* is due to set sail tomorrow morning, isn't it, Captain?"

Captain Durham nodded his assent.

"We can get Damien aboard without anyone knowing."

Her father shook his head. "He's not strong enough."

"Doctor Barkley said he would survive."

"Yes, but that was with care."

"Who can care for him better than Captain Durham?"

Her father and Captain Durham sat speechless before her father spoke another objection. "Damien will never agree to such a plan."

Olivia sighed. "No, which is why it's best if we take the decision out of his hands."

"You would send him away without his knowledge?" her father said in disbelief.

"I will do anything to save him."

Time stood still as her father and the captain absorbed the ramifications of what she proposed. Olivia continued before they could close the door on her plan.

"I'm sure Doctor Barkley already gave him a sufficient amount of laudanum to dull the pain and make him sleep. I will give him more when he wakes. I cared for Mother long enough to know how much of the opiate it will take for him to sleep. By the time he wakes, the *Princess Anne* will be far out to sea."

Her father shared a look with Captain Durham. "I don't like this, Olivia," her father said.

"Can you think of another idea that will keep Damien alive, Father?"

"When he realizes what you've done, he'll be livid."

"But he'll be alive," she countered.

"Oh, Olivia." Her father shook his head. "This isn't the decision Damien would make."

"We need time, Father. I need time to discover the father of Cassandra's babe. We need time for Lord Strathern to come to terms with his grief." Olivia turned to Captain Durham. "Where is the *Princess Anne* bound for, Captain?"

"The Indies."

Olivia swallowed. "How long will she be gone?"

"Perhaps a year. Ten months if I can get contracts for that new clipper ship your father's been talking about."

"A year," she repeated, unsure of how she would survive that long without him.

"What about Damien's estates?" her father asked. "What will happen to them?"

"We will manage them until he returns, Father. You and I."

Her father rose, then walked to the window. He was at least considering her plan. After several long moments, he turned to her. "Can you imagine the outrage Damien will feel when he discovers you've sent him away and made him look like a coward?"

She nodded. "He'll consider it an act of betrayal. And I won't blame him. But I won't give up until I convince him my decision was made out of love."

"And if you can't?"

"Then I will have to be satisfied knowing that he is alive."

Olivia awaited her father's decision, but his words echoed in her mind. What if she lost him forever because of her actions today?

In her heart, though, she knew she had no choice. To save him, she had to give him up. Not to certain death at Strathern's hands. But to hatred. Of her. Because hate her he would when he woke.

And she prayed she was strong enough to live with what she'd done.

Olivia walked beside the stretcher that carried Damien. He hadn't stirred once during the ride, nor did he wake when they lifted him out of the wagon to carry him to the *Princess Anne*. Olivia was grateful. She wasn't sure she could say good-bye if he were awake.

Doctor Barkley had looked in on him before they left, assuring her that with proper care, he would heal completely.

"My men will take Lord Iversley from here," Captain Durham said, walking down the gangplank toward her. Six sailors followed and when they reached the stretcher, they took Damien from her father's men and turned to carry him aboard the *Princess Anne*.

Olivia thought she'd been prepared to let him go. Thought she'd said her goodbyes when she'd been alone with Damien earlier, but she couldn't bear to be parted from him. Not yet. "Wait!"

The sailors stopped, and she rushed to the stretcher. When she reached it, she took Damien's hand in hers and cradled it against her breast. She didn't care that strangers were watching her.

"I'll take good care of him, Lady Olivia," Captain Durham promised.

Olivia nodded as the tears fell from her eyes, then she lowered her head and kissed Damien on the lips. If only she didn't feel as if she were seeing him for the last time. As if she were kissing him for a final time. As if she were losing him for a lifetime.

"It's time to let him go, Olivia," her father said. "We have to get him aboard before Strathern chances to find out what we've done."

She released Damien's hand and stepped back, thankful that her father's arms were there to hold her.

She stood on the dock as they carried Damien up the gangplank, as Captain Durham gave the order to raise anchor, as the *Princess Anne* sailed from the harbor. She stood until the small dot on the horizon that carried Damien away from her was no longer visible.

Olivia rode the long journey home, her heart dead yet still beating. She didn't know how she would survive. But she would, if for no other purpose than to find out the truth so Damien could come back home.

Even if upon coming home, the only emotions he could feel for her were hatred and betrayal.

Olivia lowered the pen she'd been using to work on the Pellingsworth Shipping ledgers and looked up when the door opened. It had been nearly two months since she'd sent Damien with Captain Durham aboard the *Princess Anne*. She thought by now she'd be accustomed to his being gone, but instead, she missed him more every day.

She brushed her fingers across her cheeks and hoped her father wouldn't notice she'd been crying again.

"Good afternoon, Father." Olivia walked to the tea tray Chivers had brought in just a few minutes earlier. "Would you care for some tea?"

"No, thank you, Olivia. Please, come and sit down beside me on the sofa."

Olivia looked at the strained expression on her father's face and set her cup on the table. "Is something wrong, Father?"

When she sat, he took her hand in his. "I just received this letter."

He reached into his pocket and pulled out a folded piece of paper. "It's from Captain Durham."

Olivia's breath caught. "Does he mention Damien?"

"Yes."

"What does he say?"

Her father squeezed her hands. The drawn expression on his face caused her to brace herself for what he was going to say.

"You have to be strong, Olivia."

Her father's voice broke, and the blood roared in her head as she watched his coloring pale.

"What is it, Father? Read me what Captain Durham has to say."

Her father unfolded the paper and cleared his throat.

My dearest friend,
It is with the heaviest heart that I write this letter.

Her father stopped, and Olivia found the courage to demand he continue. "Go on, Father. Read what he has to say."

I would give the world if the news I am about to tell you could be avoided, but it can't. It is best to hear the painful truth now, than hear the rumors that are certain to circulate.

Our voyage from the time we left London was plagued with unsettled seas and strong winds. Even though sailing was rough, the Princess Anne *was a sturdy ship and held up admirably. Lord Iversley improved every day. By the third week at sea, he was out of bed and had gained his sea legs, although he still tired quickly. I think perhaps the speed with which he recovered can be attributed to the anger that consumed him.*

I have to say, my friend, it is difficult to describe the raging temper the entire ship witnessed when he awoke and discovered what we had done. Although I tried to explain the reason we feared for his life, Lord Iversley was furious because we'd taken matters into our hands.

Be that as it may, during the fourth week at sea, the Princess Anne *ran into a foul storm. One of the worst I have ever seen. For three days we battled ferocious winds that broke the mainmast and mizzenmast to splinters. I knew we would be lucky to survive with our cargo intact, but prayed that when the winds ceased another ship would happen upon us. That did not happen.*

On the fourth day, a fire broke out in the hold and the Princess Anne *and her cargo sank to the bottom of the sea.*

I regret to inform you there were many casualties. A complete list will be forthcoming, and personal letters as well as monetary compensation will be sent to the families of those who perished.

And so I am at the part of this letter that distresses me more than anything I have ever penned before.

Among those who did not survive—

Her father's breath caught and the look in his tear-filled eyes swam with a pain she recognized only too well.

Olivia shook her head in denial. "No," she moaned.

Her father returned to Captain Durham's letter.

Among those who did not survive was Lord Iversley.

Olivia cried out and clamped her hands over her mouth so no more screams would follow.

Please, break the news to Lady Olivia in the gentlest of manners, my friend. I know how devastating Lord Iversley's death will be for her, for it was obvious her love for him was great.

I hope to return to England later in the year, and we will grieve together for a man I came to admire much. And love like a son.

Captain Phineas Durham

"Olivia."

It took two attempts before she could stand on her feet. Two attempts before her legs were steady enough to support her. She turned toward the door but had to reach for the back of a chair for support. Her father reached for her, but she shrugged out of his arms and weaved her way to the door. She twisted the door handle in each direction in a futile attempt to escape.

"Olivia," she heard her father say from behind her. Then louder. "Olivia!"

She crumpled to the floor as darkness overtook her.

Chapter 4

London—Three years later

Olivia made another note on the paper in front of her while Henry Lockling, Damien's steward, discussed improvements that needed to be made to several tenants' homes on Damien's property. Even though he'd been dead more than three years, no one knew it except her, her father, and Captain Durham. It was a decision she and her father had made after they'd gotten the letter from Captain Durham. *No one can know that Damien is dead. Not yet.*

The reasons had been simple. If Damien's death had become public knowledge, Lady Iversley and Damien's two sisters would have been at the mercy of a distant cousin of whom Damien had never spoken highly. By keeping Damien's death a secret, his oldest sister had been able to have a Season and find a husband. She was now happily married and expecting her first child. Damien's youngest sister, Penelope, was in the midst of enjoying her Season and, according to Lady Iversley, had caught the eye of several ideal suitors. Olivia expected to hear the announcement of Penelope's engagement by the end of the Season.

Of course, Lady Iversley was extremely put out with Damien for staying away from London for so long, but Olivia had forged several letters over the years and had had Captain Durham post them from the various ports where he stopped. Every letter promised Damien would be home soon, which only Captain Durham and Olivia knew was a lie.

She'd also used the three years to make sure Lady Iversley would be cared for when word came of Damien's death. Every quarter, she put back a portion of the profits from the estates to ensure that Lady Iversley would have an adequate amount to live on for the rest of her life. Especially if rumors were true concerning the man who would become the next Earl of Iversley when Damien's death was revealed.

Olivia took special care of Damien's estates, managing them as if he were coming back any day to run them again himself. Even though he never would be.

Just as her father would never be here to help her run Pellingsworth Shipping.

His sudden death nine months ago had left her reeling in such despair that, for the first few weeks after he was gone, she wasn't sure she'd be able to cope. But she had. There'd been too much to do to give in to her despair. Too much to take care of to lock herself away like she'd wanted and bury herself in her grief. And now, there was even more. Not only did she have the estates to look after, but there were problems at Pellingsworth Shipping.

Shortly after her father's death, the first mysterious catastrophe occurred. In the ensuing months, the shipping company had been plagued by one disaster after another.

Olivia clutched the pen tighter in frustration. If only her father were still here. Or if Captain Durham would return from his last voyage. She desperately needed someone to whom she could talk. Someone who could help her figure out what was going on.

"My lady?"

Olivia pulled herself to attention with a jolt. She looked into Henry Lockling's face and realized she'd been silent for too long a time.

Henry Lockling's thick brown hair had thinned since the first time she'd met with him three years earlier, but his shoulders were still as broad, and he carried himself with the same air of confidence she'd noted then. He was still a striking man even though his skin was more weathered and the hook to his nose more pronounced. And somewhere between the doubts he'd had of her ability to run the estates and the gradual building of their mutual respect, the two of them had become almost friends.

"I'm sorry, Henry. You were saying?"

"I was saying that other than the roofs on the Yardley and Harper cottages, the other homes made it through the winter in relatively good condition. An outbuilding or two does need repair, but most of those are minor and have been seen to already."

Olivia nodded. "What about the new barn we planned to build next to the Proctor's? It needs to be up in the next couple of months if we hope to store the wool over winter for delivery next spring."

"The lumber's already been ordered and the labor's lined up to begin construction the moment it arrives."

Olivia gave a nod of assent. "What do you hear from Iversley Hall?"

Lockling shook his head. "'Tis not good, my lady. Lord Iversley's cousin is still in residence. Lady Iversley isn't pleased that he hasn't left yet, but you know the lady. She doesn't have the heart to demand that he go."

Olivia fought the anger building within her. "What reason does Mr. Compton give for staying so long?"

The corner of Henry Lockling's lip lifted in a snarl. "He says he's concerned for his aunt. It troubles him that Lord Iversley has been gone for so long, and he's even hinted his fear that something has happened to his lordship."

Olivia knew that Damien's prolonged absence would raise questions eventually, but the last thing she needed was for people to find out why Damien hadn't returned. Not now.

Olivia rolled the pen in her fingers, then looked at Mr. Lockling. "Have you met Mr. Compton? What's your opinion of him?"

"Rumor has it young Compton cares a great deal for gaming and living the high life in London. Stephens, the butler, told me creditors have recently come to see Lady Iversley concerning Mr. Compton's unpaid bills and gaming debts. You will notice an increase in the household expenses when you go through this quarter's accounts."

Olivia lowered her gaze to the ledger Mr. Lockling had brought for her to peruse. "I see," Olivia said. She was obviously going to have to pay Lady Iversley a visit. Mr. Compton couldn't continue to mount up debts that his aunt had to cover.

"I'm sorry my news isn't better," Lockling said.

Olivia tried to smile. "You're only the messenger, Mr. Lockling. You don't have any control over the message."

"Unfortunately, no."

Henry Lockling gathered his papers and prepared to leave. He stopped his motions. "I wish you would tell Lady Iversley that you have been responsible for running the estate. The praises she offers me are totally unwarranted. They should be given directly to you."

"I don't need praises," Olivia answered. "I only need to know that Lord Iversley's estates will be in good shape when he returns."

"Is there any word on when that will be?"

Olivia halted. How should she answer? "Soon, Mr. Lockling. Within the year, I should say."

"That's good, my lady. Although you have done an admirable job running the estate, it will be good to have his lordship back."

"Yes, it will," Olivia responded. It *would* be good to have Damien back—if only it were possible for him to come back from the dead.

Lockling finished gathering the rest of his papers and rose to take his leave. Before he walked across the room, there was a knock on the door. Chivers stepped into the room.

"Lord Rotham to see you, my lady. Are you receiving?"

Olivia hesitated a fraction of a second, only because she wasn't sure she was up to a visit with the Marquess of Rotham. She wasn't ready to give him an answer, which she knew he expected. But procrastinating would do no good. It wouldn't change the inevitable.

"Send him in, Chivers. Mr. Lockling was just leaving."

Lockling bowed again and left the room. Rolland St. James, the Marquess of Rotham, entered in his wake.

When Rolland walked through the door, Olivia experienced a familiar warmth and felt tranquil and safe, as she would with an old friend. But nothing more.

She wished she felt something more for him. She liked him, admired him, and appreciated his friendship. But he could never take Damien's place in her heart. Just as Olivia could never be a replacement for the wife he'd loved and lost.

She'd known Rolland for years. He'd been a longtime friend of her father's and, as such, had been a frequent guest for dinner. She and Rolland had much in common, especially their love of the ships they both owned, so it was only natural that they were drawn to each other. And, Olivia knew that the day would come when she would have to marry. She couldn't remain a spinster forever. She wouldn't find a better husband than Rolland. If she didn't love him now, perhaps in time she would.

She watched him walk across the room and was struck by how handsome he was, how distinguished-looking. She smiled and moved from behind the desk.

Rolland took her extended hands, then lowered his head and kissed her fingers.

"Good day, Rolland."

"Olivia."

Olivia looked to Chivers who was just about to close the door. "Chivers, please have tea served."

"Yes, my lady."

"Won't you sit down, Rolland?"

"Thank you, Olivia."

He motioned for her to sit on the end of the settee, and after she'd settled, he sat in the chair opposite her.

"That was Iversley's steward who just left, wasn't it?"

"Yes."

"There's no trouble, is there?"

Olivia shook her head. "Mr. Lockling just needed to go over some work Lord Iversley had ordered be started on a piece of land that borders Pellingsworth Estate and was courteous enough to inform me before the work started. Nothing important."

"You're working too hard, Olivia," he said. His voice stayed soft but did not hide a hint of concern. "You look tired."

Olivia laughed. "Don't you know you're supposed to tell a lady she's lovely? Even if it's a lie."

"You are lovely, one of the loveliest women in all of England, but the dark smudges beneath your eyes tell me you're working too hard."

Olivia studied the genuine concern on Rolland's face while a servant wheeled a tea tray into the room. The marquess was handsome, with hair a golden blond and eyes the deepest brown. His brows angled above his eyes, giving him an austere expression that fit his station. His face was long and narrow, with high cheekbones chiseled in the same defined cut as his jaw.

Olivia poured tea when it arrived, and Rolland reached across the narrow space that separated them and took the cup and saucer from her hand. His fingers brushed against hers, keeping the contact several seconds before breaking it.

Olivia looked down. His hands were wide, his fingers long. She recognized his strength. She also knew his compassion.

Rolland's first wife had been a young, dainty beauty who was the love of his life. He'd lost her in childbirth, and during the six years since she'd been gone, some speculated he'd never remarry. This turned him into the prime catch of every Season. When he showed an interest in Olivia some year and a half ago, the *town* was abuzz with speculation.

Nearly everyone awaited the announcement of their engagement with eager anticipation. Everyone except those who favored Rotham as a prospective husband for themselves or their daughters.

Rolland took a sip of tea, then set his saucer on a table beside his chair and looked at her. "I know about the accidents with your ships, Olivia."

Olivia slowly lowered her cup and saucer to her lap. "I don't know what you're talking about."

"I'm talking about someone sabotaging your shipping company. The damaged cargo aboard the *Lady's Mist*. The faulty riggings that nearly sank the *Conquest*. The abandonment of a third of the crew that was supposed to sail on the *Viking*. Then there was the wrong cargo on the *Andora Jane* and the missed deadlines and the—"

"Enough!"

"You need my help, Olivia. Someone is deliberately trying to ruin your father's shipping company."

Olivia squared her shoulders. She refused to have anyone think she wasn't capable.

"They're just accidents. They don't mean anything."

"You're fooling yourself if you believe that. There's something more serious going on and you know it."

She lifted her chin and locked her gaze with his. "Of course I know it. How could I not? But I'm quite capable of handling it myself."

"But that's the problem, Olivia. You can't handle these problems alone. I don't *want* you to handle what's going on alone." Rolland sat forward in his chair. "Let me help you. You know how I feel about you. You know a match between us would be mutually beneficial."

"Don't, Rolland."

"I have to. I can't let you continue as you are. Marry me. Let's announce our betrothal."

Olivia's cup and saucer rattled when she moved them to the table, and she clasped her hands together in her lap. "Rolland, you are such a dear. But I can't. You know I can't. Father hasn't been gone a full year yet. I'm still in mourning. And Damien—"

"Iversley's been gone more than three years. It's quite possible he doesn't intend on ever returning."

Olivia bolted to her feet. "Don't!"

"You have to face facts, Olivia. Strathern's been dead for more than a year."

"But his son is still alive! There's still a price on Damien's head."

"When was the last time you heard from Iversley?"

"That's none of your—"

"When?"

Olivia turned her back on Rolland and looked out the window. How could she try to convince anyone that Damien would return when she knew he wouldn't?

"You're young and alone, Olivia. No one expects you to wait for Iversley. Everyone knows you've waited long enough for him to return, and that it's time you moved forward with your life."

Rolland walked to her and turned her so she faced him. "People will think you prudent and wise to marry me and let me shoulder your responsibilities."

Olivia arched her brows. "Because I'm a woman and not intelligent enough to manage on my own?"

"No, because I'm a man and it's expected of me."

Olivia shook her head. "Don't, Rolland. I can't. Not yet."

"Surely you aren't still in love with Iversley? Not after he abandoned you."

She locked her gaze with his. "Can you tell me you aren't still in love with Felicity?"

Olivia heard the air rush from him before he answered.

"Not completely. But perhaps it's time we both buried our ghosts and started again."

Rolland kept his gaze connected with hers. Olivia waited in silence, unable to give him an answer.

"Olivia, consider your position, as well as mine. I'm very fond of you."

"Fond?"

"You know what I mean." He led her to the sofa. When they were seated, he reached for her hands. "We have both loved deeply. But it's time we move on with our lives. You're twenty-six years old and nearly past the age to marry. I'm thirty-two and in need of an heir. Between the two of us, we are worth a fortune. More than either of us has need of. Without children to leave it to, what good is all we have?"

He gently squeezed her fingers as if emphasizing his next words. "I care for you, Olivia. Deeply. I want to take care of you and the children we'll have together. And you need me, too. You need me to help you run the business your father left you, as well as the properties that didn't go to your uncle. You need me to take care of Pellingsworth Shipping."

"I've managed," she said defensively.

"At what cost? Do you know the danger you're in every time you go down to the docks? A man isn't safe from the drunken sailors and thieves who roam the wharves, let alone a woman. I know your father didn't intend for you to continue like this. He encouraged an association between us. You know he did."

Olivia wasn't sure what her father had wanted for her. She knew he respected Rolland, knew he valued him as a friend and colleague, but she had no idea what role her father envisioned Rolland would play in her life.

But Rolland was right. Perhaps it was time to let Damien go.

She looked at Rolland's hands, which were holding hers, then looked up at him. "Give me a little more time, Rolland. Just until Father's will has been read."

Olivia could see the shock on his face.

"Your father's will hasn't been read?"

"Not all of it. Only the parts that involved the entailed properties. Descriptions of the land that went to my uncle, my father's younger brother."

"For God's sake, why not the rest of it?"

"Because Captain Durham is required to be here for the reading. Word was sent him when the *Angel's Wings* sailed, but he hasn't arrived yet."

"The *Angel's Wings* isn't due back for months yet."

"Perhaps two. Three if the winds are against them."

"And you've gone all this time without knowing what exactly is yours?"

Olivia felt her temper bristle. "I have no doubt my father left me well provided for. I am assuming that other than Pellingsworth Manor, which is entailed, everything else will remain in my name."

"And if it isn't?"

"I'm not worried about that, Rolland. And you shouldn't be either."

"I'm not interested in your money, Olivia. Surely you know that?"

Olivia rubbed the ache at her temples. "Of course I do. I'm just tired is all. Please, could we talk of something else?"

The look on Rolland's face said he didn't want to talk about something else, but the heavy sigh he breathed told her he'd given in.

"Very well. Do you plan to attend the Grahamshire ball tonight?"

Olivia didn't feel up to going anywhere tonight and wanted to say so but knew if she did, Rolland would have another example to throw in her face, proof she was working too hard. "Yes, I'm planning to go."

"Good. I'll come for you at eight."

He rose and walked to the door. Olivia followed to ring for Chivers. "I can see myself out, Olivia. Perhaps, though, you should find time to rest before you dress for the evening."

When Olivia didn't respond, Rolland stopped and turned to face her. "I'm only concerned, Olivia," he said. He placed his hands on her shoulders and gently held her. "I do care for you, you know."

"I know, Rolland."

"Promise me you'll give me an answer as soon as Captain Durham arrives and your father's will has been read. I don't want to wait much longer, Olivia. I can't."

"I promise. As soon as the will is read."

"Good." He kissed her lightly on the forehead before turning.

Olivia watched him walk away from her and felt a pang of guilt. Why was she putting him off?

She walked across the room and stared out the window. Damien's dark features stared back at her, his deep-mahogany hair and clear blue eyes. His strong, chiseled cheekbones and rugged strength. A renegade tear seeped from her eyes. Dear God, but she missed him. She tried again to push him from her mind. She couldn't.

Oh, it wasn't fair how he still haunted her. How he kept her from loving anyone else. But nothing had been fair since the night Strathern had burst into her engagement ball. With his damning lies, he'd shattered her dreams and destroyed her future.

Olivia hugged her arms around her middle. Maybe Rolland was right. Maybe it was time she put her memories behind her and made a new life for herself—one with a husband to care for and children to love. Maybe it was time she locked her love for Damien away in that part of her heart that had died when he did. Maybe in time she could remember again what it was like to love.

Or maybe it was already too late.

Chapter 5

Olivia stepped out of the carriage in front of Cyrus Haywood's office and walked up the three steps that led to his private rooms. She was relieved that this day was here. It had been nearly a year since her father's death, and the conditions of his will would finally be settled.

Not that she didn't know what those conditions were. Her father never kept it a secret that he considered her his heir and intended for her to have everything that was not entailed. But it would be a relief for the details to be finalized. Perhaps it would stop her uncle, the new Earl of Pellingsworth, from insinuating that her father intended for him to assume responsibility for her father's other assets, especially Pellingsworth Shipping.

Olivia entered the lawyer's outer office, and smiled at Cyrus Haywood, her father's longtime solicitor.

"Good afternoon, Lady Olivia."

"Good afternoon, Mister Haywood. Has Captain Durham arrived?"

"Yes. He's waiting for you inside."

Olivia walked past Haywood and through his outer office to the solicitor's private study. Going through her father's will wouldn't be quite so painful with Phineas with her.

"Captain," she said, rushing to take his outstretched hands. "I'm so glad you're here."

"I wish I could have been here months ago. Your father wouldn't have wanted you to be alone at a time like this."

Olivia smiled. She could smile now. Time had a way of easing the hurt. "You're here now. That's all that matters. Did you sleep well?"

"Yes, my lady. I slept aboard ship. I'm used to a bed that rocks beneath me."

Olivia smiled. "I still wish you would have accepted my invitation to stay at Pellingsworth House. Father would have been disappointed to know you'd arrived in London and not taken me up on my offer to provide you a room."

"I know, my lady. But I had much business to see to. I'm newly arrived in London. Your father would have understood all that needed to be done."

"Knowing Father, he probably would have spent the night with you. There was nothing he loved more than sleeping aboard a ship. Especially the *Angel's Wings*."

"Right you are there."

Captain Durham patted her hand then led her to one of the two leather-cushioned chairs facing the desk.

Cyrus Haywood's office was spacious, with rows of leather-bound books lining the walls. Behind his desk, a large pane glass window looked out on the London scenery. To the left, three narrow book cases were separated by two doors. The one directly to her left was closed, the door behind her partially open. Olivia assumed the doors led to private consultation rooms.

To the right, an oversized oak table took up one side of the room. Eight captain's chairs surrounded the table, and Olivia surmised that this was where Haywood met with larger groups of clients. Olivia sat in the chair before his desk and folded her hands in her lap.

Haywood took his place behind his desk and waited while a young assistant brought in tea and poured them each a cup. When the assistant was finished, Haywood started a conversation she knew was

intended to set her at ease. For several long minutes the three of them
drank their tea, keeping to the subject of the bustling tea trade. After a
sufficient amount of time, Haywood reached for a small stack of papers
and turned his attention to her. "Are you ready to begin, Lady Olivia?"

Olivia looked to Captain Durham and smiled when he reached
over to pat her hands. He gave her fingers a reassuring squeeze. She
thought it a little odd when he whispered, "Everything will be for the
best, Lady Olivia," but she didn't have time to ask what he meant.
Cyrus Haywood began listing her father's properties, investments, and
estates.

"At the time of your father's death," Cyrus said, "he held free and
clear the following properties that were *not* entailed: the townhouse
where you reside, called Pellingsworth House; Bridgemont estates in
Essex outside Witham; Homerton estate in Kent; and Fairview Manor
in Hampshire."

Cyrus Haywood took a deep breath while flipping to a new page.
"Then there is your father's ownership of Pellingsworth Shipping and
his one-half ownership in the clipper ship, *Angel's Wings*, with Captain
Durham. These holdings are separate from your father's monetary
worth, valued as of last quarter at more than one hundred thousand
pounds."

Cyrus Haywood laid down his pen and removed the spectacles
from the bridge of his nose. "Do you have any questions, my lady?"

Olivia shook her head. What questions could she possibly have?
Cyrus Haywood hadn't told her anything new. For nearly four years
she'd done the books and managed the unentailed Pellingsworth
estates, as well as Damien's estates, alongside her father. At first, he'd
suggested that she help him in order to give her something to occupy
her time as well as her mind after Damien's death. She went along with
his plan because overseeing Damien's estates was a way she could feel
connected to Damien. A way she could take care of something that had
been his. And someone had had to manage Damien's properties until

his death was revealed and the new Earl of Iversley could take over. That responsibility had fallen to her father, then to her.

She'd gone with her father to visit the estates, and gradually gone with him to oversee Damien's shipping cargoes, too. Eventually, the responsibility of managing everything had fallen on her shoulders as if her father had been preparing her for this day.

No, there wasn't one detail of her father's will that would come as a surprise, including the amount she was worth.

"You forget, Mr. Haywood. I have taken care of everything that was my father's for more than three years now. I would only question you if you informed me I was not worth such an amount."

Both Captain Durham and Cyrus Haywood smiled.

"Your father left everything I just listed to you, Lady Olivia."

Olivia's breath caught and she closed her eyes to fight the teary sense of relief that nearly overpowered her. It was over. Finally. She now had the freedom to marry Rolland—if she decided that's what she wanted. She could still care for Damien's estates and keep that little part of him as a private sanctuary. But perhaps Rolland was right. Perhaps her future lay with him and the children they would have together.

Olivia felt as if a huge weight had been lifted from her. This part of her life was at a close, and it was time to begin anew.

"But there is one condition to your father's will."

Olivia's gaze shifted to Haywood's face. His words took her off guard. He seemed paler than before. Almost hesitant. "A condition? My father put a condition in his will?"

"Yes, my lady."

Olivia turned to Captain Durham but his expression revealed nothing. She turned back and faced her father's solicitor. "Go on, Mister Haywood. What condition did my father place in his will?"

Haywood cleared his throat nervously. Olivia suddenly realized he'd done that quite often since she'd arrived. Her breathing quickened and she held herself perfectly still while Haywood picked up the papers.

"Upon the reading of this will, Pellingsworth House in London will go to my daughter Olivia, without contest, until the day of her death. She will also receive a quarterly income of two thousand pounds for as long as she lives. The estates mentioned before as well as the remainder of the . . . the . . ."

Haywood cleared his throat again. His discomfort was obvious.

"Continue, Mister Haywood," she said, releasing a breath she didn't realize she'd been holding.

"Yes. Yes. Well . . ." He cleared his throat again then read on. "The remainder of the above mentioned assets and properties, including Pellingsworth Shipping, will as of one year and one month of my death be divided into two equal shares. My daughter's share will only remain in her name upon the completion of one condition. She must, within one year and one month of my death, marry."

Olivia couldn't stop the gasp of air that cut off Haywood's words and nearly choked her. Of course she intended to marry. But her father thought to force her by putting it in his will? And then to only receive half of everything when she did? For God's sake, why? And who would control the other half?

She stared first at Cyrus Haywood, then turned to Captain Durham. She wanted to demand if he knew what her father intended, but the closed look on his face told her the answer. She spun her gaze back to Cyrus Haywood. He swallowed hard then said, "There is more."

Olivia tightened her hands into rigid fists. She was furious with her father for putting such a ridiculous condition in his will. She stared at Cyrus Haywood in numb amazement as she tried to absorb what her father had done. But nothing in the world prepared her for his next sentence.

Haywood finished in a hurry. "My daughter, Olivia, must, within one year and one month from my death . . . marry Damien Bedford, Earl of Iversley."

Olivia gasped while Haywood added even more. "If my daughter chooses not to marry Lord Iversley within the specified deadline, everything except Pellingsworth House and the aforementioned quarterly income will go in its entirety to Lord Iversley."

Olivia felt herself sway in the chair and clutched the thick leather arms to keep from reeling to the side. Surely she hadn't heard Haywood correctly. "What did you say?"

"If you don't marry Lord Iversley within the next six weeks, my lady, all the estates as well as your interest in Pellingsworth Shipping and your father's portion of the clipper ship, the *Angel's Wings,* will go to Lord Iversley. When the two of you marry, however, you will both receive equal shares of everything."

Olivia thought she might be ill. "Lord Iversley is dead," she choked out. "He's been dead nearly four years. Father knew that. Tell him, Captain Durham. Tell him Damien's dead."

She looked at the captain, expecting him to agree with her. But he remained silent.

She bolted to her feet. "Tell him! You wrote to us four years ago with news that Damien died in a fire aboard the *Princess Anne.* You told us he was dead. How could Father leave everything to someone who is dead?"

The room shifted around her, and Captain Durham rose to stand beside her. He placed his arm around her shoulder and steadied her. "Olivia. I know what you think—"

"No! Father didn't write this condition in his will. He wouldn't have. *You* must have!" She turned an accusing glare to Cyrus Haywood. "*You* must have written that condition into Father's will."

"I assure you I did not," Cyrus whispered, his tone indicating she'd insulted him.

Olivia spun around to Captain Durham. "Then you? Why? What possible purpose could you have?"

Captain Durham shook his head. "Your father wrote the condition in his will, Olivia."

She swiped her hand through the air in an act of anger. "No! He wouldn't have. He wouldn't have left everything he owned to a dead man. And he wouldn't have lied to me all these years. He wouldn't have let me believe Damien was dead if he wasn't."

"But he did, Olivia."

The strange, yet oh-so-familiar voice shattered through her control. His voice. Damien's voice.

She staggered but stayed on her feet with Captain Durham's help. A scream welled from somewhere deep inside her and her hands flew to her mouth to keep it from escaping.

Damien was alive.

Olivia took a tentative step toward him, then another. Until she was so close she could feel the heat radiate from his body. Until she could smell the clean wash of the soap he'd always used with a mixture of sea air that clung to his clothes. She lifted her chin and locked her gaze with his.

"You're alive."

"Yes. I'm alive."

"And you let me believe you were dead."

The man she'd loved more than life itself glared at her with an unreadable coldness.

Olivia pulled back her hand and slapped him.

Chapter 6

Olivia stared at him, absorbing every detail of the man standing in front of her. Time seemed to stop as her mind whirled in confusion. The emotional part of her, the part that knew how essential it was to protect her heart, said this couldn't be true. Damien couldn't be alive. The more rational part of her mind, the part that was forced to face reality, knew it was. For four agonizing years, the man she'd loved had let her believe she'd sent him to his death.

"Why? Why did you let me think you'd died?"

His features didn't change. The dark expression on his face remained closed. Missing was the warmth she'd once seen in his eyes. Absent was the laughter she'd heard in his voice. Gone was the closeness she'd felt even when he wasn't near her. Olivia kept her gaze focused on him, searching for some hint of the man to whom she'd given her heart so long ago.

That man was gone. In his place was a stranger. A man with skin bronzed from years of being out of doors. A man who was as hardened on the inside as he was on the out.

A long, jagged line ran across the left side of his face and down his neck. He let her focus on it, as if waiting for her to recoil from the sight of him. She didn't. And it angered her that he thought she would.

As if he'd given into her perusal long enough, he turned his face away. He looked across the room at Captain Durham and Haywood.

"Please excuse us," he said. His voice contained an icy chill that she'd never heard before.

He pushed open the door to the room where he'd been hiding during the reading of the will. Without a glance in her direction, he stood in the doorway and waited for her to enter.

Olivia walked past him on legs that felt weak and made her way across the room to stand in front of a window. She needed light. She needed to look out onto things that were familiar. Onto busy London streets bustling with people rushing about, doing their everyday business. She needed to watch the carriages go by on their way to planned events. She needed to see a world of normalcy instead of trying to survive in a world gone mad.

She clutched her arms around her middle and held herself perfectly still, terrified that if she let go of her rigid stiffness, she might fall apart. She nearly shattered when the door clicked behind her.

For a long time, she couldn't bring herself to face him. The silence in the room threatened to suffocate her. Olivia thought he might not want to start this conversation any more than she did. It was as if he knew, just as she did, that even the slightest move, the faintest noise would have the same catastrophic results as the first shot of a battle. And so she waited until she couldn't stand it any longer.

"Why did you let me believe you were dead?" she asked again when she realized he wouldn't be the first one to speak.

"I *was* dead. The whole world thought so."

Olivia spun around and glared at him. But his face was turned from her.

"You look remarkably well for someone who's been dead nearly four years. Did you once, in all that time, think to let me know you had survived?"

"No."

His answer stole her breath, then ignited her fury.

With his face averted, he stood as lifeless as a statue, as emotionless as a boulder of granite. She clenched her fists and faced him squarely. "Then why did you come back now?"

With a slight lift of his chin, he showed the first reaction. The corners of his lips lifted to form a cynical grin. A grin tinged with malice. "Why do you think? To get everything I should have had upon our marriage."

"My father's possessions mean so much to you? My father's land and his ships were enough to bring you back from the dead, but I wasn't?"

"You showed me the extent of your . . . concern, when you betrayed me."

Olivia sucked in a breath. "I agreed to send you with Captain Durham because Strathern wanted you dead."

"You sent me away because you didn't think I could face Strathern on my own. You didn't think I could defend myself. You sent me away because you didn't trust me enough to believe that I loved you more than your father's ships!"

"Trust had nothing to do with it. Strathern would have killed you. He'd already put—"

He slammed his fist against the top of the table. "Then he would have killed me! It would have been better than the world thinking I'd run because I was a coward!"

He glared at her, his blue eyes glowering with resentment. "Have you discovered who fathered Cassandra's babe?"

Still stunned, she shook her head.

"Did you even search for an answer? Or were you so convinced I was the guilty party you didn't even bother looking?"

"I knew you weren't the father of her babe."

"Liar! You thought it from the minute Strathern accused me. I saw it on your face."

Olivia reached out to steady herself against one of the wooden chairs around the large table. He took a step toward her.

"Well, it doesn't matter any more, does it? Strathern is dead. He went to his grave believing I was responsible for his daughter's death."

"You knew Strathern died?"

"I knew."

Olivia felt as if another spike had been driven through her heart. Strathern died less than a year after Cassandra's death—less than a year after Damien left. She pressed her fist to her stomach as if she might be ill. He'd known for more than three years that it was safe to come home.

The room suddenly lost some of its brightness. Olivia wasn't sure if the sun had gone beneath a cloud, or if the fury she felt obliterated it from her view.

Damien pulled out one of the chairs at the opposite end of the table and sat, stretching his long, muscular legs out in front of him.

"It was quite clever of your father to word his will the way he did, leaving us no choice but to marry in order to keep the ships."

She sucked in a deep breath. "Yes, quite clever. And yet not really so binding. We must marry *only* if we both intend to keep the ships." Olivia turned and leveled him with a glare filled with all the bitterness that was tearing her apart. "A choice I'm not sure I'm prepared to make."

His dark brows arched in a menacing line. "Are you telling me you would consider giving everything up?"

Olivia clutched her hands into the folds of her skirt and swallowed hard. Could she give up the estates, the land with the people she'd come to love over the years? And the ships? She'd loved the ships since she'd first stepped aboard the wooden deck of a mighty vessel as a little girl. She was never at such peace as when she was down at the docks or standing aboard one of her father's ships with the deck rolling beneath her feet and the wind whipping through her hair. How could her father expect her to give up the ships? She couldn't do it.

The ships were her solace. The harbor was where she went to feel close to her father. To Damien. The ships were what she and Damien were going to build their life around. Their future. It was a passion they both shared. Why would her father give her an ultimatum that would take that away from her?

Olivia turned her head and lifted her gaze to Damien's. She thought she saw a smile cross his face. Thought for just a moment she spied a hint of humor. A hint of smugness, as if he knew what giving up the ships would cost her. And he enjoyed her misery.

The Damien she'd loved and adored before was gone. And in his place there was a cruel and unforgiving stranger. A man she didn't even like, let alone think she could ever love again.

"Don't be too rash, Olivia. Marriage to me can't be all that bad, can it? You were prepared to do it before, and quite happy about it, if I remember correctly."

His words stung like nothing she could recall. "Why are you doing this?"

He lifted his eyebrows in feigned confusion. "Doing what?"

"Expecting us to marry. Demanding the ships."

"Because they're mine."

His eyes turned cold as ice, his voice hard as stone. "I spent four years waiting for the day I could come back to get everything you took away from me. I thought of nothing else during those long, agonizing days except returning to claim what would have been mine if you had only stood at my side and not betrayed me."

Olivia staggered under the resentment she heard in his voice. For a long moment, she could do nothing but stare at him in disbelief. Did he really believe she'd cared so little for him? But when she looked into his eyes, she knew he did.

She didn't have the strength to face his anger. She turned her back on him and walked to the window. More people bustled past. More carriages rumbled down the street. Life went on as if nothing out of the ordinary could disturb it, while here in this room, her world was crumbling around her.

She didn't turn around to face him. She didn't think she could bear to see the hard look in his eyes, the cold disdain on his face.

"I only have to marry you if I want what my father intended I should have."

"And if you don't marry me before the six week deadline is up, you lose not only the ships, but the chance to marry and have a home and family of your own."

His words were like the twisting of a knife once he had it embedded in her flesh. She slowly turned. "You are only partially right, my lord. I may lose my father's ships if I don't marry you, but you are not my only, nor my last, chance at a home and family."

His dark brows arched in a dangerous line. "Are you telling me there is someone else you intend to marry?"

"What I am planning is hardly your concern."

"Oh, it is my concern, Olivia. A groom is always concerned when his bride informs him she has plans to marry someone else."

The air she needed to breathe lodged in her throat. "When I marry, my lord, you most certainly will not be the groom. You had that choice once before and lost it."

"I did not lose it. It was taken away from me."

"No! You could have come back to claim your right any time during the last four years and chose not to. Now it is too late. It will be a cold day in hell before I will consider taking your name again. A cold day in hell before I will ever be the fool I was once."

"If anyone was the fool, it was I! And you know nothing of my reasons for not returning!"

Olivia took a step closer to him, her fury nearly consuming her. "I know you did not care for me enough to let me know you were alive. Now, it is too late for us! It was too late the minute you made the conscious decision to let me believe you were dead."

She saw the muscles in Damien's jaw clench before he rose and moved toward her. For the first time, Olivia noted an unevenness in his gait. It wasn't quite a limp, yet she could see it was an imperfection he'd become quite adept at concealing. He stopped when he was nearly upon her.

He meant to intimidate her with his towering height and broad shoulders, but she stood up to him.

"We will marry, Olivia. I will have the estates, *and* the ships, *and* you!"

Olivia reached out to the nearest chair to steady herself. Her father and Captain Durham had been right when they'd told her Damien would never forgive her if she sent him away, but she thought the love she and Damien shared could weather any disaster that threatened them.

What a fool she'd been.

She pushed herself away from the chair she clung to and stepped around him as she made her way to the door. She had to get out of here. Had to get away from him.

"We have six weeks until the deadline. I would begin making plans if I were you."

She hesitated for a fraction of a second, then threw open the door and left. For the first time since she'd put him aboard the *Princess Anne*, she wished she'd let him stay in England and take his chances with Strathern.

Chapter 7

Damien lifted the brandy to his mouth and finished the last few drops before setting the empty glass back on the table. From the moment he'd left Haywood's office, he'd wanted nothing more than to find some remote corner and get roaring drunk. But he didn't. He wouldn't. Not until he had this whole mess sorted out in his mind. Not until he was well on his way to getting his life back.

Damien thought of Olivia's boast not to marry him. She evidently had someone else in mind. Someone to whom she'd given her heart. Damien raked his fingers through his hair. The thought of her with another man made his blood boil. She was wrong if she thought he'd let her marry someone else. She was still his. Even if she didn't want to be.

He sprang from the chair in his cabin aboard the *Angel's Wings*, then grasped the corner of the table when his left leg refused to support him. He muttered an oath more vile than those he usually said when his injuries limited him, but today seemed to warrant every curse he knew. Being near Olivia again after nearly four years of dreaming about her every single day had taken its toll on his emotions. He didn't want to feel the same passion for her that he had when she'd betrayed him, but the woman he faced now wasn't the girl she'd been four years ago. The Olivia of four years ago would never have stood up to him like she had today. The Olivia from before would never have slapped him.

Damien paced the length of his cabin to stretch his legs, then sat back down in one of the two matching oversized leather chairs and rubbed his thighs. When the cramping of his muscles eased, he dropped his head back against the chair with a heavy sigh. Bloody hell, but she'd become a courageous beauty.

Damien pictured the expression on her face when she'd first seen him. When she'd first realized he was alive. The color had drained from her face, turning her creamy, clear complexion a pale white against the rich mahogany of her hair.

Oh, her hair. He knew beneath that trim, black velvet bonnet, her hair was pulled into a loose knot that, when released, would hang nearly to her waist. How many times he'd fantasized pulling the pins that held the thick, heavy lengths. How, in the months while he fought for his life, he'd envisioned twining his fingers through her hair as he held her to him, fanning it out around her as she lay beneath him.

While his breathing went in and out in a rush, he experienced an uncomfortable heaviness he swore he would never again allow himself to feel. He relived seeing her oval face turn toward him in disbelief, her huge, brown eyes staring at him in confusion. Then her upper teeth clamped against her lush lower lip, and her daintily rounded chin trembled—until she recovered and her shock changed to outrage, then open fury.

Well, now she knew what it felt like to be deceived by someone she loved. Now she knew what it meant to have her world pulled out from beneath her and be left to flounder in despair and confusion. And she'd know what it was to be helpless to control her future. He'd spent four years dreaming of this day and he would celebrate every second of it.

Only he hadn't bargained on the pangs of guilt and regret that accompanied the satisfaction.

He brushed the uncomfortable emotions aside and listened for Durham, who he had sent out to be his legs, to gather information Damien couldn't gather for himself. It was too soon for him to show his face. Too soon for his miraculous return from the dead to be the fast-spreading topic of conversation in every parlor in London. He had too much to do before he could battle the curiosity seekers and the busybodies who would vie for a glimpse at the recently resurrected Earl of Iversley.

There was his title to restore and Damien looked forward to a confrontation with his cousin with immense anticipation. If half of what Haywood told him were true, Damien was going to take great pleasure in beating the usurper within an inch of his life before he sent him packing, before he made him suffer for the advantage he'd taken of Damien's mother and her hospitality, before he made him account for every pound he'd lost gaming. But first he needed to know exactly what he was facing with Olivia. With his competition.

Damien rose from his chair and paced the cabin again. How long did it take to have a few drinks and find out a little information? Damien listened, then heard footsteps. He focused his eyes on the door and breathed a sigh of relief when the captain walked in.

Durham shook the rain from his slicker and tossed it and his hat over a hook on the wall. Then he walked to a table where three decanters sat in a deep tray. He poured liquor from one of the bottles into a glass and brought the decanter over to where Damien stood and offered to refill his glass, too.

"Am I going to need this?"

"Probably."

Damien waited for Durham to refill his glass, then cradled it in his hand. "What did you find out?"

The captain sank down onto the other cushioned chair and stretched his long legs out in front of him. After he'd taken a hefty swallow, he looked at Damien. "Olivia's name's been linked to the Marquess of Rotham. As to how serious it is, you'll have to ask someone more in the know than the blokes I bought drinks for all evening. I can only tell you the comment was made that the relationship was serious enough to cause speculation up and down the waterfront as to what might happen if there were a merger of two of the largest shipping fleets in London."

Damien felt a stab of anger fueled by a wave of something even stronger. He refused to admit it might be jealousy. Jealousy was an emotion that resulted from feelings of affection between two people. There was no affection left between Olivia and him. How could there be after what she'd done?

Damien tightened his fingers around the glass in his hand, then forced himself to relax his grip. His calm was short-lived.

"There's more," Durham said.

Damien's attention flashed to Durham's face, and he looked at the frown that covered the captain's forehead. "What?"

"Olivia is in danger."

Every muscle in Damien's body tensed. "Why?"

"According to talk at the Anchor's Down, Pellingsworth Shipping has been plagued by some mysterious incidents for quite some time."

"What sort of incidents?"

"A couple months ago, the *Andora Jane* sailed with half a cargo. And the morning the *Viking's Lady* was supposed to set sail, almost one-third of her crew failed to show. Then last week, the *Conquest* had to turn back when all the spare rigging was frayed. There have also been some shorted shipments and unexplained cancellations. And just this morning, the port authorities came to search the hold of the *Daring*."

"For what?"

"They didn't say."

"Did they find anything?"

"No. But they're suspicious now. They're the bane of every captain that sails. Hard to tell when they'll make their next surprise inspection. A little money under the table is usually the only way to keep them away."

"Did you know any of this was going on before now?"

Durham shook his head. "She didn't mention it once. Not even in the letter she sent asking me to come back for the reading of her father's will. Every time I inquired, she assured me everything was fine."

Damien rubbed his aching thighs. "When did these plagues start?"

"Evidently not long after her father died. Talk has it, though, they're happening more often of late and the mishaps are getting more serious. There was even a fire aboard the *Viking* the night she pulled into port. It could have been worse, but the first mate forgot a silk shawl he'd brought back from China for his mother's birthday and went back to get it. He saw smoke and raised the alarm before the fire did much damage."

Damien fought the familiar wave of panic at the mere mention of a fire and took another swallow of the brandy in his glass. "Does anyone have any idea who might be behind these accidents?"

"There's a lot of speculation, but nothing anyone can prove. It could be someone who doesn't think a woman should be running a shipping business. There's still more than a few superstitious old tars who think having a woman anywhere near a ship is bad luck."

"What do you think?"

Durham took another swallow of his drink and sighed heavily. "I think it sounds like someone's trying to discredit the lady. Or ruin her. Or scare her off so she'll sell."

"Competition?"

Durham shrugged his shoulders. "Possibly, but why now? Unless they think she's an easy mark now that her father's dead."

"Then it's someone who doesn't know her well, or they'd realize they picked the wrong person."

Damien walked to the other side of the cabin. His leg was more stiff than usual, although the brandy was helping the pain.

"What are you going to do, lad?"

"The only thing I can. Find out who's behind this before Olivia gets hurt."

Durham set his glass down and rose to face Damien. "You'd be wise not to let anyone know you're back. At least until your mother knows you've returned. That's not news you want her hearing through the gossip mill."

"When are you scheduled to leave?" Damien asked. Pellingsworth Shipping had signed a very lucrative contract to bring back three shipments of French wine from Bordeaux, and the captain was due to set sail soon.

"In three days on the *Wayward Lady*. They're loading cargo right now. But I'll find someone else to captain the ship. I don't want to leave you."

"No," Damien said, waving his hand. "You need to be on board. With all the accidents that are happening, we can't trust these shipments to anyone else. Besides, you'll only be gone two weeks."

"Be careful, lad. Don't take any chances you don't have to."

"I won't."

"And be careful with her, too. She's been through enough."

"Haven't we all?"

"Perhaps it would be best to forget the past and put what happened behind you."

Damien ignored Durham's comment and sat back down in his chair.

With a shake of his head Durham walked away. "I'll check on that cargo tonight. Then I'll spend the night aboard the *Wayward Lady* to make sure nothing happens. With all that's gone on, it might not hurt to keep a closer watch on things."

Damien watched Captain Durham put his slicker and hat back on and leave the cabin. He took another long swallow of the brandy and kneaded the muscles in his right thigh, which always hurt worse than the other.

The lamp burned low and soft, casting flowing shadows across the room, reminding him of shaded evenings in a gentler time. He tried not to think of her. Tried to keep his mind focused on what he had to do. On the loose ends he needed to tie up.

He couldn't rush in and claim Olivia like he'd originally intended. Revealing himself would have to wait. He needed to keep his identity a secret until he knew who was behind the accidents. Whoever it was wouldn't be nearly so careful if they thought Olivia was a defenseless female. And they'd make a mistake.

Then, when Olivia and Pellingsworth Shipping were out of danger, he'd marry her and have the life she'd stolen from him nearly four years ago.

Damien stretched his legs out in front of him and laid his head against the back of the chair. It was Olivia's face he saw when he closed his eyes. Olivia's eyes looking down on him. Olivia's lips smiling back at him. Lips he'd dreamed of kissing every night in his sleep.

Damien let his fingers trail down the left side of his face, over the wide, jagged scar that ran at an angle from his temple, across his cheek, and down his neck. The scar that pulled awkwardly at his flesh. At least she hadn't screamed in horror when she'd seen it. In fact, she'd barely seemed to notice.

Damien threw the remaining liquor to the back of his throat and rose stiffly from his chair. With a self-deprecating oath, he shrugged into his jacket and stepped out on deck. He needed fresh air. He needed something other than being penned in by four walls and a past life of memories he couldn't escape.

So he walked, without knowing where or why, in hopes he could escape the nightmares that haunted him.

Olivia glanced up from her paperwork and looked at the clock on the shipping office wall. She hadn't intended to stay here this long—hadn't even intended to come here tonight. But after her shocking afternoon, she needed to be here, in her father's office at Pellingsworth Shipping, surrounded by memories of everything that was his.

She rubbed her hand over her eyes and faced the possibility that in less than six weeks, the shipping company might no longer be hers.

Olivia leaned back in her chair and considered her choices. She could either marry Rolland and forfeit everything to Damien, or she could marry Damien and condemn herself to a life with a man who no longer loved her.

Why had her father written such a stipulation into his will? He knew how much she loved the harbor. Knew how much she loved coming to the shipyards to oversee the comings and goings of ships and the cargoes they carried all over the world. And her father had essentially given it all to Damien, leaving her no choice but to marry him to have a connection to it.

She lunged forward in her chair and slammed her fist against the top of the desk. She would not marry Damien. She wouldn't marry a man who didn't love her. A man who'd let her believe he was dead. A man who only wanted her now because of the wealth that would come with her.

No. She would never marry Damien.

She would marry Rolland. He wanted to marry her, had pressed her to marry him more than once. But love would never be part of their marriage. He was still in love with his first wife. Just as she was still in love with Damien. And probably always would be.

The choice came down to the ships. To how badly she wanted to keep them. To what she was willing to do to keep them.

She laid down her pen and looked outside at the darkening sky. It was past time for her to leave. Johns, her driver, would no doubt be worried. If she didn't get home soon, Cook would be upset with her again tonight for having to hold dinner, and Mrs. Dawes would scold her for staying down here after dark.

After her disturbing afternoon, she needed to keep her mind as busy as possible. She grabbed some paperwork to take with her and stuffed it into a leather folder. There was enough here to keep her busy half the night. It was the only way to keep Damien from infiltrating her memory. The only way to keep the pain of what he'd done from hurting worse than it already did.

She took her pelisse from the closet, then locked the door behind her and hurried toward her waiting carriage. Before she could reach it, a hand grabbed her. Strong fingers wrapped around her neck, squeezing the air from her body. Olivia tried to scream but couldn't get any sound past her throat.

The man held her from behind so she couldn't see him. The harder she fought, the closer he brought her up against him, the tighter he held her. She tried to kick him, but he moved far enough away to get out of her reach.

He was a big man, with arms so muscular she couldn't span them with her fingers. And he was tall. As tall as Damien if not taller, because the top of her head barely reached his chin. He laughed. He was enjoying this. Enjoying the dominance he had over her. It was almost as if he were playing with her, tormenting her, like a cat torments a captured mouse.

She heard his laughter in her ears, felt his body vibrate against her back. She struggled again, and he laughed even harder at her feeble efforts. Olivia was terrified. For the first time ever, she was afraid for her life.

"Fighting won't do you any good, little lady. You might as well relax and enjoy yourself. It doesn't matter if my women are willing or not when I take 'em."

Olivia struggled harder. She tried to scream again, but his hand clamped tighter over her mouth. His other hand moved over her body, down her throat and across her breasts, touching her as no one ever had. She reached above her and felt satisfaction when she raked her fingernails down his cheek.

The giant holding her bellowed in pain, but his grasp didn't ease.

Instead, he spun her around, and with a swift blow, brought his fist down across the side of her head.

Lights flashed behind her eyes, and she shook her head to clear the confusion that made everything go dark around her. With almost no effort, he pushed her against the side of a building and leaned into her.

Olivia knew what he intended to do, and fought him, clawing and scratching whatever exposed part of him she could reach. Her feeble efforts would have been comical if the situation weren't so desperate. And suddenly, her attacker's weight lifted from her.

Olivia collapsed to her knees and tried to catch her breath.

Two men were fighting. The man who'd pulled her attacker away slammed his fist into her attacker again and again. The attacker stumbled, but recovered with more speed and agility than she'd thought someone of his size could possess. He spun around, a knife in his hand gleaming in the moonlight.

Olivia hadn't seen her rescuer reach for a weapon, but he, too, held a knife. With lightning speed, he slashed his blade through the air and grabbed the attacker's right hand, causing his knife to fall to the wooden planks. Her champion slashed out again, and she heard a loud groan.

She knew her attacker had been wounded a second time because he staggered behind a large barrel stacked along the buildings.

Her defender picked up the second knife and lunged forward, then darted to the side when the injured man picked up the barrel and heaved it toward him. Her rescuer recovered quickly and swung out with the knife; her assailant turned and ran.

Olivia moaned a weak cry of relief.

"Are you all right?" he asked.

"Yes. I'm fine."

Strong arms held her, then lifted her off the ground. Olivia looked up and stared into Damien's face.

The breath caught in her throat, and she pushed away from him. He let her go.

"What the hell are you doing down here alone?" he bellowed, his voice loud and angry. "Don't you know not to come here after dark?"

"I had work to do," Olivia answered, her legs trembling beneath her, but she refused to let him see how frightened she still was. "A shipping company doesn't run itself, you know."

"No wonder your father set up his will like he did. The sooner you can worry about guest lists for afternoon teas instead of shipping cargoes the better."

"How dare you!"

Damien closed the gap between them until he loomed over her. "I dare because it's my right."

"It will never be your right to tell me where to go and what to do."

"Your father gave me that right four years ago."

"No! My father gave that privilege to a man he once admired. And only because he thought to protect me. You, sir, are a usurper who is taking advantage of the good my father thought to do."

Olivia felt him stiffen before her and thought her words had made an impact. Until he spoke.

"Be that as it may, Olivia, the facts remain. You are still my responsibility and I don't want you to come down here again."

Olivia clenched her hands into fists to keep from hitting him. "Where I go is no longer your concern, my lord."

With her chin high and her back rigid, she turned and walked away from him for the second time since he'd come back.

This time it was easier.

Chapter 8

Damien crept through the shadows in an alley behind Pellingsworth Shipping and watched as two men scaled down the rope ladder on the side of the *Conquest* and dropped into a waiting dinghy. He hadn't seen them climb aboard, nor did he know what they'd done while they were there, but he knew that whatever it was, it wasn't good.

It had been three days since Olivia had been attacked. He'd come down each night to watch, but nothing had happened since. Except that Olivia still had come to the office twice despite his order.

His temper raged when he thought of how she'd so blatantly ignored his warnings. He knew her stubbornness was what motivated her. That and her pride. He knew she had no intention of giving in to him. Of submitting to him in any way. At least she hadn't come alone tonight, but had been smart enough to bring her man, Chivers.

Damien moved his thoughts from Olivia back to the two men tying the dinghy to the wharf and climbing onto the walkway. He wrapped his fingers around the knife in his pocket and waited for them to come closer.

One of the men was tall and bulky, his weight as much muscle as fat. He walked with a lumbering gait that made him appear clumsy. The other was short and squatty. He sported a scraggy red beard and had a black knit hat pulled low on his head.

Damien evaluated the two and thought the shorter man looked the more dangerous. He wore a patch over one eye, and the way he carried himself said he was a man used to fighting battles.

Damien rubbed away a pain in his leg and waited as they approached. When they were near enough, he stepped out from the shadows between the two buildings and stood in front of them, blocking their paths.

"Good evening, mates. I was wondering if you'd like to explain what you were doing aboard the *Conquest*?"

Both men pulled knives from their pockets and slashed the blades through the air. Damien had anticipated their attack. If he were to survive, one of the men would have to die. He didn't much care which one. He needed answers and only needed one of them alive to give them to him.

The two men separated and surrounded him. Damien moved so he could see them both. He couldn't afford to let this go on too long. He didn't have the stamina he'd had before the fire and had to make short work of them if he wanted to live.

The shorter man lunged forward, and Damien ducked out of his way. In a quick move, Damien spun around and brought his knife upward. The blade caught the taller man on the arm and he growled a loud curse.

Damien swiped his blade through the air again, and the shorter man attacked a second time. Damien moved with the instincts he'd developed living the last years in ports much more deadly than London's. He darted to the left and shoved his knife upward. He struck the taller of the two beneath the ribs and the man doubled over. Blood gurgled deep in his throat as he fell lifeless at Damien's feet.

Before Damien could pull the knife from the first man's gut, the second man arched his blade through the air. Damien felt a hot, burning pain run across his waist at his back. He sucked in a painful breath and spun around to face his attacker.

This assailant was smaller, but his tactics were more aggressive. He circled Damien as though he'd figured out Damien's legs were weak and thrust out the knife from every direction. Damien parried the thrusts, his aim sure enough to keep most of the attacks at bay.

Damien noticed the shorter man kept his head at an angle, his sightless right eye a hindrance. Damien moved to the right and the man turned his body to keep Damien in view. Damien moved more, and the man turned faster. When Damien was out of the man's line of sight, he charged forward. He came up behind the man and wrapped his arm around his neck.

The man struggled, thrusting his elbow back and hitting Damien on the side where he'd been injured. Damien sucked in a hard breath. His shirt clung to him, wet and warm with his blood. He tried to keep his hold but was engulfed by white-hot shards of pain. It took every ounce of his strength to keep from going down. But before he could gain control of the man, the attacker raised his foot and brought it back against Damien's leg.

Damien doubled over as the agony of a thousand fiery saber strikes consumed him. His arm fell from around the man's chest. Damien's knife dropped to the boards with a dull thud, and his legs gave out from beneath him. He had nothing with which to protect himself and knew he was powerless to stop the man from killing him.

Damien rolled to the side, blindly reaching out to find anything with which to arm himself. The man sprang toward him, and Damien rolled farther, trying to ignore the throbbing that ripped through him. The man raised his knife, then stopped short when a voice bellowed from behind them.

"Hey! What's going on there?"

Damien rolled to the edge of the walkway nearest the water, desperate to escape the man trying to kill him.

The short man with the patch pulled away. With an angry grunt, he turned and ran in the opposite direction. Damien dropped silently into the cold, murky water.

"Where'd they go?" a voice asked while Damien tried to keep his head above water without making any noise. He wanted to pass out from the wound at his side, but instead, took huge gulps of air and prayed he wouldn't lose consciousness and sink to the bottom of the sea.

"One ran down that way," another voice said.

"I thought there were two of them."

"There were. Here he is. He's dead."

Damien stayed in the cold, frigid water until the two sailors left to get the authorities. It wasn't that anyone cared what had happened to the man, or that they'd search for the man who'd killed him. Deaths were all too common at the docks. The men who died were not worth worrying about. But the body did have to be removed, after all.

Damien waited until all was quiet, then stretched his left arm out in front of him. He needed to put distance between himself and the man he'd murdered. His right side burned like a white-hot poker was still embedded in his flesh, and Damien felt a strange lightheadedness with which he was all too familiar. He knew he had to get somewhere for help before he was no longer able.

⁓

"My lady?"

Olivia bolted upright in bed and stared at her maid. It was the middle of the night and Tilly stood at the side of the bed, clutching the front of her robe together with one hand and holding a lamp high in the air with the other.

"What's wrong, Tilly?"

Olivia blinked her eyes as she struggled to focus, then took a deep breath, trying to keep her heart from thundering out of her chest.

"It's Chivers, ma'am. He sent me to fetch you."

Olivia threw the covers back and took the wrap Tilly held out for her. "Did he say what was wrong?"

"No. He just said to have you come."

Olivia pulled the tie around her waist and followed Tilly down the hall. "Where is he?"

"In your father's room, ma'am. He asked for you to wait outside."

Tilly knocked on the bedroom door, and they waited in the hall until Chivers came out. He quickly closed the door behind him, and he and Tilly shared a look before the maid scurried away.

"What's wrong, Chivers?"

"It's . . . Lord Iversley, ma'am. He's come with information concerning the *Conquest*."

"At this hour?"

Chivers nodded. "He says it's imperative you send a message to the captain to tell him something's wrong aboard ship."

"What is it?"

"He doesn't know. He saw two men leaving the *Conquest* in the night and knows they were up to no good."

Olivia looked at the door Chivers was guarding, then stepped forward. Chivers didn't move. "Where's Lord Iversley?"

Chivers hesitated, then answered. "He's inside, ma'am."

"Let me pass."

"I'm afraid Lord Iversley gave express orders to keep you out."

Olivia fisted her hands at her sides, but it was fear racing through her body more than anger. "I'll not be told which rooms I can enter in my own home. Please, stand aside."

Chivers released a heavy sigh. "He's been hurt, my lady."

Every nerve in Olivia's body went numb. "How badly?"

"Bad enough."

"Have you sent for the doctor?"

"Lord Iversley refuses to have a doctor. I've sent Johns for some bandages and a needle and thread. I've had a little experience sewing, and Lord Iversley assures me he'll be fine."

"Step aside, Chivers."

"But Lord Iversley said—"

"I don't care what Lord Iversley said. This is still my house, and I'll decide which rooms I can and cannot enter. Not Lord Iversley."

"Yes, my lady. I told the earl as much."

"And he said?"

"I couldn't repeat what the earl said, my lady."

"I imagine not."

Olivia took a step forward, and Chivers reached for the door. He stopped with his hand on the knob. "Please be warned. The earl's not in the best of spirits."

"He's been no other way since he's come back," Olivia said, as she stepped past him.

"Yes, my lady."

Chivers rushed to open the door, and Olivia marched into the room. She stopped when she saw Damien lying on the bed.

He was stretched out on his side, facing her. His eyes were closed and a sheet covered him to his shoulders. A deep circle of blood had seeped through the white linen.

She took another step into the room. His eyes snapped open, and his hand reached out as if searching for a weapon. With reflexes so swift they startled her, Damien swung his feet over the side of the bed and sat up.

His torso was naked from the waist up, his skin a deep bronze, his chest matted with dark hair. He still wore his breeches, and Olivia was thankful for that, but it wouldn't have mattered. All she could focus on was his broad chest and muscled shoulders.

A sheen of perspiration covered his entire body, and the taut look on his pain-ravaged face tore at her heart. She stepped closer to him, even though the fury she saw in his eyes told her she wasn't welcome.

"Damien?"

"Get the bloody hell out of here!"

Olivia wasn't cowed by his temper. She'd been warned. She was shocked, though, by the vehemence in his voice, the fierceness of his words.

"Chivers! Get her the hell out of here!"

Olivia took another step closer. "Chivers is still in my employ, my lord. He takes his orders from me."

Damien flew to his feet, then reached out a hand to support himself. He nearly crashed to the floor before he regained his balance. Olivia rushed forward, as did Chivers, but Damien's harsh demand stopped them both.

"Leave me alone!"

Olivia watched in helplessness as he held them off with an outstretched hand and a glaring look. His knees seemed to buckle beneath him, and the arm he had braced against the bedside table trembled in weakness.

"You're hurt, Damien. Let us take care of you."

"No! Get out. Chivers will take care of me."

Blood seeped from the wound at his side while perspiration shone on his body. His face grew paler by the minute.

"Damien, let me—"

"Olivia," he breathed in a rush as his legs buckled beneath him. "Get—"

He lost his balance, his body staggering before it sank downward.

"Damien!"

Olivia and Chivers rushed forward, supporting Damien on either side. They sat him on the bed, then laid him down. Olivia reached for a cloth while Chivers turned him to his side.

She hadn't glimpsed his back until now. Hadn't seen what he was trying so desperately to hide from her. The horrifying scars ran diagonally from shoulder to waist and lower, pulling and knotting his flesh in grotesque designs.

Her stomach rolled. Not at the horrendous sight before her, even though it was gruesome. But at the pain he must have endured. At the agony he must have suffered.

Tears welled in her eyes, and she bit her lower lip to hold them back.

"You've seen it. Now get the hell out."

His voice jolted through her like the shock of a needle pricking her skin. It was all she could do to keep her voice even.

"Yes, I've seen it. Now get ready to have another mark added to your flesh. This wound needs tending."

Olivia reached for a wet cloth and wiped the blood from Damien's side. His muscles were hard beneath her hand, not the corded hardness one associated with strength and power, but the tight, bulging tenseness that came with pain and humiliation.

Johns rushed into the room carrying a bucket of water, a tray filled with salves and bandages, and a needle and thread. Chivers told Olivia where to press, where to wash, and what to hand him next, while Johns held a bright lamp high so Chivers could sew the jagged flesh together. Damien lay with his face turned from her, his left side shielded, his eyes averted.

Olivia hurt so much she thought she might die.

She let herself look again at the horrible scars marking his beautiful body while tears flowed silently down her cheeks. The wall she'd erected to protect herself from his anger and resentment cracked, then crumbled.

This was the result of the fire she thought had killed him. This is what he'd wanted to keep hidden from her. In her attempt to protect him, she'd caused him to suffer.

Chivers finished sewing the long gash at Damien's waist and when he was done, she pulled the fresh covers over him and drew the drapes to keep out the early morning sun.

His eyes were closed. Whether it was because he slept, or because he refused to look at her again, she didn't know. She sent Johns to warn Captain Durham that there was something wrong aboard the *Conquest*, then she gathered the soiled linens and quietly left the room.

Her resolve to keep from breaking down before she reached the solitude of her own room weakened with each step she took. The pain pressing against her chest was almost more than she could bear, and by the time she closed the door behind her, she wasn't sure she could survive under the weight of such guilt and hopelessness.

Chapter 9

Damien squeezed his eyes shut tight and sucked in a harsh breath. He turned in the strange bed and felt a renewed stabbing of pain, then lay still and quiet. Bloody hell, but he hurt. He felt worse than he did after a night of drinking and brawling.

His mind worked feverishly to recall what he'd done last night to make him hurt so. Then reality dawned, and he realized he wasn't in the Indies any longer, but in London. And he remembered the fight.

He prayed he'd feel the gentle rocking of a ship on the ocean and find himself aboard the *Angel's Wings*, but knew he wouldn't. He wasn't sure why he'd come here except . . . Now he wished he hadn't.

He lay still and silent, refusing to awaken fully. He heard her soft breathing and smelled the sweet lilacs and roses that she'd always used to wash her hair. Her presence was so overpowering he could imagine her in his mind's eye. He knew if he looked, he'd find her there.

He slowly turned his head and opened his eyes.

She sat curled in the chair, her feet tucked beneath her and a quilt thrown over her. Her mahogany hair hung down around her shoulders and curled softly at the ends. Her thick, dark lashes rested daintily against her cheeks. She was so beautiful the sight of her made him ache.

Her lips were full and dark, her nose small and upturned, and her skin soft and clear. Everything about her was perfection, a perfection he remembered loving all those years ago when the world was easy and carefree and he thought he must be the luckiest man alive. A time before his world had crashed down around him and he'd lost everything he held dear.

He didn't want her to wake up. Didn't want to see the worry he'd seen on her face last night, the concern he'd glimpsed in her eyes. He only wanted to remember her betrayal. The world she'd stolen from him. The life he vowed to get back.

She moved. First, only her arm stretched out lazily from beneath the cover. Then her hand pushed the cover down, exposing her white eyelet gown, and the pale peach satin wrap she wore over it.

Her head moved and she winced, as if she'd lain too long in one spot and felt some discomfort. She sighed. Then she opened her eyes and her gaze locked with his. And he saw not pity exactly . . . but regret in her eyes.

She'd seen him. Not all of him, not the worst of him, but enough to know he was no longer whole.

For a long time, neither of them spoke. There really was nothing more to say. Nothing that wouldn't embarrass either of them. So they said nothing. Until the silence was too unbearable.

"Did you send word to the *Conquest*?"

"Yes. The men you fought had cut the ties that fastened the cargo in the hold. The first rough seas would have tossed the crates around like matchsticks. The cargo would have been a complete loss."

Damien stared up at the ceiling, thankful his left side was turned away from her. "Why haven't you gone to anyone for help? These problems didn't just start."

She pushed her feet out from beneath her and sat up in her chair, her back rigid and straight. "I have gone for help. I alerted the port authorities and hired investigators to look into what's happening. But they haven't been able to discover anything that might lead to who is responsible. I don't know what more you expect me to do."

"Don't you? How long do you think it will be before someone is seriously injured?"

With her chin high, she turned her face away from him.

Damien blew out a harsh breath. "Do you have any idea who might be behind your problems?"

She shook her head.

"Have you received any threats? Anything in writing?"

"No. Until recently, everything that's happened has been more an inconvenience than anything. Costly, but nothing more than destructive pranks. And nothing serious. Until the fire last week and the—" She stopped.

"The attack the other night," he finished for her.

"We can't be sure that was even related. It could have just been coincidence."

Damien didn't answer her, and as if his silence said more than words, she rose from her chair and walked away from him. He watched her cross the room.

He wanted her to go away and leave him. Instead, she opened the drapes to let in the early morning sunshine, then pulled the rope to ring for a servant. A few minutes later, Tilly opened the door.

Olivia turned to issue orders. "Tell Chivers Lord Iversley is awake. Then have Cook prepare a tray."

"Yes, my lady."

Tilly left and Olivia came back to the bed and straightened the covers.

Damien bit back a curse. He didn't want her here. He didn't want her fussing over him, staring at him. Seeing him for what he really was. What he'd become. There'd be time enough for that after they were married, but he wasn't ready yet to see the shock on her face, the revulsion. Or God help him, the pity.

It had been a mistake to come here, but he'd had no choice. If the attack the other night was any indication of the danger she was in, she'd need someone close by to protect her.

She moved to the other side of the bed and poured a glass of water. He fisted his hands at his sides and turned away from her. He heard her sigh of frustration at his refusal of her help, then a heavy thud as the glass hit the top of the bedside table.

"Chivers will be here soon," she said. Her voice held a tinge of anger and her movements conveyed her annoyance as she straightened the covers on the other side of the bed. "You'll be more comfortable after we've changed the bandage."

"I want to be alone, Olivia."

"I'm sure you do." She stopped rearranging the covers and glared at him. "Why did you come here?"

"To tell you about the two men I saw leaving the *Conquest*."

"You could have sent a message."

Damien's temper warmed. "I couldn't risk someone recognizing me."

"Why?"

"Because whoever is doing this thinks you are completely vulnerable. That you have no one to protect you. The minute the assailant finds out you're not alone, he might change his tactics."

"And become more dangerous?"

"Yes."

"But why did you fight them on your own? You could have been killed."

"I wasn't."

"But you could have been. You should have—"

"Enough, woman!"

A wave of pain hit him. Damien clutched his side and waited until the spikes of pain lessened. He closed his eyes and tried to look as if he was falling asleep in hopes she'd go away. Didn't she know how her nearness affected him? He wasn't fit enough to battle her right now.

When he'd put his cold demeanor safely back in place, he opened his eyes and looked at her. "Have you set a date for our wedding?"

He almost laughed at the speed with which her hostile gaze darted to his. At the strained tone to her voice.

"There will be no date to set. There will be no wedding between us."

"But there will, Olivia. The sooner you accustom yourself to it, the easier our existence together will be."

"There will never be an . . . *existence* between us. You have changed too much."

"Because of you! You are the one who caused the change in me. And you will live with the results."

He watched her face pale from his brutal accusations and heard her suck in a shaky breath. His intended barbs had hurt her, and he wasn't sorry. The anger and thoughts of revenge he'd lived with for nearly four years came back with a raging force. "Now leave me alone."

She recovered enough to respond with more hostility than he thought she could muster. "You forget, sir. This is my home. I'll not be ordered out of any part of it."

Damien was still glaring at her when Chivers came with fresh bandages. Every muscle in his body tensed. It was one thing for her to see him in the darkness when his mind was foggy with pain. Another matter for her to see his disfigured body in the bright morning sunshine. He couldn't bear it.

"Leave," he said, making sure his voice was harsh and his word a command.

"I saw the damage last night. There's no need to—"

"Fine! Then stay. Take a good look at what I've become."

Damien saw her blanch, saw her recoil from his attack. He hoped he'd been cruel enough that she'd run from the room in tears. The old Olivia would have. The young, naïve woman-child he'd left nearly four years ago. The woman he'd come home to didn't back down so easily. He saw her lift her chin in defiance and with an angry snap to her movements, she reached for the salve on the tray Chivers had brought.

"Hold Lord Iversley still," she ordered Chivers. "This is bound to hurt. And we wouldn't want him to tear his stitches open."

Damien prepared to receive the brunt of her anger. He'd goaded her, insulted and antagonized her enough to be on the receiving end of her resentment. He was ready for her abuse. Welcomed it. He'd add this to the other transgressions he'd compiled against her. The long list of sins he didn't want to forgive . . . or forget.

Chivers lifted Damien's shoulders and steadied him. He removed his shirt first, then helped him move to his stomach with his arms bent at the elbows. Damien's palms were flat against the mattress at either side of his head and he fisted his hands into tight balls. Sunlight poured through the open windows, exposing every ugly inch of him. He expected to hear her gasp with revulsion when she saw him. Instead, she removed the bandage at his side, her touch soft and gentle, then cleaned the wound with such tenderness he hardly realized she was caring for him.

"You did an excellent job stitching Lord Iversley," she said to Chivers, her fingers moving over him with rapid attentiveness. "I'm sure in time the mark will be barely more than a scratch."

"Thank you, ma'am," Chivers answered.

She rinsed her cloth, cleaned the wound, dried it, then put on more salve before she covered it again with a clean bandage. He swore her fingers lingered on his flesh several moments after the bandage was in place, but he must have been mistaken. It probably took every ounce of her courage just to look at him, let alone touch him.

She gathered up what she'd used and put it on the bedside table.

Damien watched from the corner of his eye and noticed that her hands trembled when she set down the jar of salve. Her cheeks had a flush much more pronounced than could be explained by the exertion it took to change his bandage. She stepped back from the bed, nervously wiping her palms against the front of her wrap. When she spoke, her voice contained a certain breathless quality.

"Chivers will help you with anything you need. After I've dressed, I'll return with your breakfast, and we'll discuss at length how quickly you can be gone from here."

"You'd kick an injured man out onto the streets?"

"If *you* are that injured man, yes. I have no intention of letting you get too comfortable here."

"You forget I used to live here, Olivia. And, according to the stipulations in your father's will, will probably live here again when we're married."

He heard her breath catch before she answered.

"The chances of you living here ever again are so negligible they aren't even worth considering. I would encourage you to recover quickly, my lord. My hospitality will last only so long."

"I'll anticipate your return, then," Damien said, dropping back against the mattress. "I always look forward to anything you have to say."

He heard the sharp swish of her clothing as she turned away from him. The door closed with a firm thud. Thick tension remained long after she left.

Damien lay without moving, waiting for the hostility of her presence to calm. Chivers finally broke the spell she'd left in her wake.

"Would you care to rest for a moment before we begin? I think a shave might be in order if you feel up to it."

"Yes, Chivers. Thank you."

Chivers silently moved toward the door, and Damien stopped him before he'd turned the handle. "Chivers, would you consider it a traitorous request if I asked you to send someone to the *Angel's Wings* to gather my belongings?"

Chivers hesitated a moment. "Everything, my lord?"

"Yes, Chivers. Everything."

Chivers pondered longer. "No, sir. I would consider it a controversial means to a necessary end. Having you in such close proximity may make her choice easier."

Chivers kept his gaze focused on Damien's. Damien thought he'd noticed a hint of warning in Chivers's tone, then realized . . .

Chivers hadn't indicated whether having Damien so close would tilt the scales in his favor . . . or against it.

Chapter 10

Olivia threw down her pen and shoved her chair back from the desk where she'd been working since leaving Damien's bedside hours earlier. Damn him. Damn him.

Damn him!

She walked to the large bay window that overlooked the well-tended garden and tried to soak in the beauty of the flower beds in full bloom. She needed something to soothe her, to ease the hurt. Something that would soften the knowledge that he didn't love her. That he only wanted to marry her because of the ships. While she . . .

A small stabbing pain clenched inside her breast. God help her, she still loved him with every beat of her heart.

She pounded her fist against the window frame. How could she stop loving someone she'd loved her whole life? If only he'd leave. If only she hadn't taken care of him. Hadn't touched him. The minute she'd placed her fingers against his warm flesh, sparks of emotion nearly took her to her knees. Why hadn't the feel of him beneath her fingertips been as heartless as the words he spoke, or as cold as the glare in his eyes?

Instead, he set her on fire. From the tips of her fingers to deep in her belly. She'd been jarred by emotions she swore she'd never feel for him again. And hurt by the resentment she saw in his eyes.

Olivia wiped away a renegade tear that dared to spill from her eye, then stiffened at the soft knock on the door.

"Excuse me, ma'am. The Earl of Pellingsworth is here to see you. Are you receiving?"

Olivia felt the air leave her chest. *The Earl of Pellingsworth.* It was a title reserved for her father. A title he'd held proudly, but was now given to her uncle, her father's younger brother.

"Yes, Chivers. Show the earl to the blue salon. I'll be there momentarily."

"Yes, ma'am."

Olivia waited until the door closed behind Chivers, then took a linen handkerchief and dabbed at her eyes. It would do no good to let her uncle think she was a simpering female. And she couldn't let him know the real reason for her tears. She couldn't reveal Damien's miraculous return from the dead to anyone. Not until they knew who was sabotaging the ships. Damien was right about that. She did need his help. Even though he was the last person on earth to whom she wanted to turn.

Olivia smoothed her skirts, then walked down the hallway. She'd always been fond of her uncle and was happy that someone who was so much like her father had inherited the title after her father had died. Unfortunately, when her uncle died, that title as well as the entailed properties would pass on to her uncle's eldest son, Richard, who was, without a doubt, one of the most repulsive people she'd ever met. She didn't want to imagine what the Pellingsworth name would stand for when Richard assumed the title.

She suddenly wished her uncle a very long, healthy life.

Olivia shook her head in chagrin at the thought as she stepped through the open door and placed a smile on her face in greeting.

"Lord Pellingsworth. How nice of you to drop by."

Her uncle popped up from the sofa, his thick graying hair sticking out on either side of his head as if he'd been caught in a windstorm, even though the day outside was sunny and calm.

He rushed forward to take her hands, and Olivia gave his a gentle squeeze.

"Olivia, my dear. I apologize for being so remiss in coming to see you. It's been far too long. Your father would scold me for neglecting my duty."

"Nonsense, uncle. I've been perfectly fine." She pointed to the chair next to the sofa. "Won't you sit down?"

"Thank you."

Her uncle took his seat as a downstairs maid brought in tea and a tray of cakes. Olivia poured, then handed him a cup of tea with cream and no sugar as she remembered he liked. He took one swallow, then set the cup and saucer on the table and scooted forward in his chair.

"I'll get right to the point, Olivia. There's no sense delaying the purpose of my visit over small talk."

Olivia lifted her startled gaze to his and noticed for the first time that her uncle seemed a bit agitated. As if he were on a mission, and the mission was not a pleasant one. "Is something wrong, my lord?"

"I'm afraid there is, my dear. I don't want you to think I'm interfering, nor do I want you to think I'm trying to tell you what to do. But I can't just sit back without coming to your aid."

Olivia knew what was coming and didn't want to hear it. "My lord, please don't—"

He held up his hand to stop her. "I've just learned of the problems you've had with your ships and cargoes. Oh, Olivia. I am so sorry, but I was afraid of this."

"Afraid of what?"

"Afraid that once certain men your father considered competition realized a mere woman was running Pellingsworth Shipping, some of them would take advantage of your helplessness."

Olivia wanted to smile. Her father had been the only one who considered her more than qualified to run Pellingsworth Shipping. "I'm hardly helpless, uncle."

"You may not think yourself so, but I'm afraid that isn't how you appear. Just consider your situation: you're young, you're inexperienced in the shipping world, you're—"

"I'm not inexperienced," Olivia said in defense. "I worked with Father in the shipping office nearly every day of my life."

"That may be so, but you could have worked with your father for several lifetimes and certain members of my set would still consider you incapable of running a shipping company. You're a woman, Olivia."

Her uncle said the last sentence as if being female were a regrettable condition.

"Be that as it may, my lord, Pellingsworth Shipping has seen a steady increase in shipping contracts over the last four years, as well as a commendable income."

"But not over the last twelve months, if rumors of the accidents and unfortunate problems are accurate. It's impossible to accrue the same profits while paying for the repairs and damaged cargo you've been forced to cover. And next year will be worse."

"You are assuming that the men I have hired won't discover who is behind the mishaps."

Her uncle shook his head. "Whoever is behind your mishaps won't give up, Olivia."

"And neither will I."

Something inside her forced her to show her strength. It was as if she needed to prove to her uncle that she could manage this latest onslaught of tragedies.

"But I don't want to see you in danger, Olivia. I would never forgive myself if something happened to you. I would always think that if I had stepped in, I could have alleviated any risk to your person, as well as to Pellingsworth Shipping."

"And what do you suggest doing, that I'm not already doing, to eliminate the dangers?" she asked, trying to keep her temper in check.

"You could get rid of the shipping company."

Olivia couldn't hide her shock. "You expect me to sell my father's shipping company?"

"It's the only way, Olivia. The accidents are only going to get worse, the disasters more catastrophic, until someone gets seriously injured or killed."

She clenched her hands in her lap. She couldn't sell Pellingsworth Shipping. She wouldn't even consider it.

"No."

"It would be better to sell it than lose it. How long do you think you can run at a loss? How long before an entire ship and cargo is destroyed? How long before lives are lost?"

Olivia abruptly rose from the sofa. "Surely you aren't implying it will go that far?"

"It will, Olivia. You know it will."

Olivia looked at her uncle. "And to whom do you suggest I sell my ships?"

"To me. I will give you a more than generous price for them. By selling the shipping business to me, it will always remain Pellingsworth Shipping."

A surge of anger raced through her, and she sucked in a shaky breath. "No, my lord. I won't sell the ships. Ever."

"At least think about it, my dear. You don't have to make a decision now, but at least promise me you'll think about it. As I said, I couldn't live with myself if something happened to you."

Olivia shook her head, then gave in because she knew he wouldn't give up until she did. "I'll think about it, but I can guarantee you the answer will remain the same."

Lord Pellingsworth rose from his chair and wiped his palms against his jacket. "I know how hard it would be to sell the ships. But selling would be better than having the deaths of innocent men on your conscience. Think over my offer, Olivia. It will be best for all concerned."

Olivia watched her uncle leave the room. When she was alone, she walked to the sofa and sat with her hands clenched in her lap. *Sell Pellingsworth Shipping?* She couldn't imagine it. She couldn't imagine giving up something her father had spent his life building.

But that's exactly what might happen if she didn't marry Damien. Perhaps that's why her father had put the stipulation in his will. He knew how difficult it would be for a woman to venture into a world where men dominated. He understood better than she the problems that would arise. So he'd boxed her into a corner where she had no choice but to enter into a loveless marriage—for Damien would never love her. Or remain single four more weeks and let Damien inherit everything by default.

Olivia ground her teeth in frustration. She may not like the choices before her, but she had choices. And she would make the choice she could live with.

And marriage to Damien wasn't one of her options.

Olivia sat curled up in a huge floral wingback chair by her bedroom window and listened to the mantel clock downstairs chime four. The moon peeked through her window, casting bright rays of light that gave a glow to the room almost as if it were day. In the corner of the room sat her bed, which was hidden in the shadows. Olivia had lain in the darkness as long as she could stand the isolation, then moved into the light where she wouldn't feel so lonely.

Olivia leaned her head against the side of the wingbackchair and closed her eyes. Damien's wound was healing quickly, and he'd left earlier tonight. Tilly had let that bit of information slip when she was helping Olivia get ready for bed. But he'd returned. She'd seen him from her bedroom window. He'd sneaked in the back through the garden gate a little after three.

She didn't know where he'd gone or why, but when he'd returned, he had had a bundle in one hand—clothes perhaps, and a bottle in the other. His gait had been unsteady, and Olivia thought he might have been drunk, but she couldn't be sure. His gait was always uneven now, as if he'd sustained an injury to his legs. But his staggering this evening could also have been blamed on the bottle in his hand. She thought drunkenness more likely the cause because he'd bumped into the walls as he'd climbed the stairs. He'd entered his bedroom and tripped over something that crashed to the floor.

Now, all she heard were the soft snoring sounds of a man deep in exhausted slumber.

Olivia sat forward in her chair. A noise. Low and eerily haunting.

She rose from her chair and put on her slippers and robe. The moon was bright enough that she didn't need a lamp, and she stood in the center of the room and listened. She heard it again. From outside her room. Down the hall.

Damien.

She rushed from the room and ran down the carpeted hallway. She heard it again. A low, keening sound, the cry a wounded animal made when caught in a trap. And the moan grew louder.

Olivia opened Damien's door and stepped across the room. Silvery beams of moonlight shone down on the bed. His covers were wadded in a crumpled heap from the thrashing of his arms and legs. A heavy film of perspiration covered his forehead and cheeks, and the tortured expression on his face distorted his features. It was the intensity with which he fought his unknown demons that frightened her. The fierceness with which he battled horrors only he could see that was the most terrifying to watch.

"Get it . . . off me! Off! Oh, God!"

Olivia leaned over him, not knowing whether to touch him or not. It wasn't that he was naked as some men were when they slept. He was completely covered, a white nightshirt covering his torso and dark satin pants on the bottom. What gave her pause was the viciousness he represented, the danger. Even though he was submerged in a deep, dark sleep, she knew his dreams were deadly as he fought his demons.

"Damien?"

"Oh, no . . . No more . . . No more . . ."

Olivia extended her hand and touched his shoulder. "Damien, stop. You're going to tear open your—"

With lightning speed he reached out and grabbed her. He clamped his hand around her arm and pulled her toward him. Olivia flew through the air, over Damien's body, and down on the mattress beside him as if she weighed little or nothing. She landed on her back, and before she could yell for help, he had his fingers around her neck and was squeezing.

"Damien." She choked out the word but knew he hadn't heard her.

She struggled, pulling at his hands. She scratched and dug her fingernails into his flesh, praying he'd wake up enough to realize what he was doing. His eyes were open but she knew he wasn't seeing her.

"Damien!"

His gaze cleared, and with the same speed as he'd attacked her, he pulled off her.

"Olivia?"

She rolled away from him, gasping for air.

"Olivia! Bloody hell."

She rolled into a tight ball on the edge of the bed and hugged her arms around her middle. She didn't think he'd intentionally hurt her. But she was frightened.

Her head pounded as she struggled to breathe, and her heart thundered in her breast. She moved farther away from him.

"Are you all right?" He turned her over and looked down on her. His eyes were wide with fear, his breathing harsh and labored. His hands moved over her with frantic urgency. "Are you all right? Did I hurt you?"

"No. I'm fine." She coughed.

He ran his fingers over her face and down her arms. He touched her gently, then brushed her hair back from her face.

"Ah, bloody hell! Do you know what could have happened to you?"

He ran the callused pads of his fingers down her neck, touching the spots where his fingers had clamped against her. He jumped from the bed with only the slightest stumble and rinsed a cloth in the cool basin water. He came back to the bed and laid the cloth over her neck.

There was still a look of panic on his face. "What the hell were you doing in here?"

"You were having a nightmare," Olivia choked out. "I came to wake you."

"Don't *ever* do that again! I could have—"

He rinsed the cloth in the water again and laid it back on her skin. Their gazes locked and held. Neither of them could look away.

"I'm fine, Damien. You just frightened me, that's all."

"You're going to have marks in the morning."

"I'll wear something high that covers them."

His voice grew quiet. Softer. "Why couldn't you have left me alone?"

He stared at her, his breathing still harsh and jagged. Then he leaned over her. His body angled across hers, his hip touching her, burning her. He braced his left arm on the other side of her at her waist, his nearness more disturbing than she could fight.

For just one moment, Olivia was certain Damien no longer remembered the scar that ran the length of his face. For just one moment he'd forgotten his vow not to love her. For just one moment she forgot he would never love her. And that kissing him would be the biggest mistake of her life.

He lowered his head, and it was too late.

His lips pressed against her with a desperation that stole her breath. He wanted her. She could feel it in the pressure of his mouth against hers, in the way his lips moved over hers.

Again and again he kissed her, long, hard, deep. Until his breathing was a part of her. There was no gentleness in his taking of her. None of the refined passion he'd shown her in their youth, but a raw, needy demand that left her weak. Then his mouth opened atop hers, and his tongue entered her mouth.

She was on fire, burning from a desire she'd harbored in desolation. She wanted him. Wanted him with a need that was all-consuming.

Olivia wrapped her arms around his neck and gave in to him. His tongue sought her out, touching, finding. And she welcomed him with every ounce of her being. She needed him. Couldn't get enough of him.

Low, earthy moans echoed in the heated darkness, hers, his, their frantic breaths a part of each other. She'd never known such desire.

She reached for him, holding, touching, rubbing her hands over his shoulders, down his arms. She couldn't get close enough to him, and with each kiss of desperation, she knew he battled the same desires that raged through her.

His hands touched her breasts as his mouth drank from her lips. Olivia arched into him, the fiery need inside her building until it was nearly out of control. And he kissed her again. And again. His tongue working her to a mindless frenzy. She held on to him, fearful she might drop from the frightening height where they'd flown together.

She wrapped her arms around his broad shoulders then moved her hands up and down his body. He was so strong, his muscles hard and knotted beneath her fingers. She moved her hands over the corded ripples across his shoulders, then cupped the sides of his face in her palms and—

He pulled her hands away from him and pinned them to her sides. "Don't touch me. Not there."

Olivia felt the air leave her body. The realization of what they were doing—of what she'd allowed him to do, filled her with a deep-seated anger. She was such a fool.

"Please, get off me."

He didn't move. "Why? So you can pretend this didn't happen? So you can pretend you don't want me?"

"I don't want you."

She gasped for air. Her chest heaved as she struggled to breathe. What had she done? She was in shameful disarray, her gown up around her thighs and her wrap gaping to reveal her exposed breasts. She fought to free her hands from his grasp, then pushed her gown down as she rolled away from him and slid from the bed. The moment her feet hit the floor, she pulled her wrapper closed and covered herself. When there was some semblance to the way she looked, she walked silently to the door.

"It's no use, Olivia. You enjoyed what just happened."

Her hand froze on the door handle and the blood roared in her head. "Not as much as I regret what just happened. Not nearly as much as I regret it." And she opened the door, stepped out into the hallway and left him.

The hallway was dimly lit, the carpet thick beneath her slippers. Her heart thundered with each step away from his room. By the time she was back in her own room, she felt as if the weight of the world had been placed on her shoulders. As if the painful heaviness pressing against her breast had grown ten times.

And she knew she would remember the kiss they'd shared until her dying day.

Chapter 11

"The Earl of Rotham to see you, my lady."

Olivia looked up from the papers she was working on and glanced at Chivers standing in the open doorway to her study.

"Are you receiving?"

Olivia laid down her pen, then shoved her chair back from the desk. "Yes, Chivers. I'll see the earl in the morning room. Please see that tea is served."

"Yes, my lady."

Chivers left the room and Olivia rose to her feet. Even though Rolland didn't know it, she was eager to see him. Her whole future seemed at risk, and she thought Rolland held the key. Especially after the way Damien had kissed her the other night. She needed Rolland's predictability so she could erase Damien's demanding turbulence.

Olivia followed Chivers down the hall, trying to forget the memory of Damien holding her, of his lips moving atop hers, of his tongue invading her mouth. For two days, she'd done everything in her power to avoid him. Everything to keep herself hidden. And during the daylight, she'd been successful. It was during the long, sleepless nights that his memory haunted her, that she lay awake, thinking of him, listening for him. And when she could take no more, she'd get up and sit in the dark and watch for him to come home.

She didn't know where he went or whom he saw, but he left each night after dark and didn't return until the wee hours of the morning.

Only once since that night had she heard noise coming from the room down the hall, and knew he was in the throes of another nightmare. But she didn't go to him again. She didn't want to risk a repeat of the other night.

Olivia's cheeks fanned with heat as she walked through the door to where Rolland waited for her. The concerned look on his face when he turned to her forced her to forget Damien's kisses, but her fingers flitted across the fluted chiffon she wore at her neck, arranged just high enough to cover the ugly bruising.

"Olivia. Are you all right?"

The Marquess of Rotham rushed across the room and clasped her hands in his.

"Yes, Rolland. I'm perfectly fine. Is there something wrong?"

Rotham led her to a sofa and sat down beside her. He kept her hands clasped in his.

"Why didn't you tell me you'd been attacked the other night?"

Olivia wanted to laugh. She'd nearly forgotten about the attack. So much more had happened since then. So much that was far more monumental than a mere attack. "Because nothing happened. It was just a drunken lecher," she lied, "intent on stealing what little coin I had with me."

"But you could have been hurt."

"I'm fine." She looked down at her hands nestled in his because she couldn't look him in the eyes. "Someone came to my rescue."

"Olivia, I've been far too lenient with you. But this last attack leaves me no choice."

Rolland released her hands and stood, towering over her like an avenging angel. "Olivia, I forbid you to go to the docks unless I go with you."

"You what?"

"You heard me. It's for your own good. I don't want you to go down there again if I don't accompany you. And never after dark."

Olivia was stunned. "And if you aren't available to escort me?"

"Then you will postpone going until I am available."

Olivia tried to stamp down her temper. She took several deep breaths like she'd learned to do over the years. But this time it didn't help.

"I have a business to run," she said through clenched teeth. "I have to go to the docks."

"Olivia, it's not safe."

She couldn't handle this. Not with everything else. "Rolland, please. I don't want to argue."

Lord Rotham sat back down beside her and turned so his knees touched hers. "Neither do I, Olivia. I care for you. You already know that. We've discussed it repeatedly. Just as we've discussed the advantages of a marriage between us."

Rolland took her hands in his and held them.

Olivia let her fingers rest in his, let the cool touch of his palms seep into hers. Then she pulled her hands from his grasp and walked away from him.

"What is it, Olivia? Something's wrong. What is it?"

Olivia knew what she wanted to do, what she *had* to do. She wiped her damp palms against her skirt and slowly turned to face him.

"Could I ask a favor?"

"Of course. Anything." Rolland slowly rose from the cushion and walked toward her. There was a frown on his face, a look of concern. She felt a twinge of guilt, but was far too nervous for it to bother her.

"What do you need, Olivia?" he said, placing his hands on her shoulders.

It was a friendly gesture, a familiar, yet proper gesture that couldn't be mistaken in any manner as being intimate.

He was a tall man, as tall if not even taller than Damien, and as broad. But that is where the similarities ended. Rolland was as fair as

Damien was dark; as straightforward and readable as Damien was closed and mysterious; as easygoing as Damien was explosive. And he offered her everything Damien withheld from her.

"Olivia. What is it?"

Olivia swallowed. "Would you please kiss me?"

Rolland dropped his hands from her shoulders as if she'd burned him, and took a step back.

"What?"

"Would you kiss me?"

Olivia saw the shocked look on his face and stumbled to explain herself. "You've never kissed me—other than a light touch on my forehead when bidding me good night." Olivia twisted her hands in front of her. "You've asked me to marry you, even demanded it," she said with a shaky smile, "but you've never kissed me. Would you kiss me now?"

He stepped closer and smiled. "Of course. It would be my pleasure."

And he kissed her.

His lips were warm and smooth atop hers, his kiss perfect in execution, with just the right blend of heat and emotion. There wasn't a hint of unrestrained passion, but that of a quiet giving, of a sharing of emotions while holding passion in check. And yet, Olivia thought she felt a deepening of desire simmering just beneath the surface. A passion she was sure would develop into something more than friendship. And he kissed her again.

Rolland wrapped his arms around her. He pulled her closer and deepened the kiss. And Olivia gave in to him, kissing him back, shoving Damien far back in her memory and giving Rolland as much as she could. And it was there, a stirring deep in her belly. The awakening of emotions she thought had died when she thought she'd lost Damien. The relief she felt was indescribable. The delight of knowing that physical pleasure would be part of her marriage to Rolland.

He kissed her once more, then lifted his mouth from hers and stared down at her.

"Thank you," she whispered, her breathing rushed, yet controlled.

He ran his fingers down the side of her face and nodded. "Neither of us are under any delusions, Olivia. We have both found the loves of our lives and lost them. I don't expect to find the love I had with Felicity ever again, and I know you don't expect to find what you had with Iversley. But that is not to say that something special will not grow between us. We are already more than comfortable with each other. I am confident in time a strong fondness will develop."

Olivia sadly agreed. She didn't expect a grand passion from her marriage to Rolland. His words forewarned her of that. But she could have something else. She would have happiness. She would have a home. She would have a companion with whom she would always be comfortable. And in time, perhaps even come to love deeply.

And she would have children. The love she needed would come from them. The love she had inside her would be given to them. She would be content.

"I will call for you tonight at eight. Lady Conover is hosting a musicale featuring an evening of Mozart. I know how fond you are of that composer's music."

Olivia smiled again and gave Rolland her hand. He kissed her fingers, then lifted her chin and kissed her gently on the lips.

"We'll talk later," he said and turned to walk out of the room. He stopped before he reached the door. "Oh, I almost forgot. Felicity's aunt, Lady Chandler, and cousin Prudence are in town for a few weeks, and I promised to show them around. Felicity and Prudence were the closest of friends, and we have stayed in touch even after Felicity's death. Would you mind if they joined us for the Conover musicale?"

"Of course not. I'd be delighted."

"Thank you, Olivia. I'll see you tonight." And Rolland left.

Olivia watched his retreating back, and when he was gone, she walked over to the far side of the room and stared out into the garden.

"That was a foolish thing to do."

Olivia spun around to see Damien standing in the open doorway. He wore no jacket or waistcoat, but was dressed in a loose white shirt that he'd tucked into buff breeches. He leaned casually against the doorjamb and studied her with his arms crossed over his chest and one booted foot over the other. There was a dark look on his face, and her breath caught in her throat as if she'd been caught doing something she shouldn't.

"What are you doing here?"

"I came down to talk to you but noticed you had a visitor." Damien picked up a small hand-painted vase and studied it closely. "You shouldn't have let him kiss you."

Olivia felt her temper rise. "How dare you."

"Aren't you going to ask why?"

"No."

He set the vase back on the table and stepped closer to her. "It's not wise to compare two lovers' kisses."

"I see."

Olivia watched him for a long while, then moved toward him. She cocked her head at an angle, and he turned so the left side of his face wasn't so exposed. She didn't let that deter her. "Well? Aren't you going to ask?"

"Ask what?"

"Which kiss I enjoyed more. Yours or Rolland's."

"No."

"Ah. How confident you are."

Olivia took another step closer to him. Her toes nearly touched his as her wide skirts wrapped around his legs. His face was completely exposed to her, and she knew he wanted to take a step away, but his pride wouldn't allow it. Instead, he angled his head slightly so the scar wasn't in her line of view.

"You are assuming, my lord, that I found Rolland's kiss inferior to yours."

"And you didn't?"

"I honestly can't say. Yours was evidently not that memorable. I barely recall it."

She thought she saw a smile lift the corners of his mouth, but before she was certain he turned away from her, not giving her a clear view of his face.

"Then perhaps a reminder is in order."

He reached for her, but she pushed him away. "No. I don't want you to kiss me again."

"Because you're afraid this time you won't be able to stop?"

"No. Because I find your kisses too assuming. As well as offensive."

She heard the intake of his breath.

"There was a time you didn't."

She spun on him, her glare burning. "There was a time you had rights you no longer have."

Damien smiled, then walked through the room. He stopped and filled a glass with a small amount of brandy, then sat in one of the two chairs angled in front of the fireplace. He stretched his legs out in front of him as if he belonged here, as if he were lord of the manor.

Olivia closed her eyes and pushed aside the growing ache in her chest. Oh, there was a time when she'd imagined Damien sitting here like this, when a vision of him stretched out before a fire was everything she'd always dreamed. But no more. Not now, knowing what she did. Knowing there would never be a word of affection spoken between them. Knowing he wanted her because he thought he had a right to her.

The anger she felt was like a sharp knife through her heart. She wanted him gone. She didn't trust herself near him. Not when she remembered how easily she'd given in to his kisses.

She took a step closer to where he sat and faced him. "I see you're nearly healed. How soon before you leave?"

"Are you in a hurry to have me gone, Olivia?"

"Yes."

He smiled. "Well, I'm not in a hurry to leave. I enjoy your hospitality. I enjoy being with you."

"No, you don't. You enjoy tormenting me. You enjoy threatening me. And you enjoy the idea of punishing me for the grave injustices you think I've committed. Injustices you consider beyond redemption. But you do not enjoy being with me."

He took a sip of brandy, then tipped his head back against the cushion and stared up at the ceiling. All the while, he rubbed his right thigh, kneading the muscles as if loosening painful knots.

"You're not entirely right, Olivia. I hardly think I've tormented or threatened you, and I don't consider it punishment to come back to claim what should have been mine."

"Then what do you consider it?"

His head slowly turned until his unyielding gaze was locked with hers. "Retribution. Something justly deserved. I have come back to take what should have been mine four years ago. What your father agreed I should have." He turned his head and looked at her. "What you took from me."

Damien's words struck her with the force of a fist aimed at her gut. She nearly sank to her knees. "You'll never believe I put you aboard Captain Durham's ship that night to save your life, will you?"

"No, Olivia. Never that. You forget. I saw the doubt in your eyes when Strathern barged into our ball with his accusations. The look of condemnation on your face. The look of disappointment." He tightened one hand into a fist. "If only you would have faced society with me. If only you would have given me a chance to prove that I loved you more than your father's ships. But you didn't."

Damien sat forward in his chair and drained the little that remained in the bottom of his glass. "And now we will both live with the choice you made."

The painful pressure in her chest tightened. "And do you blame me for the scars, too, for everything that happened to you?"

Damien slowly stood, his legs unsteady at first, then seeming to gain strength. He didn't look at her, but walked to the window and stood with his arm braced against the wood while staring out at the carriages rumbling past the front of the house. He was quiet for several long minutes. Finally, he spoke.

"No, Olivia. The fire wasn't your fault. You didn't start it, and I'm sure if you would have known the *Princess Anne* was going to burn, you would have chosen another ship to take me."

That, at least, was something. And yet the relief of knowing he didn't hold her accountable for his pain made her want to cry.

"Well," he said, pushing himself away from the window. "Although I've enjoyed our little talk immensely, I have much to do."

"Such as?"

"I still have estates to run . . ." He smiled a sinister grin that sent a shiver down her spine. "I've neglected them far too long. And I need to see my mother and sisters and tell them I've returned. Then, I need to dispose of my worthless cousin. And, of course, there's the matter of finding out who's trying to sabotage our shipping company."

"Is that where you go, Damien? To the waterfront? Is that why you leave in the middle of the night?"

He turned his head, his dark brows arching, the right side of his mouth lifting, almost as if he'd found something she'd said humorous. "I didn't realize you were so interested in my affairs."

"I'm not. I'm only concerned when people come and go from my house at all hours of the night. It's hardly something I'm used to."

"That will change as soon as I can risk going out into the open."

"When do you anticipate that will be?"

"Soon. We have less than a month before we must marry."

Olivia's heart flew to her throat. "I don't have to marry you."

"Yes, you do. Oh, I know you'd like to think you have a choice. That you could consider marrying Rotham. But you can't, Olivia. You know your father didn't intend for you to marry anyone but me. That's why he stated his will as he did. Because he intended for Pellingsworth Shipping to remain with us and be passed down to our children. In order for you to obey his wishes, we have to marry." Damien laughed. "It will be one of life's small injustices, Olivia. An ironic twist of fate that's beyond laughable."

He walked across the room and opened the door, then stopped. "We will both finally get what we dreamed of four years ago, and what neither of us want today. It's quite humorous, don't you think?"

He didn't wait for an answer, but walked away from her, closing the door behind him.

Chapter 12

Olivia sat in the carriage at Rolland's side. Prudence and her mother, Lady Chandler, sat opposite them. They were returning from Lady Conover's musicale, and for reasons Olivia couldn't explain, she was as tense as a longbow pulled taut and ready to fire.

The cause couldn't be the music or the performance. Lady Conover's musicale had been exquisite, the performers having done such a magnificent job with Mozart's mastery of lyric melodies and pure harmonies, Olivia was still in awe.

Nor was it the company. Lady Prudence and her mother had been ideal companions. Prudence was warm and open, and a stunning beauty in her polite, quiet way. Olivia was drawn to her the moment they met.

It was something else. And Olivia knew where the blame lay. At Damien's feet.

Ever since they'd had words this afternoon, she'd battled an intense fury because he'd been so presumptuous to assume he knew what she had to do. And guilt because she knew he was right—*if* she intended to keep the ships.

Even though her father had left the choice to her of whether or not she would marry Damien, she knew he'd been positive of what her decision would be. She knew her father had always intended Damien to take charge of Pellingsworth Shipping, as well as the investments and lands he'd left her. That it would all be passed down to her heirs some day. But . . .

Surely her father would understand why she couldn't do it.

". . . isn't he, Olivia?"

Olivia turned her head to the side and stared at Rolland in confusion. "I'm sorry. Isn't he what?"

"My, but you're in a strange mood tonight. We were discussing Mozart. His talent."

"What? Oh, yes. Remarkable."

"I agree," Prudence said, showing a burst of enthusiasm. "Last year when we came to London, we heard a performance of his Symphony in G Minor, and I'm embarrassed to admit I couldn't keep the tears from falling. It was one of the most exciting pieces I had ever heard."

Olivia nodded. "Yes. That's one of my favorites, too."

Prudence breathed a dainty sigh and sat back against the squabs. "Can you imagine what he might have left the world if he hadn't died at such a young age?"

Olivia nodded. "It would have been stunning."

Olivia spun the maudlin conversation to a more jovial tone. She turned to Lady Chandler. "How long do you and your daughter plan to stay in London?"

Lady Chandler smiled. "A month, at least. Prudence and I get to Town so seldom we have to make the most of it once we arrive."

"Yes. Mother has spoken of nothing but the chance to attend the opera. And next week a dear friend of hers, Lady Fortinier, is hosting her annual ball. It's always the highlight of our visit and is so well attended there is always quite a crush. Are you and Rolland planning to attend?"

"Yes. Everyone looks forward to Lady Fortinier's ball."

"Good. Perhaps we'll see you there."

"Better yet," Olivia said, smiling at the excitement on Prudence's face, "why don't you and your mother join us?"

"Are you certain?" Prudence asked, her flawless manners showing some hesitancy as she glanced at Rolland to make sure she wasn't intruding.

"Of course," Rolland chimed in. "We'd like nothing better than to have you and your mother as our guests."

Prudence looked at her mother, and when the elder lady nodded her approval, Prudence smiled. "Oh, that would be wonderful."

"We'll pick you up around eight then," Rolland instructed, as the carriage slowed in front of Lady Chandler's townhouse.

Rolland disembarked first and helped Lady Chandler down the steps. Prudence slid to the edge of her seat then stopped. "I can see Rolland is quite fond of you, Olivia," Prudence whispered, placing a gloved hand gently on top of hers. "I want you to know how pleased I am you have helped him take the step he needed to continue his life."

"I assure you, I did nothing."

"Oh, but you must have. I was afraid after Felicity's death he would never come out of mourning to make another attempt at life. Rolland is the most wonderful man I have ever met and has so much to offer a wife." She squeezed Olivia's hand then looked into her eyes. "I'm truly happy for both of you. You are exactly what he needs."

Prudence rose quickly, and Olivia watched her step out into the street.

While Rolland escorted Prudence and her mother to their open front door, Olivia sat in the semidark carriage. Had she just imagined tears in Prudence's eyes when she spoke of Rolland? Had she just imagined a hidden sadness when Prudence voiced her congratulations?

Olivia pushed the thought to the back of her mind and smiled as Rolland opened the carriage door and joined her inside.

"So what do you think of Prudence?"

"She's wonderful. I can see why she and Felicity were such close friends."

"Yes," he said thoughtfully. "I'm so glad the two of you have met."
Olivia could only smile.

He sat forward as the carriage rumbled through the busy London streets on its way to Olivia's townhouse, then slid across the seat to sit next to her. "But I don't want to talk about Prudence right now. I'd rather talk about us and the date we need to set."

Olivia's heart lurched, then settled to a surprising calmness. Yes, they needed to set a date. She had less than a month to marry; less than a month unless she intended to marry Damien.

And she did not. She could not.

But she could not go into a marriage until everything was out in the open. Until Rolland knew about Pellingsworth Shipping and about Damien.

Olivia lifted her chin and looked into Rolland's expectant gaze. "Yes. We need to set a date. But there is something I need to tell you first. And when I do, I won't hold it against you if you decide you don't want to marry me."

She clenched her hands in her lap, unable to go on.

"What, Olivia? Why on earth would I not want to marry you?"

Olivia cleared her throat. "Pellingsworth Shipping will not come with me when we marry."

There was a slight pause while Rolland digested what she'd said. Then he laughed.

"This has all been about Pellingsworth Shipping? Your nervousness, the worry on your face, the circles beneath your eyes? All because you think I only want to marry you for your ships? Oh, Olivia."

He reached out and took her hands in his. He brought them to his lips and kissed the backs of her fingers. "I have many vices, as I'm sure you already know, but greed is not one of them. I have enough ships of my own. I'm not marrying you to obtain more."

Olivia breathed a shaky sigh. "It's not just the ships. It's . . . it's . . ." She needed to tell him. Before they set a date, she needed to tell him Damien was alive. That Damien would get the ships. That Damien would get everything. But the words were so difficult to say.

"I didn't know Father had willed his ships to . . . to . . ."

"It doesn't matter who, Olivia. Although I can guess readily enough."

Olivia's gaze darted to Rolland's. No, he didn't know. He couldn't even guess.

She shook her head and pulled away from him. There was no way he could have known that Damien had been alive all this time.

"Olivia, it's all right. No one is going to fault your father for leaving Pellingsworth Shipping to Captain Durham. It was widely known they were not only the best of friends, but business partners as well. It's only natural he left the ships to someone he valued so highly."

Olivia nearly choked as she gasped for breath. Suddenly the truth was even harder to say. She pulled her hands out of his grasp and wrapped them around her middle to ward off the tremor that shook her. "No" was the word she tried to form, but the sound barely made it past her lips.

Rolland reached for her again. "It doesn't matter to whom your father left his shipping company. Captain Durham is an admirable man. Your father couldn't have entrusted his ships to a better person."

"No. He didn't—"

Rolland placed his finger against her lips to stop her words.

"It doesn't matter, Olivia. I don't care about them."

"Oh, Rolland," she said, the truth so painful it made her tremble.

"You haven't changed your mind, have you?" he said, the expression on his face turning serious.

Olivia's hesitation was only slight, yet long enough to give Rolland pause. When the expression on his face turned blank, she quickly shook her head. "No. I haven't changed my mind."

"You're sure?"

"Yes."

Even though her voice sounded reassuring enough, her body betrayed her by shivering. "Don't worry, Olivia. The ships aren't important."

"Oh, Rolland. Would you mind if we married soon? Very soon?"

"Of course not. If that's what you want."

"It is. Yes. We can marry three weeks from today."

Even in the shadowy carriage, Olivia couldn't miss the surprise on Rolland's face. "Very well. I will apply for a special license."

Olivia leaned over to kiss him lightly on the cheek. "Thank you."

"Yes. We'll announce our engagement at the Fortinier ball on Tuesday next, and be married two weeks later on the last Wednesday of the month. That will be three weeks from today."

"Thank you, Rolland," she said again. "I know this isn't how you envisioned our wedding, but it will be for the best."

"It's not my wedding I'm so concerned about. I've already gone through a big wedding with all the pomp and hundreds of guests. It's you. You've never had the wedding of your dreams."

"It hardly matters. The day will be special no matter how many people are there to witness it."

"Yes, that's true," he said, as the carriage slowed in front of her townhouse.

Rolland jumped down onto the street and held out his hand to help her. Olivia wanted to look him in the eyes and tell him the rest. The part she'd omitted. The part she knew he'd never understand when he found out she hadn't told him. But she couldn't. Not yet. Not until after their engagement was announced, and it was too late for anyone to do anything about it.

Because there would be all kinds of hell to pay the minute Damien found out what she intended to do.

"Olivia?"

She shook her head and turned her attention back to Rolland.

"Are you all right?"

"Yes. Of course."

"Until Tuesday then."

"Yes. Tuesday."

Rolland jumped down from the carriage and escorted her to the house. Olivia looked out the window and watched the man she was going to marry leave in his carriage and felt a painful tug.

Instead of the elation she felt the first time she'd agreed to be someone's wife, Olivia was overcome by a sadness that was indescribable.

She handed Chivers her wrap and walked to the stairs. "Is Lord Iversley home?" she asked, stopping halfway up the winding staircase.

"No, my lady," Chivers answered from below her. "He went out over an hour ago."

Olivia continued on her way up the stairs, thankful Damien wasn't there. Facing him tomorrow would be difficult enough. Facing him tonight would be impossible.

She'd already lost him once. On Tuesday, she'd lose him a second time. Only this time it would be forever.

Chapter 13

Olivia pulled the shutters closed on the windows at Pellingsworth Shipping and blew out the lamp, blanketing the outer office in total darkness. She stepped into her father's office and closed the door, so that to any observer, it would look as if Pellingsworth Shipping was empty.

She knew she was taking the coward's way out again, knew she was putting off the inevitable. But for at least one more day, she'd avoided seeing Damien. She'd avoided his blatant insistence she set a date for their wedding. She'd avoided telling him again she refused to marry him but intended to marry the Earl of Rotham. She'd avoided the pain she felt when he looked at her as if he enjoyed the dilemma she was in.

Pain gnawed inside her when she recalled his confidence that her conscience wouldn't allow her to marry someone else. And sometimes she didn't think she could go through with marrying Rolland. Then Damien would say something or do something to remind her his only reason for marrying her was to get what he thought he deserved and make her pay for stealing it from him four years ago.

Olivia pulled out a folder of cargo receipts and began the tedious job of entering them in the ledger. This was a task she could have done at home, but she was less likely to run into Damien here, especially if she made it appear as if the office were abandoned for the night. She'd even sent her driver home with instructions not to come back for her for two more hours. Only Captain Durham knew she was here. He'd just returned with a cargo of wine from Bordeaux that morning. She'd talked to him earlier this evening, but made him promise he wouldn't tell Damien she intended to work late.

The captain was scheduled to leave again in two weeks for the second shipment of wine. Perhaps if she asked, he'd stay another day or two to stand in for her father when she married Rolland.

The thought weighed against her like a heavy burden pressing against her heart, but she refused to allow it to bother her. She shoved any reminder of the wedding she'd looked forward to four years ago far back in her memory and concentrated on the figures she needed to enter into the ledger and the lists of cargo she needed to add to Pellingsworth's inventory.

At first, she didn't realize how uncomfortable the office had become, how closed-in she felt, how difficult it was to breathe. She rubbed her eyes and thought that exhaustion was the reason the numbers swam on the pages before her. But when she lifted her head to pour a glass of water to soothe her burning throat, she noticed the dense haze that darkened the room and the acrid smell that burned her nose.

Her heart pounded in her breast as she shoved back her chair and raced across the room toward the door.

Thick, black smoke now billowed beneath the door, filling the room so that she could barely see. She reached to open the door, but pulled her hand away from the blistering metal knob and stepped back.

Escape from the front was impossible. There was a small side door on the opposite side of the room that exited to the warehouses—if she could reach it. But when she turned around, the room was engulfed in smoke; thick, black, billowy clouds that choked the air. She couldn't even see her hand in front of her face.

She stumbled across the room, certain the door was in front of her, but instead ran into the table where her father kept his collection of maps. She'd gone the wrong way. She turned around and went back, praying she was headed in the right direction.

Her eyes burned until the tears ran down her cheeks and her lungs felt as if they were on fire. She couldn't breathe. She couldn't think. The room spun around her and she sank to her knees on the floor.

Olivia inched her way across the room, trying desperately to find the door, but nothing was where she thought it should be. And the longer she tried, the more lost she became. Finally, she was too exhausted to try any longer. Even breathing took too much effort. And Olivia curled up in a tight ball and let the smoky darkness consume her.

Damien stormed through the empty house for the second time, searching for Olivia in every room. She wasn't there.

"Chivers!"

The servants avoided him as if he were an invading army come to rape and pillage. Only Chivers was brave enough to venture near him, although not with relish if the fearful look on his face was any indication.

"Did you need something, my lord?"

"You know damn well what I need," Damien bellowed, maneuvering the stairs after checking in Olivia's empty bedroom. "Where is she?"

Damien stopped at the foot of the stairs and waited. Chivers's gaping silence indicated he knew, but was debating whether or not to divulge the information. Damien clenched his fists. Chivers would tell him, or by the time Damien finished with him, he'd wish he had.

For two days, she'd avoided him as if he had the plague. Every time he got close to her, she escaped through a rear door or the servants' exit, going through every back hallway and stairway. But he wasn't about to give her one more day. Not one more hour.

Not one more bloody second!

"Where is she, Chivers? It's already dark outside. Tilly admits she didn't have an engagement tonight, so wherever she went, she left here to avoid me."

"Perhaps she had an errand to run, my lord."

"How did she get there? Her carriage is still in the stable and that idiot driver of hers refuses to say where he took her."

"I'm sure she'll return shortly, sir."

Damien glared at him. "After all that's happened, you know as well as I she might be in danger."

An anxious look crossed Chivers's face. "Perhaps she doesn't wish to be disturbed, my lord."

"I'm sure she doesn't. But I don't much care."

Damien's temper rose another notch. What was she trying to prove? He wanted this over. He wanted a date set. And he wanted his ring on her finger.

It wasn't as if she didn't still love him. If the kiss they'd shared was any indication, she still did. So why was she being so bloody stubborn? Surely she didn't expect him to forgive her so easily for betraying him? Surely she didn't think things would be like they'd been before she'd sent him away?

He'd learned a lot in the four years he'd been gone. He'd learned that love wasn't an emotion to be given away lightly. That loving someone meant giving them a special part of your heart and soul. And when the person you loved trampled on what you gave them, the pain never went away.

And he'd learned another valuable lesson. He'd never love Olivia that deeply ever again. He'd never give her that much power over him. Never risk that much of his heart. Especially when she'd already proved she could never love him as deeply in return.

"Where is she?" he bellowed at Chivers, and this time he left no doubt he'd do the man bodily harm if he didn't get an answer. "Where!"

Damien watched the expression on Chivers's face change and knew the moment he capitulated.

"She went—"

But before Chivers finished his sentence, the front door flew open and one of Olivia's footmen burst through the opening.

"Fire! There's a fire. Everything's in flames!"

Chivers caught the gasping footman before he collapsed into a chair beside the door. "Where, Willy? Where's the fire?"

"At the warehouse," the footman choked out. "I followed Lady Olivia . . . like you said. And waited to make sure nothing . . . happened to her. And all of a sudden, the whole place was in flames."

"Where's Lady Olivia now?" Damien asked, his feet already carrying him across the foyer to the stable.

"She's inside! I tried to reach her, but the fire's too bad."

Damien froze for a fraction of a second, then raced down the long hallway and out through the kitchen exit. His mind refused to believe this could be happening. But the fear mounting inside him knew it could.

A groomsman threw a bridle on his horse as Damien grabbed the reins and hurdled onto the gelding's bare back.

The ride to the waterfront was the longest few minutes of Damien's life. A fire. Olivia was inside a burning building. He fought the overwhelming fear that consumed him. He knew how quickly a fire could devour everything in its path. Knew how terrified Olivia must be. Every muscle in his body trembled as he pushed his horse harder.

Breathing became more difficult, whether from remembering the horror of being trapped beneath burning beams aboard the *Princess Anne*, or from the heavy smoke that filled the air as he neared the Pellingsworth Shipping office. Damien rode as close as his horse would take him, then jumped to the ground and ran the rest of the way.

A long line of men were passing buckets, throwing water on the front of the building. Captain Durham had taken control and was issuing orders to the crew of sailors, but Damien knew it was too late. The whole front of the building was clearly engulfed in flames, and no amount of effort would save it. Damien raced through the downpour of glowing ashes to get to him.

"Where is she?"

Captain Durham turned around when Damien yelled. He had a confused look on his face. "Where's who?"

"Olivia! Where is she?!"

Damien looked around, frantic to find her. To see her sitting off to the side. He didn't. Damien started to run toward the burning building, but Durham stopped him.

"You can't go in there," Durham yelled through the thundering noise. "It's too late to save anything. The fire's too far gone."

"But Olivia's in there!"

"She can't be. The building was dark. It was empty."

"She's here!" Damien said, rushing forward. "Her footman said she didn't get out."

Fear and terror darkened Durham's features, and he threw down his bucket. "The back! There's an exit to the back."

Both Durham and Damien raced around the side of the building. Smoke billowed from beneath the closed door, but Damien couldn't see flames.

"Get the men over here. Maybe we can stop it from this side."

Durham ran a few steps back, then turned. "Don't go in, Damien. Wait until I bring help."

"Go!"

Damien raced for the door. He had to get to her. If the fire hadn't reached her, the smoke had. And that could be just as deadly.

Damien pulled his cravat from around his neck, then kicked open the door that led to Olivia's father's office. A rush of choking smoke came out at him, blinding him.

"Olivia!"

Nothing.

"Olivia!"

When he heard no answer again, Damien put his cravat to his nose and rushed in. He couldn't see her, the room was too dark, so he went by feel.

His legs trembled beneath him. His nose and throat burned so that taking a breath was nearly impossible. He remembered that night aboard the burning ship. The night he'd nearly died.

Damien pushed himself farther into the room, over to where Pellingsworth's desk sat. Empty.

He worked his way to the right and bumped into the table where the earl had kept a collection of maps. He moved his feet, praying he'd find her lying on the floor, then dropped to his knees and crawled. Dear God. Where could she be?

"Oliv—" he tried to yell, but his throat was so raw he barely made a sound. He got back to his feet and moved to the other side of the room. His lungs burned with every breath he took, and Damien knew from experience it wouldn't be long before the smoke suffocated him. Or the flames reached him.

He looked upward as long, licking flames shot across the ceiling and knew it was too late.

In frantic desperation, he swiped his hand across the floor in great arcs. Nothing.

She had to be here. She had to!

He crawled to another spot, this time in front of Olivia's father's desk and swept his arm in front of him again. Nothing. He moved and felt again. His hand came into contact with something soft. A piece of material. The hem of her gown.

Damien crawled closer and followed the fabric with his hands. It was Olivia. She was huddled in a tight ball with her face buried in her arms. Damien scooped her up and walked with her to where he thought the door should be, but couldn't find the exit.

"Iversley!"

Damien stopped to listen.

"Iversley! Here!"

Damien heard Captain Durham's voice and made his way toward it. Fresh air hit him like an updraft on a clear, cold night at sea. Strong arms steadied him as he stumbled from the building with Olivia tight against him. He took in one huge gulp of air after another, then sank to his knees and cradled Olivia in his lap.

"Olivia! Liv!"

Damien swiped his fingers over her face, pushing her hair from her eyes.

"Is she breathing?"

"I don't know. Liv!"

"Here."

Someone handed him a cold, wet cloth and he placed it on her forehead, then ran it down her cheeks. "Liv. Can you hear me?"

Damien placed his hand on her chest, praying he'd feel her chest rise as she struggled to take a breath. Nothing. Next, he placed his hand on her stomach and pushed. Nothing. He pushed again. Harder.

Olivia's stomach lifted and she took a narrow gasp of air. Damien lifted her so she could breathe easier and she flailed her arms, struggling with more strength than he thought she had. Then the wracking coughs started. Damien sat her up straight and pressed his hand against her back while she coughed to clear her lungs.

"Easy, Liv, easy. You're safe now."

"Get her away from the building, lad," Captain Durham said. He leaned down to help Damien to his feet. "She needs to get out of this smoke."

Damien rose with Olivia in his arms. His legs screamed in pain, and he nearly stumbled when he took the first step.

"Let me carry her," Durham offered.

"No," Damien answered, limping away from the blaze. "I should never have let her out of my sight."

Damien looked down. Olivia's complexion was ashen pale. Her

eyes remained closed, and when she did open them, he was struck by the terror he saw there. A terror he remembered all too clearly.

The realization of what could have happened loomed larger with each step he took away from the blazing fire. By the time he reached the carriage Chivers had driven, Damien's temper was flaming in a raging fury. What the hell was she doing down here? How many times had he forbid her to come alone? Bloody hell! She could have died.

Damien stopped when Olivia sucked in a labored breath, then she drew her knees in as another spasm wracked her body. She gasped for air, her body tensing in fear. How he remembered doing the same. The panic that consumed him because he couldn't take in enough air to breathe. Struggling against the unbelievable pain.

Damien stood frozen to the spot while Olivia trembled in his arms. Going into that burning building was like enduring the terror and the pain all over again.

Damn her! She could have died!

"Iversley."

Damien heard the captain's soft voice from behind him and felt the man's steady hand resting atop his shoulder. He'd relied on Durham all those months after the fire, when all he wanted was to die. It was Durham who had rubbed his aching legs when the muscles knotted and cramped. And Durham who had sat with him when the pain was so bad Damien was on the verge of taking his life.

Damien looked from the concerned expression on Durham's face to Olivia's fragile body in his arms.

Her eyes were open, and she looked at him with huge tears threatening to spill over her lashes.

"I didn't discover the fire until it was too late," she gasped.

Damien realized how fragile she was and fought another surge of terror for what she'd gone through. "What the hell were you doing down here anyway?" he hissed. "You could have been killed." He ground his teeth and said in anger, "And it would have served you right."

Damien wanted to take the words back the minute they left his mouth, but it was too late. Her face paled even more, and with a ragged breath she uttered, "Yes. I could have made everything so much simpler."

She closed her eyes, and the tears he was sure she didn't realize were there seeped between her lashes and ran down her cheeks.

"You need to get her home," Durham said softly.

Damien nodded and walked to the waiting carriage. Chivers had the stairs pulled down and Damien stepped up with Olivia in his arms.

"Please, put me down," she said, her voice ragged and hoarse.

Damien ignored her and leaned out the window. "Hurry, Chivers. Take us home."

Damien watched Chivers rush to the front and climb atop. Before the carriage lurched forward, Captain Durham approached the window. "I'll take care of things here," he said, glancing back at the smoldering shipping office, "and see if I can find out anything. Maybe the person responsible left some evidence."

Damien nodded, then leaned back against the cushions as the carriage took off. His legs ached mercilessly, and when Olivia struggled to get off his lap, another shot of pain spiked through his thighs. He sucked in a heavy breath and pulled her firmly against him. "Sit still, dammit!"

She went stiff in his arms, and he inwardly cursed himself. He'd never felt such terror as he had when he realized Olivia was inside the building. Never felt such helplessness as when he couldn't find her. Never knew such devastation as when he feared he might be too late. And instead of letting her know how much her safety meant to him, his fear came out in the form of anger.

Damien breathed a deep, shuddering breath and wrapped one hand around her middle. He placed the other around her shoulder and pressed her shivering body close to his. She held herself away from him for what seemed an eternity, then gave into exhaustion and burrowed deeper against him.

In the darkened silence of the carriage, he rested his chin against the top of her head and tried to make sense of the war his emotions were waging inside him.

~~~)

Olivia scooted up in the bed and leaned back against the mound of pillows supporting her back. Breathing was easier sitting upright than lying down. She pulled the down covers about her chest and took in as deep a breath as her lungs would allow.

She'd already endured a thorough examination by Doctor Barkley then the ministrations of a very anxious Tilly and the rest of the staff. They'd helped her bathe and wash her hair, then helped her into a fresh nightgown to remove the last hints of soot and the smell of smoke. The drapes in her room had been opened wide at Damien's insistence, then Cook had sent up a cup of special tea guaranteed to soothe her aching throat.

She'd tried to play down their fussing, but from the moment Damien had carried her into the house, she'd been hovered over until she begged to be left alone. Alone so she could sort out what had happened after the fire. Alone so she could come to terms with Damien's reaction. A reaction that frightened her nearly as much as being trapped in the fire.

A part of her wasn't ready to face the harshness of his feelings. A harshness he'd made more than obvious. Another example of the hostility he hadn't tried to conceal from the moment he'd come back. And no matter how hard she tried, there was no way she could excuse his anger for anything but what it was. She was an inconvenience to him, a bothersome irritation he'd just as soon do without. Except he couldn't. Because she was the means to his end.

Whether she wanted to face it or not, the facts did not lie. Whatever they'd shared had been destroyed when she'd put him aboard the

Princess Anne. She may not have lost him to death, but she'd lost him nonetheless.

Olivia wrapped her arms around her bent legs and rested her chin atop her knees. She felt so alone. So confused. So frightened.

She brushed her fingers across her damp cheeks, then stiffened when the door opened.

"I thought maybe you'd be sleeping."

She heard Damien cross the floor and dabbed the corner of the coverlet to her cheeks before turning to face him.

"I'm not sure I want to sleep."

"It's common to feel that way at first. Closed in. Like someone has sealed you in a small jar."

"Is that why you ordered the drapes left open?"

"It helps. The fear you feel now will go away in time."

"As yours has?"

"Yes, well . . ." Damien pulled a chair close to the bed and stretched his legs out in front of him. "The nightmares are better than they used to be. They come less often."

He leaned forward and reached out his hand to touch her cheek. She pulled away.

"You're bruised."

"Am I?"

"You must have fallen against something."

"I don't remember."

"Olivia, I don't want you to ever—"

"Do your legs pain you much?"

Olivia knew what Damien was going to say and wanted to avoid his demands. She knew from the stern look on his face he intended to lecture her again for going to the shipping office without telling him where she was going or taking him with her. She knew he was angry with her, but she wasn't up to hearing him scold her like she was an errant child and he the taskmaster.

And, she didn't want to waste her energy trying to break down the hostility that sprouted between them without warning. Or struggle to pretend a part of her wasn't dying inside because the man with whom she'd been so in love her whole life couldn't forgive her.

"Do they? Still pain you, that is?"

His hands stilled atop his thighs and an unreadable expression covered his face. "At times. More so in the evenings or when I . . ."

"Or when you overexert yourself, such as you did tonight," Olivia finished for him.

"Don't let it concern you. It's not important."

But she was concerned. More than she wanted to be. "What do you do to ease the pain?"

He cast her a sideways glance that contained no softness, making sure at all times to keep the scarred side of his face turned away. Then he lifted the corners of his mouth in an expression that was a long way from being a smile. "Sometimes I drink until I can't feel the pain. Sometimes Captain Durham works the muscles until the cramping goes away. Are you worried you will be saddled with a cripple for a husband, my lady?"

There was no mistaking the antagonism in his voice or the sharpness in his words. Yet another example of the punishment he intended to mete out. A reminder of the futility of thinking they could have a future together. Olivia clutched her hands around her middle to buffer the pain. "No. I'm not worried."

Damien sat forward in his chair and looked at her. It was one of the first times he'd faced her squarely and his whole face was exposed to her. She thought the movement was purposeful, as if he'd wanted to force her to see the whole of him to gauge her reaction.

"How did you get the scar on your face?"

He lifted the corners of his lips to form a smile. But it wasn't a smile. There was something indifferent in his look. "Does it repulse you?"

"Do you intend for it to?"

His smile broadened. "You've changed," he said. "The Olivia from four years ago would never have answered my question with such a forward question of her own."

"What would she have done?"

"She would have apologized for having offended me."

"And were you offended?"

Damien shook his head.

"Then I see no need to apologize." She kept her gaze locked with his. "And you still have not answered my question. How did you get the scar?"

"It happened during the fire. I'm not sure exactly what struck me. Perhaps parts of the rigging. The masts and yardarms shattered into smithereens, most of them as sharp as rapiers."

"Is that when your back and legs were damaged?"

He hesitated. His body reacted as if her words had been a whip. His hands tightened to fists at his sides and his midnight-blue eyes hardened. "Yes, that's when I was *damaged*."

"I see," Olivia said, realizing this was another item on the long list of sins that he intended to make her pay for having committed.

"Enough about reliving our past," he said. "We have other, more important things to discuss."

Olivia braced herself for what was coming next.

"We have two days and three weeks left before the deadline. We have to—"

"Not now, Damien."

"If not now, when?" There was a harshness in his tone.

She closed her eyes to block out the intensity of his gaze. "Later."

"It's for your own good, Olivia. We have to marry or you'll lose the ships."

"Perhaps the ships don't mean as much to me as you think."

An uncomfortable silence separated them. Then, a slow, lazy smile lifted his lips. "I know better than that. And I expect an answer."

Olivia sighed. "Very well. You'll have your answer."

"When?"

"In two days. You'll have my answer in two days."

Damien gave her a look she didn't try to understand.

"Very well. I'll wait until Tuesday. I will have to arrange for the special license soon after."

She slowly turned to face him. "You're very sure, aren't you?"

His dark brows arched in a most menacing manner. "Sure of what, Olivia? That you'll marry me?"

Damien stood and looked down on her for a fraction of a second, then walked to the open window. He didn't seem interested in the goings on outside, but merely stared into the predawn sky.

"Your father was as close to me as if he were my real father. He took me in and raised me as if I were his own. He instilled in me a pride for everything he owned because he intended that I would some day have it. That I would care for it as he had done. You understand that as clearly as I do. He instilled that same pride in you. And you love everything that carries the Pellingsworth name as dearly as I do."

Damien dropped his hands from either side of the window and walked to the foot of the bed. "You will marry me because you won't give up the ships. And I will marry you because you are mine. I won't give you up."

"Because you love me?"

He looked at her, his gaze searing her flesh.

"I did once."

And he turned and left her.

Chapter 14

Lady Fortinier's ball was, as promised, one of the most well attended events of the Season. There was hardly one member of Society absent. Which meant everyone would hear of her engagement to Rolland before the stroke of midnight.

Everyone except Damien.

She didn't doubt he'd be standing in the foyer waiting for her to come home. At least by then her betrothal to Rolland would have been announced, and it would be too late for him to do anything to prevent it.

Olivia forced a smile on her face and tried to appear calm, even though she was quivering inside. She tried to imagine Damien's reaction when he heard she intended to marry Rolland. He'd be furious, no doubt.

"Is something wrong, Olivia?"

Olivia snapped her gaze to where Prudence stood at her side and focused her attention on what was going on around her. "I'm sorry. What were you saying?"

"I was just commenting on the crush of people. I thought it was crowded before, but even more people have arrived. There's such a crowd one can hardly hear oneself think. I'm glad Mother found a chair earlier, or she'd be forced to stand until we go down for dinner."

Olivia looked around the room. "Yes. Everyone is here."

She cast a glance into the crowd and saw Rolland wend his way through the guests with a footman following him, carrying a tray of filled punch glasses. Prudence must have spotted him at the same time.

"Here comes Rolland." She smiled and her eyes glowed when she spied him.

Olivia was struck by the open look of adoration on Prudence's face. A look that was impossible to miss.

She considered how she'd feel if another woman looked at Damien like that, and she realized it would anger her to the point of wanting to harm her. It saddened her to realize she wasn't angry with Prudence. The love she saw in Prudence's eyes was something Olivia was incapable of giving Rolland. A love he deserved to have.

"He's ever so handsome, isn't he?"

"Yes, he is," Olivia answered, unable to hide her reaction to Prudence's admission. Prudence's face turned a deep shade of red.

"Oh, I shouldn't have said that."

"What? That Lord Rotham is handsome? But he is. It's very plain to anyone who looks at him."

"But I shouldn't have said it out loud. I'm terribly sorry. Please forgive me."

"Nonsense," Olivia said, squeezing Prudence's arm in reassurance.

"It's just that we've known each other for so long, and consoled each other through such sadness. I forget myself sometimes. But I'm glad to see him so happy now. Truly I am."

"So am I," Olivia said, focusing on Rolland walking toward them.

"He looks quite pleased with himself, doesn't he?" Prudence said teasingly when Rolland was near enough to hear. "As if getting mere glasses of punch were some amazing feat."

"You wouldn't say that if you'd been the one battling such a crowd," Lord Rotham answered good-humoredly, handing Olivia a glass first, then one to Prudence. He took two off the tray for himself and drank one immediately. "It's a good thing Lady Brockbury didn't come armed, or she'd have dueled me for your punch," he said, placing the empty glass back on the tray. "She tried to trip the footman with her cane the way it was."

"Oh, she did not." Prudence giggled behind her fan. "You're exaggerating."

"On my honor," Rotham said, holding his hand over his heart. "She did."

Rolland and Prudence both laughed with ease. Olivia tried. She truly did. But when her gaze met Rolland's, she knew he saw her fear. His smile faded.

"Would you excuse us a moment, Prudence? I'd like a few words with Olivia."

"Of course. I need to check on Mother to make sure she has everything she needs."

"Let me escort you over. Will you be all right until I return?" he said, looking at Olivia.

"Of course."

Prudence took Rolland's arm and he led her across the room to Lady Chandler. After saying a few words to her, he wound his way back across the room to where Olivia waited.

"Would it be too cool for you outdoors without a wrap?" Rolland asked.

"No."

Olivia walked with him across the room, then exited through the large double doors that led to the patio.

"Let's step over here," he said, escorting her to the cement stairs and down a flagstone path. "We won't be bothered."

A small curved stone bench sat off the side of the path, overlooking a beautiful bed of flowering azaleas. Olivia sat down and found herself looking at the flowers rather than Rolland.

"Second thoughts, Olivia?" he asked, sitting beside her.

Her gaze darted upward and met his. "No. No second thoughts. You?"

Rolland sucked in a deep breath that expanded his shoulders, making him appear even more magnificently handsome than ever. For just the briefest second, Olivia was consumed by a wave of guilt she didn't want to try to understand.

She should tell him about Damien. Should be honest with him before he announced their betrothal. Before the world found out Damien was still alive, and Rolland would forever question why she'd married him.

"No, Olivia. I'm not having second thoughts."

Rolland stood with his back to her. "I won't lie to you and tell you I'll never think of Felicity again, or continue to miss her. But I've mourned her long enough. It's time I got on with my life. I'm ready to marry. Ready to begin again."

He turned to face her, his gaze not leaving her face. "But I'm not sure you are."

Olivia looked down at her hands, clenched in her lap.

"Something's wrong, Olivia. I've known it for days. Since the reading of your father's will. Are you sure there's nothing I can help you with?"

Olivia's heart leaped to her throat. This was her opportunity to tell him. Her perfect chance, and it would only take a few words.

Damien's alive and he wants to marry me.

Olivia opened her mouth to say them, and closed it. How could she explain to Rolland the reason she couldn't marry the man she'd always loved? How could she expect Rolland to understand she was choosing friendship over love?

She couldn't. She didn't have the words to make him understand.

"No. I'm fine."

"Would you rather I wait to make the announcement? It doesn't have to be tonight, you know."

Her heart thundered in her breast. She couldn't imagine waiting any longer. Couldn't imagine risking that Damien would find out.

"No," she said hurriedly. "I'd rather we make the announcement tonight."

A frown darkened Rolland's face. "Very well."

She reached for his hands and held them. "I'm just being silly, Rolland. I want to marry you. Truly, I do. And I'm looking forward to starting a life with you." She kept her fingers clasped with his and offered him a warm smile.

"Then we'd best go back in."

Rolland held out his arm and she rose to take it. Olivia walked back into the ballroom at Rolland's side. Where she intended to be for the rest of her life.

The crowd had grown even larger, if that were possible, and Olivia went with Rolland to the far side of the room where Prudence stood with a group of acquaintances.

"This dance set is almost over," he whispered in her ear as they weaved their way through the people. "I'll make the announcement just after. Unless you tell me differently."

He was giving her one more chance. Olivia looked back over her shoulder and smiled. "I won't."

Olivia felt Rolland's hand press more possessively at the small of her back. She filled her lungs with a deep, fortifying breath. She was doing the right thing. She had to believe she was. Or maybe she was doing the only thing she could. It hardly mattered. The end result would be the same. She would be Rolland's wife. Not Damien's. Damien would have the ships and be rid of her.

Olivia fought the tightening in her chest. They would both be happy. Just not with each other.

Olivia lifted her gaze to Rolland. She tried to look happy. Truly she did. And she would have been successful except . . .

The music had stopped.

Rolland reached for her hand and gave her fingers a gentle squeeze, then excused himself. With his head high and shoulders back, he headed toward the dais where the orchestra was set up.

Blood roared in Olivia's head with each step he took and the room spun around her.

Olivia forced herself to stay quiet instead of yelling for him to stop. She couldn't breathe. Instead of the excitement she'd experienced the night her father had announced her betrothal to Damien, she was consumed by an overwhelming sense of doubt. How could she do this to Rolland? How could she marry him when she knew she could never love him?

He walked up the two steps and turned around to face the crowd. Slowly, person by person, they gave him their attention and the room was silent.

"Ladies and gentlemen, if I may?"

There was the soft shuffling of feet and the gentle swishing of satin skirts as everyone shifted positions so they could see him. Rolland waited a little while longer to give his interruption import.

Olivia felt the tension mount. Felt her panic grow.

"I have an announcement to make. A very special announcement."

Someone at the other end of the room hollered, "Here, here, Rotham. About time!"

When the cheers and applause died, Rotham continued. "I know this announcement is a long time in coming, but making a decision this important is like choosing a bottle of fine wine. It cannot be done in a hurry. And so," he said, sweeping his gaze over the room, "it is with the greatest pleasure that I announce that I have found the rarest of all—"

He stopped.

"Go on, Rotham," someone yelled from the crowd. "Don't be shy."

But he didn't go on. Instead, his eyes locked on something at the top of the stairs behind her. Then, ever so slowly he shifted his gaze to Olivia.

A growing eruption of muffled pandemonium broke out around her.

"Olivia?"

Olivia felt a hand on her arm, heard Prudence call her name, but she couldn't give Prudence her attention. All she could do was concentrate on Rolland and fight to keep from being swallowed by the din of gasps and shouts that swelled as the guests turned to look to the top of the stairs.

Olivia didn't look. She couldn't bring herself to. She knew what she'd see.

"Oh, Olivia."

Olivia gasped for air as her body was sucked into her worst nightmare. She knew who everyone was gaping at in shock. Knew from the look of disbelief on Rolland's face that he was living the same tragedy as she.

"Turn around, Olivia," Prudence said, clasping her fingers around Olivia's arm.

Olivia knew Prudence was trying to comfort her, but there was no comfort to be found. She knew Prudence thought Olivia would be ecstatic to know the man to whom she'd once been betrothed was still alive, but she wouldn't be. There would be nothing but an unimaginable chain of horrific events the minute she acknowledged the man everyone was staring at.

Olivia didn't turn around. She was too focused on Rolland. Too focused on the words he would never say. The words that if never spoken would change the rest of her life.

"Turn around, Olivia."

This time Prudence's voice was a more forceful command instead of a gentle whisper.

Olivia gave Rolland one last glance. Instead of the proud look he'd worn before, his expression had hardened. There was a cold look of wide-eyed disbelief that told her he knew now what she should have told him in the garden, what she'd tried to tell him. And she knew he'd never forgive her for leaving it unsaid.

She moved from the mixed look of embarrassment and anger on his face to the ashen complexion of Prudence's and knew it was too late to fix anything.

The room quieted, and still Olivia wasn't brave enough to turn around.

She kept her gaze focused on Rolland, on the confusion she saw on his face from the furrows on his forehead to the narrowing of his eyes. Then she saw deep inside him. He stood before her like an open book, vulnerable and exposed before the world. She saw the hurt, the embarrassment, the betrayal.

When she could look at him no longer, she closed her eyes and turned around.

Her gaze locked with Damien's, his expression closed and unreadable. He was dressed in formal, black evening attire, and her breath caught when she looked at him. If anything, he was more breathtakingly handsome than ever.

Only now he sported a scar that ran down the left side of his face.

He towered above them with his hands at his sides and his legs braced wide. His satin shirt and cravat shone snowy white against his bronzed complexion. He held himself with regal stillness, his back straight, his chin lifted proudly, and his demeanor stoic and aloof. He'd cut his hair, the rich mahogany she'd always ached to run her fingers through gleaming beneath the hundreds of candles lighting the ballroom.

Olivia fought the effect he had on her and let her gaze scan his towering length. His massive height was daunting; the high, rigid cut of his cheekbones and the chiseled angle of his jaw emphasized his strength. Every separate part of him combined to make him more formidable than ever.

He stood as was his habit since he'd come back, with his face turned at a slight angle so the left side of his face was obscured from view. Olivia wondered what he would do now. There was no way he could hide his scar from so many people. No way he could shield himself from the mass of people that crowded the ballroom, staring at him. And in the next breath, she found out.

Damien slowly turned his head, breaking contact with her for the first time, scanning the room from the left to the right, giving every person there a clear view of his face.

Olivia listened to the gasps of shock, the sighs, the sharp intakes of breath. Muffled voices whispered Damien's name throughout the ballroom, and Olivia felt a thousand eyes bore in on her. Everyone waited with bated breath to see her reaction, to witness the display of emotion, as if watching the drama of a play unfold.

Olivia wished swooning were in character for her, but it wasn't. She was left to face whatever would happen with her eyes wide open and a show of bravery she far from felt. And she was suddenly consumed with fury. All of which was directed at Damien.

Damn him for coming here. Damn him for choosing tonight to show the world he was still alive. Damn the luck that he'd discovered that Rolland was going to announce their betrothal tonight.

She didn't know how he'd found out. But her mind didn't have to travel far to realize half the household staff probably knew what was afoot. It was impossible to keep a secret of this magnitude, and she should have known he was too adept at sticking his nose into her business to miss her plan.

Olivia locked her gaze with Damien's and saw a victorious gleam in his eyes. He thought he'd won. Thought he'd left her with no choice but to come to him as the long lost love of her life. Damn him.

Damn him!

Olivia cast Rolland a hasty look of regret, then turned and walked toward the open patio doors. People stepped aside to let her pass as she walked with regal aloofness through the crowd. She needed to escape. Needed to get far away from Damien and the chaos he'd caused. Needed to be where Rolland's look of betrayal didn't burn through her heart.

Olivia made her way across the flagstone patio and down the steps that led away from the house. She turned to the left rather than follow the path that would take her to the same spot where she and Rolland had been earlier.

Trees and bushes blurred past her as she made her way farther from the house.

"Olivia!"

Her heart pounded in her breast, and tears streamed down her cheeks.

"Olivia, stop!"

The path split. One way led to a wooden gazebo, the other to a small lake. She unconsciously chose the path to the gazebo and picked up speed to escape him.

Leaves and flowers swam around her as tears blurred her vision. She stumbled and would have fallen if Damien's strong fingers hadn't clasped her arm and steadied her. He brought her to a halt, then turned her around and pulled her to him.

Olivia wrenched his hands off her with as much force as she could gather, and stepped away from him. "Get away from me."

"That's enough, Olivia."

"Leave me alone!"

"I can hardly leave you alone. All of Society is waiting with bated breath for me to rescue you and bring you back inside. They are all convinced you ran because the shock of seeing the man you were once engaged to marry was too much for you."

"I'm not going back inside with you. I won't—"

"Enough!"

Olivia heard the anger in Damien's voice and forced herself to stay rooted to the spot. Forced her gaze to remain locked with his. Every instinct warned her to step away from him. To look away from him.

"Is it true? Did you really intend to announce your betrothal to Rotham tonight?"

"Yes!"

Olivia saw the muscles in Damien's jaw clench. Through sheer force of will she didn't back down when he stepped closer, but held her ground.

"Does he realize you won't bring Pellingsworth Shipping with you?" Olivia bristled with anger. "Yes. And he wants me anyway."

Even in the dark, she saw the fury darken his visage, turning his eyes from midnight blue to nearly black. The hard tone of his voice left little doubt as to his temperament.

"You would give up Pellingsworth Shipping?" he asked incredulously. "Gladly!"

He stepped back as if she'd slapped him. "Then I'm glad I arrived when I did. I saved Rotham from embarrassing himself by announcing his betrothal to a woman who's already promised to another man."

Olivia breathed past the tightness in her chest. "Any promise I gave you was nullified the moment you made the decision to let me believe you were dead."

Anger flashed in his eyes and without warning, Damien reached out and grasped her shoulders. "You won't marry anyone but me, Olivia. You're mine. Mine!"

Olivia tried to twist out of his arms, but he held her tighter. She opened her mouth to demand he release her, but before she could utter the first word, his mouth came down on hers.

His kiss was hard and demanding, his lips grinding against hers with unyielding fierceness.

Olivia tried to turn her head, but he refused to let her go. One of Damien's arms wrapped around her waist, pulling her closer. The other reached around her back at the shoulders, his hand moving upward to cup the back of her head, making it impossible for her to turn away from him.

His fingers raked through her hair, loosening the pins and letting them drop to the ground. Her hair cascaded down her back in wild disarray, as wild as the emotions raging through her.

She tried again to twist out of his arms, but he kissed her again, his kisses relentlessly consuming. He wanted so much, demanded so much, took so much. And Olivia knew if she gave in to him for even one second, she'd be lost.

She fought him as long as she could, but her efforts were as futile as they'd been when he'd kissed her before. Her resolve weakened and a visceral fire fanned deep inside her. She knew if she didn't stop him now it would be too late. She made one last valiant attempt.

She flattened her palms and pushed against his chest, but her efforts only increased his determination. He held her tighter and deepened his kisses.

She moaned, whether a feeble attempt to scream for help or a result of the passion building inside her she wasn't sure, but he opened his mouth over hers and took in the sound.

"You're mine," he whispered, lifting his mouth. "Mine." Then he lowered his mouth over hers again and ground his lips against hers. And her body betrayed her.

She wanted him, needed him, would die without what he was giving her. She was on fire, completely consumed by a raging inferno and each kiss only stoked the fire. She molded against him as if she were part of him, wrapped her arms around him in an effort to get closer. And he took advantage of her weakness. He thrust his tongue into her mouth with only one goal in mind—to dominate. To conquer. To control.

And he succeeded.

His mouth possessed hers while his hands moved over her, down her back, over her hips, cupping her backside and tucking her close against him.

Olivia was past thinking, past possessing the strength to fight him, or having the willpower to resist him. And deep inside her, she knew she didn't want to. She didn't want him to ever stop kissing her. Didn't want him to stop touching her. She wound her arms around his neck and gave in to him.

Their kisses turned desperate, their passion a wild frenzy of taste and touch and feel. Olivia gave in to what Damien wanted, what he demanded; and she took with equal abandon. Took until neither of them could breathe on their own. Until the very feel of him touching her, holding her, cupping her breast, moving over her flesh caused a thousand explosions to erupt inside her like a magnificent fireworks display. At that moment, with his hands working their magic on her body and his mouth taking her to the edge of sanity, she knew she'd lost.

With her arms wrapped around him and her mouth pressed against his, she gave way to the despair and faced the realization that she'd given up everything she swore she'd never let him have. She'd allowed him to use her body to destroy her soul.

That thought caused a cry to go up from the very depths of her being. A cry of desperation, of defeat.

She grew limp in his arms, her arms no longer clinging to him in wild abandon, but hanging at her side. Her mouth no longer seeking his kisses with insatiable need. Her body no longer alive at his touch.

Olivia knew the moment Damien realized she was no longer carried away by her emotions. He lifted his mouth from hers and looked down at her. Then, with a tenderness that surprised her, he wiped the tears that spilled from her eyes.

"You're mine, Olivia," he gasped, his voice raspy from the demands of their kisses. "Mine."

Olivia wanted to argue, but how could she when she remembered how effortlessly he could possess her? When she remembered how quickly she lost control of her determination to fight him? When she remembered what a willing partner she'd been even though she swore otherwise.

Olivia shrugged out of his arms and turned in desperation to get away from him. Then stopped short.

Rolland stood on the walk just a few feet away from them, a spectator to her blatant betrayal.

His face was void of expression, and only the clenched firmness of his jaw and the tight fists at his side gave any evidence of what he might be feeling.

Olivia fought the panic building inside her. "Rolland, it's not—"

Rolland held up his hand to stop her words. With a proud lift of his chin, he said, "It's all right, Olivia. I see you've made your choice."

Then he turned and walked away from her.

And Olivia knew her future had been sealed.

Chapter 15

Damien hovered in the shadows while he waited outside the Lady's Knight, one of London's most renowned gaming hells. A hall well known for having made paupers out of more than one of Society's wealthiest nobility. His cousin Brian, numbered among those currently losing money, expected Damien's mother to repay his debts.

This wasn't how Damien had imagined confronting his cousin, nor was tonight the time he'd chosen to make an appearance. But Brian had taken advantage of Damien's mother long enough. And Damien no longer had an excuse to keep his identity hidden. Olivia had taken that out of his hands when she'd forced him to make an appearance at the Fortinier ball.

Blast! She actually planned to marry someone else! She was prepared to give up her ships rather than take him as her husband.

Damien mopped at the cold sweat that had gathered on his forehead. He couldn't believe how close he'd come to losing her. If Chivers hadn't inadvertently let it slip that the house was in turmoil because of the mistress's upcoming wedding announcement, he'd have never known what was taking place until it was too late. It was a miracle he'd walked in when he had.

Damien rubbed his thigh and leaned his hip against a wooden crate in the alley where he'd been hiding, then breathed a harsh sigh.

Damn her! Didn't she know he'd never give her up? Didn't she know she was his? He'd spent every hour of the last four years dreaming of her. Dreaming of holding her in his arms, of kissing her, and having her beneath him. Of being inside her.

Damn him for the fool he was, but he wanted her. Wanted her more now than he had before she'd betrayed him. And she'd belong to no one but him. Never. Even if he never let himself love her, he couldn't deny he desired her.

Damien raked his fingers through his hair and looked at the door to the Lady's Knight. He wished his cousin would get the hell out of there. Damien was itching for a fight. And every minute the wastrel spent inside darkened Damien's mood. It had been more than three hours now, and the carousing blackguard would be lucky if Damien didn't kill him for what he was doing.

The door to the Lady's Knight opened and Damien studied the men leaving. It had been a long time since he'd seen his cousin, nearly four years to be exact, but Damien had watched him for two days now, and other than his cousin aging slightly, he hadn't changed much. Damien looked at each of the men and breathed a sigh of frustration. None of the men leaving were him.

He settled back onto the crate and waited. And let his mind travel to how he'd left Olivia just hours earlier.

He'd taken her out of the Fortinier's garden by a back gate, her hair still hanging loose, the bodice of her gown torn where he'd pulled at it. And her face void of expression. She'd followed him without a word, as if the shock of seeing Rotham walk away from her had stolen her ability to speak.

Was she in love with Rotham? Surely she couldn't be. Surely her betrayal didn't include that, too.

A fresh wave of fury washed over Damien as strong as a tidal wave crashing to shore, leaving only destruction in its path. He needed to get this over with and get back to her. She was his. She'd said herself she'd always known it. She once told him that she'd loved him from the day her father had brought him to live with them. She'd spoken the words just before Strathern had destroyed their lives. And if what happened each time he kissed her was any indication, nothing had changed.

Damien pushed himself away from the crate and raked his fingers through his hair in frustration. He looked up as the door to the Lady's Knight opened, and his cousin walked out. From his unsteadiness as he staggered down the walk, he wasn't going home sober.

Damien watched him stop to light a cigar before he crossed the street toward him. Damien waited in the shadows until his cousin was close, then stepped out of the alley and grabbed him none too gently by the collar. Before Brian could steady himself, Damien shoved him into the alley and threw him up against the side of the building. Brian reached into his pocket and Damien clamped his hand down on his cousin's wrist.

"I wouldn't try it," Damien whispered, pushing his forearm upward beneath his cousin's chin.

"What do you want?" Brian sputtered, still struggling, but not so much anymore. "If it's money, you're too late. I don't have as much as a crown left."

"And you're about to lose even more, Brian."

Damien's cousin stiffened. "How do you know my name? I've never seen you before in my—"

Damien pushed himself away and stood his full height. He moved to where the bright moonlight would help light his face and glared at his cousin. It only took a moment before Brian's jaw dropped and his eyes widened. Then he tipped his head back and laughed.

"I don't believe it! You've returned."

"Obviously," Damien answered.

His cousin laughed again. "Just my luck. I would have bet you'd never return."

"Well, you lost your bet. And the streak of wild spending you've done at my expense has come to an end."

Damien stepped forward, just enough to let his menacing height and breadth intimidate his cousin. "You have until noon tomorrow to remove yourself and your belongings from my mother's home and leave London."

Damien's cousin staggered. "And my debts?"

"I'll cover them if you're gone before noon. If you're not, I'll let your creditors take payment from your hide."

Damien spun away from Brian. The sight of his wastrel cousin turned his stomach.

Damien had only taken a step away from Brian when he heard a shuffling of feet. His cousin was an idiot. He wasn't smart enough to take the gift Damien had offered him and run as fast as his drunken body could carry him. Instead, he thought to challenge him. As if someone who hadn't done an honest day's work in his lifetime was any kind of match for a man who'd spent the last four years laboring aboard a ship.

Borne from instinct, Damien pulled the knife he kept in his pocket and turned. He slashed it through the air in a downward arc that caught Brian across the bicep. With lightning speed, Damien grabbed his cousin by both arms and threw him against the side of the nearest building. "Get the hell out of my sight before I kill you."

"You're a madman," his cousin hissed.

Damien glared at his cousin as long as he could stand the sight of him, then released him and let him slide to the ground.

Damien walked over to his driver. After stepping into his carriage, he tapped his walking stick to the ceiling, and the carriage lurched forward.

Damien leaned back against the cushions. Something bothered him about his appearance at the Fortinier ball, and about his confrontation just now with his cousin, but he couldn't put his finger on it. Something wasn't right, but he didn't have time to spend thinking about it. He had other, more important things he needed to do.

He closed his eyes and rubbed his aching thighs while he formulated a list of items to take care of. He needed to meet with his solicitor first thing in the morning, then send someone to the country with a message for his steward to come to London right away. He didn't have time to visit the estates in person, at least not until after he was married, so he'd have to rely on Henry Lockling to give him a report of everything that needed to be taken care of. Then, he and Olivia would go to the country, and he'd have plenty of time to repair and care for everything that had been neglected over the last four years.

He thought of what condition the estates were probably in and his anger toward Olivia intensified. It was her fault he hadn't been here to care for the land and the people.

A myriad of emotions twisted and turned inside him, and Damien suddenly realized what was at the heart of the anger he harbored for Olivia. His *pride*. She'd assumed responsibility for him and taken away his choices. By sending him away, she'd made him appear a coward. Why couldn't she have trusted him enough to let him fight his own battle?

He had to admit that although he wanted to hate her for what she'd done, he couldn't. He still had feelings for her. His blood raced every time he held her in his arms. His body reacted each time he kissed her, and deep inside, he knew he still loved her. He just wasn't sure he could ever forgive her for what she'd done.

The carriage slowed and he was glad the ride was over; he didn't want to have to consider what exactly he felt for Olivia any longer.

Damien stepped out of the carriage and walked aboard the *Princess Anne*. It was late, and he knew Captain Durham was no doubt asleep, but he needed answers to too many questions that only Captain Durham might have. He didn't knock when he reached the captain's cabin, but walked in.

It didn't take long after Damien lit a lamp for the captain to wake. "What the . . . ?"

"I need to talk to you."

Captain Durham sat upright in his bunk and swung his legs over the side of the bed. "At this hour?" he said, not caring that his night-shirt rode up around his thighs.

"It's important."

Captain Durham raked his fingers through his graying hair. "It had better be. I just got to sleep. I was keeping watch in case whoever's causing trouble tried again tonight."

"Did they?"

"No. It was quiet."

Damien pushed a chair closer to the bed and sat. "I had an interesting day."

"You woke me to tell me about your day?" the captain bellowed.

"Yes." Damien stretched his legs and rubbed his thighs. "I went to see Mother this morning. She's in London with my sister. She brought Penelope for her Season."

"How delightful," the captain answered, his voice filled with sarcasm. "And is your sister enjoying her Season?"

"I didn't wake you to talk about my sister's Season."

"You didn't?" The captain's mouth opened in a gaping yawn. "Oh, then it must be to tell me what cakes and little sandwiches your mother served with tea."

"Hardly," Damien answered. "It's to tell you her reaction when she saw me."

"What? She wasn't glad to see you?"

"Of course she was glad to see me. She was surprised that I was home."

"Then what's your problem, lad?"

"My problem is that she was surprised that I'd returned, but she wasn't surprised that I was alive. And, she did a damn good job of scolding me for staying away so long." Damien paused. "She treated me as if she hadn't heard that I was dead."

The captain got to his feet and crossed the cabin. When he reached a cupboard on the other side of the small room, he opened a door and pulled out a bottle. He poured a little of the amber liquid in a glass and took a swallow. "She's your mother, lad. Maybe she'd heard that you were dead, but just refused to believe it."

Damien watched the captain's features change. After four years of being with Captain Durham every day, he knew when he was hiding something. "Then tonight I made an appearance at the Fortinier ball."

Captain Durham took another swallow from his glass. "I bet that caused quite a stir."

"Oh, yes." Damien rose to face his friend. "But mostly because I interrupted Lord Rotham announcing his engagement to my fiancée."

The glass in Durham's hand stopped midway to his mouth. "Lady Olivia intended to marry Rotham?"

"You didn't know?"

"No."

"What struck me as odd was that no one at the ball was surprised that I was alive." Damien waved his hand through the air. "Oh, they were surprised that I'd returned. I'd even call their reaction shock. But they weren't surprised that I was still alive."

The captain lowered his gaze. "Perhaps they forgot."

"Then my cousin must have forgotten, too. Because when I met him a little while ago to tell him to get the hell out of London before I sicced his creditors on him, he said, 'I don't believe it. You've returned,' not, 'I don't believe it. You're alive.'" Damien took a step closer to Captain Durham. "Why would he say that? You thought I died in the fire and sent word to Lord Pellingsworth to tell Olivia that I was dead. And when you found me alive, I asked you not to tell anyone that you'd found me."

"That's exactly what I did, lad. I informed Lord Pellingsworth that you were dead. At the time, we all thought you were. And when I found out you'd survived, I didn't send word. Just like you demanded."

"Then why was Olivia the only one who thought I was dead?"

The captain turned away from him and walked back to the cabinet. When he'd refilled his glass, he took a swallow large enough that it drained half the liquor in his glass.

"Why!" Damien asked again, only this time the word came out not as a question but as a demand.

Captain Durham slowly turned. "Because she thought you were dead but kept your death a secret."

Damien staggered backward a step. "Why? Why would she let everyone believe I was still alive?"

"To protect your mother and your sisters, I assume. To protect your property."

"Protect them, how?"

Captain Durham walked toward him and poked his glass to Damien's chest. "For a smart lad, you sure are ignorant at times."

"Then explain things to me."

The captain sat in the chair behind his desk. "She never said, but I assumed she intended to keep your death a secret until your sisters were both married, and she'd put enough money back for your mother to live comfortably for the rest of her life."

Damien felt as if the *Princess Anne* were trying to ride out a hurricane. The floor shifted beneath his feet and he had to reach out for the nearest piece of anchored-down furniture to steady himself.

"What if I never returned?" he said when he found his voice.

"Then Lady Olivia would have gone to her grave still thinking you were dead. And she probably would have told your mother and sisters, and they and the rest of London would have thought you were dead, too."

Damien shook his head to try to clear it. "Why? Why did she let everyone believe I was alive and would come back someday?"

"You saw your cousin. You know what he would have done to your estates and your wealth if he had inherited your title. He wouldn't have given a tinker's damn about your mother or your sisters. They would have been at the mercy of that no-good excuse for a man. And they would have been penniless. They would have lived in poverty and want. Along with your estates and your tenants, and everything else he could get his hands on."

"Oh, hell," Damien said.

"I expect she would have told your mother the truth after your younger sister was safely married. I'm sure she'd want your mother to come to terms with your death—even if she couldn't herself."

Damien looked at Durham. "What do you mean by that?"

Captain Durham shook his head. "That's something you'll have to figure out on your own." The captain rose to his feet. "Now, get the hell out of here so I can get some sleep."

Captain Durham walked past him and climbed into bed. He pulled the covers up over his shoulders and turned his back on Damien. "And douse the lamps before you leave," he growled.

Damien doused the lamps before leaving the captain. He wasn't sure if the captain would get any sleep tonight, but Damien knew he wouldn't.

Chapter 16

Damien stepped out of the carriage the minute it stopped and walked through the door Chivers held open for him.

"I'm afraid Lady Olivia isn't receiving yet," he said, as he put Damien's hat and gloves on the foyer table. "She's still in her rooms."

Damien stopped with his hand on the banister. "Did her maid say how she slept?"

"I believe Tilly said the lady had a restless night."

"I see," Damien answered.

"She seemed a little upset when she came home last night. Cook sent up a glass of wine to help her sleep."

Damien clenched his fingers around the railing and slowly climbed the stairs. "Thank you, Chivers. I'll see myself up. Would you send up a tray with coffee?"

"Yes, my lord."

Damien climbed the rest of the stairs, then walked down the long hallway. Only when he was sure Chivers could no longer see him did he give into the pain and limp toward his room.

Olivia's room was the third door to his right, and as if his feet had a will of their own, they didn't slow until he reached her bedroom door.

He should have let Chivers announce him, but he knew if he had, she'd refuse to see him. He knocked twice, then turned the knob and opened the door.

Damien stepped inside the room and closed the door behind. He found her on the far side of the room, sitting on the cushion inside the recessed window.

At first he didn't think she intended to speak.

"Did you need something?" Her acerbic tone made the sharpness of her words so caustic he thought they might burn his flesh.

"I came to make sure you were all right."

"How considerate."

Damien ignored the sarcasm in her voice and walked across the room. His first step hurt like hell and his left leg buckled slightly beneath him. He gritted his teeth in pain and kept walking. He stopped when he reached her.

She sat on a cushioned window seat with her legs tucked close to her chest and her arms wrapped around her knees. The early morning sunlight filtered through the windowpanes, the bright rays casting a glow to her hair, giving it a golden shimmer. Her complexion was pale; the healthy color she usually wore was gone.

He held his breath and looked into her eyes. At least they didn't glimmer with unshed tears like he feared they would. He understood her better now. Understood why she'd made the decisions she had. To know she'd been crying would have been more unbearable because the blame would all be his.

She turned her face away from him and looked out the window. "I've been expecting you," she said, lowering her cheek to rest against her knees.

"Is that why you're hiding here in your rooms instead of waiting to receive me downstairs?"

"I wasn't going to receive you."

"I anticipated as much."

"I wish you'd leave. You shouldn't be here. It's not proper."

"We're betrothed."

"No, we're not."

Damien smiled. "Oh, but we are."

Damien heard her heavy sigh before she said, "Do you think because you stopped me from becoming engaged to Rotham that now I'll be desperate enough to marry you?"

"Were you really going to let Rotham announce your betrothal? For God's sake, why? You would have lost everything."

He saw her shoulders lift in a silent sigh. "Perhaps the ships weren't worth having, since marrying you would have been part of the bargain."

"You consider marrying me that much of a tragedy?"

"I consider marrying you a farce. A farce in which I wasn't prepared to play a part."

Damien felt like he'd been slapped. Even his cheek stung from the impact of her words. The sunlight streaming through the window gave more than enough light for Damien to see the stoic expression on her face. For him to see the hollow look of resignation. She turned her face from him and lowered her cheek to rest on her knees as she again stared out the window. An eon seemed to pass before she spoke.

"Do you think," she said turning to face him, "that some day it might be possible for you to forgive me, Damien? Or is that too much to hope for?"

Damien felt as if she'd plunged a knife through his chest. Her face was void of expression, her voice steady and calm, while her words, on the surface so innocent, dripped with sarcasm. He felt as if he were truly facing his most formidable enemy, more dangerous—more life-threatening even than Strathern.

He knew her attack for what it was. Recognized the insincerity in her soft words so demurely spoken. She knew he could never forgive her. And if she didn't, she'd find out once they married. Her question wasn't sincere. It was a challenge. She was challenging him to forget what she'd done. Challenging him to forgive her. But that would never happen. He hadn't been the one to strike the first blow. Or the second. She had. When she'd sent him away. When she intended to announce her betrothal to Rotham. Well, he accepted her challenge and vowed to give her the battle of her life.

"You sound as if you think I carry a grudge, Olivia. As if my intent to marry you is to enact some sort of punishment. It's not. Far from it. Marrying you is merely the only option left to either of us—a business arrangement. I have an obligation to fulfill. Both to your father and to myself. To . . . care for you, as well as your father's ships and estates."

"You aren't obligated to marry me. Father didn't make that a stipulation of his will. He only stipulated that *I* marry *you* in order to keep Pellingsworth Shipping."

"I don't see the difference. Your father didn't want you to lose Pellingsworth Shipping any more than I do."

"Of course not. And by marrying me you will have accomplished two lofty goals: your conscience will be clear because of the debt you feel you owe my father for raising you as his son; and I will constantly be near you so you can remind me of my unforgivable betrayal."

Damien closed his eyes. "Believe what you want, Olivia. What matters is that your father intended for us to marry. If he hadn't, he wouldn't have put that stipulation in his will. He would have left Pellingsworth Shipping to you with no strings attached. He knew how much you wanted it. He was evidently quite sure you'd forgive me for letting you believe I was dead."

"Well, he was wrong."

"Perhaps partially. But in time . . ."

Damien stopped. He was too tired to think of the future, and his leg ached too much to contemplate the life he and Olivia would face together. There were other, more important things to worry about, such as the identity of the person responsible for all the *accidents* at Pellingsworth Shipping. Until they knew who was trying to cause damage to Pellingsworth Shipping, no one was safe. Especially Olivia.

Damien sat up in his chair and turned toward Olivia. "The *Commodore* arrived in port today. Captain Durham wants to make a thorough check of the cargo before we release it, in case our friend's been at work again."

Olivia swung her legs over the side of the bench and leaned forward. A glimmer of excitement shone on her face. "I'll go with you and—"

"You're not going to the docks, Olivia. I can check the cargo. I'll make sure everything's all right and send word to you."

"You can't stop me from going."

"I can and I will. Have you already forgotten you nearly died by being so reckless?"

Olivia had the good sense to hold her tongue and look at least a little contrite. Damien rose to his feet and stood over her. "I'll issue an invitation to Captain Durham to call on you as soon as he has time. He'll only be in port another week before he has to leave again for France. I assume you'll want him here for our wedding. I'll get the special license so we can marry without reading the banns, and we'll say our vows before he leaves."

Damien saw her shoulders lift. The gown she wore accented the brown of her eyes. He clenched his fingers around the arms of the chair to keep from reaching for her. To keep from touching her.

He pulled his gaze away from her and pushed himself to his feet. His movements were stiff and slow, and he tried to ignore the pain as he stepped away from her. He didn't like the way his body reacted to her. The urge he felt to take her in his arms, to hold her, touch her, kiss her. The desire he felt for her was a weakness. A weakness that gave her too much power over him. That left him too vulnerable.

Damien clenched his teeth hard. Hadn't he learned his lesson? Wasn't the shattered heart that stuttered inside him reminder enough?

He walked to the door and opened it, then turned around to look at her. He saw the angry glare in her gaze and ignored it.

"We need to appear in public so people get used to seeing us together. What function did you plan to attend tonight?"

She didn't answer.

"Which one, Olivia?"

"The Maddenly ball."

"Fine. I'll come for you at five. We'll take a ride through the park where we'll be noticed. Then, I'll return around nine so we can make an appearance at the Maddenly ball."

"Damien, I won't—"

He didn't let her finish her sentence, but stepped out of the room and closed the door behind him.

He needed a drink to dull more than just the pain in his legs.

Chapter 17

The door opened and Olivia looked up from her desk in the makeshift workspace where anything that could be salvaged from the fire at the Pellingsworth Shipping office had been taken. She breathed a sigh of relief when she saw that it was Captain Durham.

She'd come to the wharf shortly after Damien had left the house and had been sorting through piles of papers and half-charred ledgers for more than two hours. She felt as if she'd made very little progress. It was going to take months before she could make sense of some of the scraps of invoices and partially burned bills of lading. Thank goodness she'd taken the most important ledgers home with her the night before the fire, and they'd been spared.

"Here's the complete cargo inventory from the *Commodore*," Captain Durham said, closing the door behind him. "The men are doublechecking everything as they unload it, and I put extra guards on duty until the cargo is delivered tomorrow."

"That was probably wise," Olivia said, then laid down her pen and reached for the stack of papers he handed her. It was twice as thick as the stack she'd just entered into the ledger. She'd be lucky if she finished in time to rush home and be ready when Damien came to pick her up.

"Did you see any sign of Lord Iversley?" she asked, trying to sound nonchalant.

"No. He was here earlier but left shortly before you came." There was a slight pause before he added, "That couldn't have been planned now, could it?"

Olivia lowered her gaze again to the papers in front of her, refusing to let Captain Durham know she'd overheard Damien issue orders to Johns that he wanted to be picked up at precisely ten o'clock because he had an appointment with his solicitor that would probably take until midafternoon.

The captain didn't move, but stood in front of the desk until Olivia looked up at him.

"This isn't what your father intended, you know. He was certain when the two of you saw each other, you'd both forget everything that had happened before and realize how much you loved each other."

Olivia wanted to laugh. "Well, Father was wrong."

"Give him time, my lady. The last four years weren't easy for him."

Olivia shoved back her chair and bolted to her feet. "And they were for me? He let me believe he was dead! He let me believe I was responsible for his death!"

"No! What happened wasn't your fault. No one thinks that."

She swallowed hard. "He does!"

"He doesn't blame you for the fire. He doesn't blame you for what happened to him."

"But he can't forgive me for sending him away." Olivia stared into Captain Durham's eyes, then smiled at the confirmation she saw on his face. But she felt no happiness, only complete despair. "You warned me not to put him aboard. You said he wouldn't thank me for it, but I couldn't think past the fear. All I could think of was the ten thousand pounds Strathern had put on his head."

"You should have told him. If he had known—"

"It wouldn't have mattered. He would have been more determined than ever to stay. He was too proud to run."

"But at least he would have understood why you sent him away."

Olivia shook her head. "No. Nothing I could have said or done would have changed his mind. I was so young and scared. I was so afraid I was going to lose him. So afraid one minute he'd be alive and the next he'd be dead. I knew I couldn't live the rest of my life without him."

Olivia walked away from the captain so he couldn't see the hurt on her face. "But I lost him anyway. As irrevocably as if he had died."

"No, you haven't," Captain Durham answered, but there wasn't the conviction in his voice that made her believe he was right.

"Why did he let me believe he was dead? Why did *you* let me believe he was dead?"

"I had to. He wouldn't let me tell you the truth."

"Why?"

Captain Durham breathed deeply. "If you could have seen how badly he'd been hurt, you'd know the answer. When I wrote you that letter informing you Lord Iversley was dead, I honestly believed he was. Then, when I found him, I didn't think he'd survive. No one did. Not even the doctors."

"But he did."

"Yes. He did. And it took him nearly two years before he took his first step."

Olivia's stomach lurched. "Two years?"

"Two flaming yardarms fell on him before the ship went down, one across his back—he said you saw the scars the night he was injured—the second across the backs of his legs."

Captain Durham filled a glass from the decanter on a small side table and lifted it to his mouth. "His legs were burned so badly the doctors wanted to amputate them, but Lord Iversley wouldn't let them. I agreed with him. He was so close to dying, I couldn't see putting him through more."

Captain Durham took another swallow. "I lost track of the times I thought we'd lost him. The pain was so intense, the only way he could handle it was with alcohol and drugs. He lived on laudanum for months."

"He's still in pain," Olivia offered, the knot in her stomach twisting until she thought she might be ill.

Captain Durham nodded. "It's mostly his legs now. It wasn't that long ago he couldn't even walk, and he's still building strength in them. When he's on them too much, or overdoes it, the muscles knot."

"He said you knew what to do to help him."

"There was a man, a healer of sorts, who the locals considered a miracle worker. He was Chinese, so none of the English would go to him."

"But you took Damien to him?"

The captain nodded. "The doctors did all they could for Lord Iversley, but the pain was still so bad at times I was afraid he'd—"

"He'd what?" Olivia asked, when Captain Durham stopped.

"Afraid he wouldn't be able to take it much longer."

Olivia's heart skipped a beat. "You were afraid he'd take his own life?"

"There's a point for each of us when we can't go on. I was afraid Lord Iversley wasn't far from reaching that point. So I took him to the healer."

Olivia sank down on her chair. "Did he help Damien?"

"Yes. I'm not sure exactly what he did, and I wouldn't expect you to believe all of it if I told you, but the wounds that wouldn't heal before, slowly healed. And his mind healed as well."

Captain Durham walked over to the small-paned window on the opposite side of the room and stared out of it. "From the moment he turned the bend toward recovery, he was obsessed with getting home."

"Father obviously knew he was alive. Why did he keep it from me?"

"Because he knew you'd want to go to him. He knew you'd sail to India on the first ship that left England. And I knew Iversley wasn't ready to face you."

"He hated me that much?"

"He was still too angry and hurt to know what he felt. And still in too much pain." Captain Durham took another sip from his glass.

"Then news came that your father had died, and there was no stopping him from returning to London."

Olivia sat back down and reached for the pen on the stack of papers in front of her. She gripped it until her fingers ached. "So he could claim everything he thought I'd taken from him."

Captain Durham turned back toward her. "That's not the only reason, my lady. This is his home. It's where he belongs. It's where you are."

Olivia couldn't hide the look of surprise. "I hardly think I was the reason he was so eager to come home, except perhaps to exact punishment for all the pain and suffering I'd caused him."

Captain Durham paused. "I'm not going to lie to you by telling you what happened between you and Lord Iversley didn't affect him. It did. But he loves you. He always has."

How she wished she could believe the captain. How she wished she could feel a glimmer of hope that Damien could ever love her again. But nothing made sense where she and Damien were concerned. And with each confrontation, he drove her further away from him.

Olivia shifted the papers on the top of the desk. She'd worried enough about Damien. She'd let him consume every waking hour, and it was time she thought of something else. Something she could control. Like who had started the fire and wanted to drive her out of Pellingsworth Shipping.

"Do you have any idea who might be trying to discredit Pellingsworth Shipping, or sabotage our shipments?"

Captain Durham shook his head and crossed his thick arms over his massive chest. "I wish I did. I'd hang the reprobate from the tallest yardarm and let the birds pick his bones clean."

Olivia tried to keep the smile from her face, but her lips lifted at the corners. Then her expression froze when the door flew open. It hit the wall with such force it nearly took the door from its hinges.

Damien stood in the opening, his face creased with anger, his stance as formidable as an avenging warrior's. Fury invaded the room.

It pushed through the open doorway in a great rush that enveloped her like a heavy cloak. Even Captain Durham stepped to the side to give way to Damien's temper.

"What the hell are you doing here? I told you to stay home. You're not safe here."

Olivia stood on legs that trembled beneath her but refused to back down. "I wasn't aware you had the right to tell me where I could go or where I had to stay."

"Don't start that. Not now. You know damn well you're not safe—"

"What I know *damn well*, is that for ten more days, Pellingsworth Shipping is mine. I am responsible for it as I have been from the day my father died. I am also accountable to no one for my actions. I alone will determine where I go and when. You, Lord Iversley, may issue orders as long and as feverishly as you'd like, but I am under no obligation to listen to them or abide by them."

Olivia watched Damien's features turn even harsher. Even Captain Durham must have felt the tension because he took another step away from the desk and quietly left the room.

Damien stared at her for several long, interminable seconds, each one stretching to what seemed hours. Olivia fought to keep her composure. For weeks she'd been tossed about in an emotional wind tunnel. The stability she counted on to maintain her equilibrium had been ripped from her grasp, leaving only confusion and frustration in its wake. And the cause of her turmoil stood before her, glaring at her with an expression riveted with censure and disbelief. Olivia wasn't sure whether she wanted to run to him or run away. So she clutched the edge of the thick, oak desktop and prayed it was enough of a barrier to protect her from herself as well as him.

Olivia watched Damien's shoulders drop as his virulent temper lost its fury. When he spoke, she heard a blatant tone of regret in his voice.

"What has happened to you, Olivia?"

Olivia sucked in an angry breath of air. "I have become what you made me."

He shook his head, and one strand of dark hair dropped onto his forehead. Olivia wanted to reach out and push it back. She wanted to thread her fingers through his hair like she'd done years ago with such inexperienced naiveté. The coldness in his voice stopped her.

"I didn't turn you into what you have become."

"And what is that, Damien? What is there about me you do not like? My independence? The fact that I have a mind of my own and use it? Or is it that I have removed you from that lofty pedestal where mere mortals couldn't compete with you? That I no longer look at you with stars in my eyes and open adoration on my face?"

Olivia stormed around the corner of the desk and stood toe-to-toe with him. "For four years I mourned you. I took care of the properties you'd left unattended, because it was the only way I could feel a connection to you. And when father became so ill he couldn't leave the house, I ran Pellingsworth Shipping as well as your estates."

Olivia clenched her fists and glared at him. "Yes, I've changed, Damien. Do you honestly think that shallow, love-struck female you were going to marry could have managed seven estates and an entire shipping fleet without changing? All that was important to me when I thought you would always be there to take care of me were the latest fashions and which ball I was going to attend. So," she said, drying her damp cheeks with her fingertips, "if you don't like what I've become, you do not have to connect yourself with me. There's a ship sailing at dawn. You're welcome to leave anytime you—"

Before she could finish the sentence, Damien clasped her by the upper arms and covered her mouth with his.

His kiss was harsh and demanding. As if he were punishing her for another injustice he thought she'd committed. As if kissing her was the only way he could exert his control over her.

His kisses contained no passion, only dominance. It was as if she'd affected some baser part of him, and he wanted to chastise her for it. As if he wanted to destroy her independence and the woman she'd become.

Olivia knew she should fight him, knew she should struggle to escape his grasp, but she didn't. She couldn't. She wanted to be held in his arms. She was desperate to feel his towering strength pushing against her. Desperate to feel his touch sear her flesh.

He deepened his kiss, all the while moving his hands over her. He ran his fingers across her shoulders and down her back. He wrapped his arms around her as if afraid she might escape his grasp, then moved his hands over her arms again.

His hands spanned her waist, then his fingers began their movement around her, over her, stopping only when they covered her breasts.

A strangled moan echoed in her ears, whether hers or his she couldn't tell, didn't care. The rasps of their breathing were a foreign sound that thundered in unison, one gasp meshing with another. And she wrapped her arms around Damien's neck and gave in to him.

He deepened his kisses, opening his mouth atop hers, demanding she grant him entrance, forcing her to yield to him. And she did. Not because she had no choice, but because she didn't want another choice. She couldn't deny him something she was so desperate to have. Something she'd craved from the first time he'd kissed her.

Olivia hated herself for her weakness. Hated herself for yielding with such abandon.

His tongue entered her mouth with the determination of a conquering army, touching the innermost reaches of her mouth, battling with her, then mating with her. A thousand fiery spirals swirled to the pit of her stomach, churning and churning until her legs weakened beneath her. And he kissed her again.

And again.

Olivia fought to regain control of her senses. Fought to stop the desperate cries coming from deep within her. Fought to keep from giving in to him so completely. And failed. With his mouth on hers, his hands kneading her breasts, and her hips pressed hard against his, she welcomed every demand he made of her.

Then, with an agonizing roar, he dropped his arms from around her and pulled away from her as violently as he'd first taken her.

Olivia stumbled as if the ground had shifted beneath her feet. She braced her hands against the corner of the desk. Her legs no longer had the strength to support her while her chest heaved with one ragged gasp after another.

She wasn't sure what had happened. Wasn't sure how they'd reached the point they had.

With as much dignity as she could find, she pulled her gaping bodice together. Her gown was open to the waist, her cotton chemise unlaced, exposing her breasts. Breasts that still tingled from his touch. With trembling fingers, she pulled the thin material together, then fastened the satin buttons of her gown. Her cheeks burned with humiliation. What had she let him do?

She slowly lifted her shoulders and nervously straightened the twisted folds of her skirt. When she had some hold on her composure, she turned around. Facing him was hard. Seeing the regret on his face would only add to her shame. But she would not back down from him. She would not cower. She hadn't started what had just happened. She hadn't been the one to precipitate the kiss. With chin high, she turned.

He'd stepped to the other side of the room where he stood with his back to her. His hands were braced against the wall as if he needed support to help him stand. His head hung between his outstretched arms and his legs were braced wide. The dark material of his jacket stretched taut over his shoulders and his whole torso heaved from exertion. He hadn't recovered yet and she waited for his breathing to calm.

She would not be the first to speak. She would not be the first to make excuses for what had just happened, or point an accusing finger. He alone would have to come to terms with the mistake he'd made.

"You need to go home, Olivia," he said, his voice strained, rife with emotion. "You need to get out of here," he whispered from the far corner of the room. "I'll pick you up shortly before five. I've promised you a ride through Hyde Park, and we still need to attend the Maddenly ball."

"I haven't finished entering—"

"Just go," he ordered. "I'll enter them."

Olivia shuddered at the anger she heard in his voice. She suddenly wanted nothing more than to take herself as far away from him as she could.

She grabbed her cloak from the hook by the door and whirled it about her shoulders. Her fingers trembled when she fastened the satin frog at the base of her throat and her legs shook beneath her. She walked to the door and stopped with her hand on the knob.

"The girl you thought to marry four years ago is dead, Damien. Just as the man I dreamed of marrying is. It is impossible for either of us to resurrect what we had before. And useless to try."

With her heart in pieces, she walked out into the dreary, afternoon gloom. A light mist was falling but Olivia hardly noticed. How could she care about a little rain ruining her bonnet when she'd just lost so much more?

Chapter 18

The Maddenly townhouse was filled to overflowing for their annual ball. There were more guests than usual, many of whom had come only to see if Damien and Olivia would make an appearance. They'd nearly been disappointed.

Damien had waited for Olivia to come down for more than an hour, and finally, when he'd had one more drink than he should have had and his patience was long gone, she'd joined him.

She was stunning. Her gown of emerald green perfectly complemented her coloring. The décolletage was lower than he might normally approve, revealing more of her lush, creamy breasts than he thought necessary, but its cut enhanced her figure. The shimmering satin hugged her narrow waist to reveal curves he wasn't sure he wanted the rest of the world to realize she possessed. Her thick, dark hair was loosely pulled back from her face and hung down her back in spiraling curls, partially concealing the flesh at her shoulders that her gown didn't cover. Her features were the same: a heart-shaped face of creamy clear complexion, huge dark eyes, high rosy cheekbones, and dark, lush lips just begging to be kissed. He couldn't deny she made a magnificent picture.

As long as one didn't look at the lifeless stare in her eyes or the dark circles rimming them.

She'd spoken little on their way through the city, answering only the questions directed to her, and with the briefest reply possible. She'd spoken to him even less once they'd arrived, directing her attention to those around her. It wasn't lost on him that she chose the first opportunity to escape him. Or that she hadn't returned.

Damien looked across the room where she stood with a circle of friends. She nodded her head as if someone were pulling strings to make it move, and she wore a dull smile that appeared as if it had been painted on her face. Then she laughed, the sound forced and hollow. Damien could take no more.

"Excuse me," he said to the group of men who surrounded him, eager to gather any bit of information as to where he'd been the last four years.

Damien wended his way through the crowd, stopping only long enough to not be rude when spoken to, then pushed his way to where Olivia stood. She had her back to him, and when he approached, everyone saw him but her. Their wide-eyed reaction was one to which he had become accustomed. Not many in polite Society could view his scarred face without showing some sign of surprise.

Damien knew the second Olivia realized he was close. Her shoulders lifted and her back stiffened as if she were being forced to face something—or someone—unpleasant.

"Excuse me, ladies. I hope you don't mind if I steal Lady Olivia from you. I've gone without her at my side far too long."

The ladies all sighed, but Olivia ignored their reaction by saying, "But Lady Warren was just telling us who—"

"I'm sure Lady Warren can tell you later, my love. I, unfortunately," he said, placing his arm around her shoulder in a most possessive grasp, "would like for us to greet my mother, who looks like she's most anxious to speak with us. Then, I'd like to view Lady Maddenly's garden."

Damien didn't give her a chance to argue further, but hooked her arm through the bend of his elbow and walked to where his mother was visiting with several of her friends. When they neared, she held out her hands to welcome them.

"Damien. Olivia."

Lady Iversley kissed him on the cheek, then greeted Olivia with the same affection.

"Oh, Olivia. I can't tell you how happy I am to have Damien home again and to know the two of you can pick up where you were before Damien was forced to leave London. I can't wait for you to set a date. You've had to wait far too long as it is."

"Yes," Olivia answered, "it has been a very long time."

Olivia's restrained response was polite and respectful, but her voice contained none of the warmth of the girl he remembered from four years ago. The hollow look in her eyes exhibited none of the exuberance from before. Damien wondered if he were the only one who noticed.

Olivia smiled, her expression cordial, even pleasant, and Damien doubted his mother noticed the detached expression on Olivia's face, or her lack of color. His mother was too excited by the possibility that her remaining children might marry within mere months of each other. She was so elated that Penelope seemed to have captured the attention of the Marquess of Tumbledon that she didn't notice that Olivia wasn't as happy about Damien's return as everyone assumed she would be.

Damien held Olivia next to him for a few more minutes while his mother gushed over how perfectly everything had worked out for her family, then he and Olivia took their leave. He escorted Olivia across the room toward the patio door, then stepped with her onto the terrace.

"That was unnecessary," she said when they reached a quiet corner of the garden. "We hardly need to appear so companionable for your mother. She's already convinced nothing has changed between us."

"And if you continue to ignore me, it won't take long for my mother, as well as the rest of Society, to realize a lot has changed."

"People see what they expect to see. And they expect to see two people still in love with each other."

"And we're not?"

That brought her first reaction. "Don't mock me." She glared at him, her full lips pursed in a show of anger.

Damien smiled. "I seem to recall a kiss we shared earlier that—"

"Do not confuse love with lust, Damien. There is a vast difference between the two emotions."

"You are an expert on the difference?"

She took a small step closer to him. "I was a participant in that kiss. There was a goodly measure of dominance and control. There was even more anger. And there was an unbelievable amount of lust in what we shared." She lifted her chin and glared at him. "But there was no affection. Only a foolish lack of control on my part. As well as your own. It shouldn't be hard for us to make sure it doesn't happen again."

"It shouldn't?"

"No."

She turned and took a step away from him. "Now, I'd like to go in, if you don't mind. I've been looking for my uncle, the Earl of Pellingsworth. I'm not sure he knows you're back. I need to talk to him. Perhaps soften the news."

"Why should my return concern him?"

Olivia smoothed her hands over her skirts then clutched them together in front of her. "It's not your return that will concern him. It's the news that Father left you Pellingsworth Shipping. He's shown quite an interest in it for the last few months and has made an offer to buy it."

"He wants to buy Pellingsworth Shipping? Why didn't you tell me?"

"Because I had no intention of selling. I just want him to know the ships are no longer mine to sell so he doesn't think there's a chance I'll change my mind."

Damien felt the first wave of unease. "Why does he want them?"

"I don't know. Perhaps because he carries the Pellingsworth title. Perhaps because they were Father's, and he doubts my ability to run them proficiently as Father would have." She glared at him with more intensity. "Perhaps because he is a man and can't abide the thought of a woman intruding into his world."

She turned her head to the side and looked away from him. "I want to make sure he hears how your return will affect him from me, and not from someone else."

"Very well," Damien said, extending his arm. He wanted to argue with her, to comment that not all men felt as she thought they did, but he didn't. Talking to her uncle was more important. She took his arm and made her way back into the ballroom without giving him the slightest notice.

All eyes were riveted to them as he'd expected, but before they'd taken many steps into the ballroom, Damien knew something had changed. Olivia's footsteps faltered before she quickly recovered. He looked down, expecting to find her faux smile firmly in place, and he wasn't disappointed. But her gaze wasn't focused on him. Instead, she stared at a small group of guests on the opposite side of the room.

The Marquess of Rotham and the woman he was with were the center of attention. The marquess laughed at something someone said, then reached for a very pretty woman's hand and brought it to his lips. They laughed again, and the look the two shared was more than mere friendship.

Damien tore his gaze away from them and looked down at Olivia in time to see her erase the look of despair from her face. Even though the smile on her face hadn't faltered, the color in her cheeks had. She was even paler than the day he'd walked back into her life.

Damien refused to give a name to the strange emotion that surged through him. He refused to acknowledge the fury raging inside him. He knew some might call it jealousy. But that's not what it was. Because if one side of the coin was jealousy, the other side was love. And Damien had endured four years of living hell because of love. He knew better than to walk into the same trap again.

They took another step closer to the couple, and Rotham lifted his gaze and noticed them. His reaction was the same as if he'd just spied a very dear friend. He took the arm of the woman next to him and brought her with him to greet them.

Damien now had a physical reason for the discomfort he felt. Olivia's fingers clamped around his arm with the biting strength of a vice, and another surge of fury belted him in the gut. It was past the time of giving what he felt any name other than what it was.

Damien glanced back to Olivia's pale face and thought for the first time that the price he might be forced to pay to have her could be more than his heart could afford.

Olivia forced herself to look calm and smile as she watched Rolland reach for Prudence's hand and bring her with him to where she and Damien stood. He was as stunningly handsome as always, and Olivia was struck by what a perfect couple the two of them made.

She was happy for Rolland, truly she was. She wished him all the joy in the world. One only had to see the happiness in Prudence's eyes to know that she'd be a much better wife for Rolland than Olivia would have been. The peaceful contentment that emanated from them was further proof that they were much more compatible than she and Rolland ever were.

She tried to keep from trembling as Rolland made the introductions, greeting Damien as if the two of them were well-formed business partners instead of two men who'd both intended to marry her. Blood roared in her head until she couldn't think. She must have swayed because Damien's arm wrapped around her waist and he pulled her closer to him for support.

". . . so happy for you, Olivia," she heard Prudence say, and Olivia shook her head to clear it.

"Thank you," she answered when Damien's touch tightened. "I think I must still be in shock."

"And I must take full responsibility for that," Damien added. "I thought it would be easier if I broke the news of my return in person rather than Olivia hearing it in a message. Now I'm not so sure. It was quite a shock for her."

"I'm sure that no longer matters," Rotham said, as his gaze locked with hers. "For I know the lady never stopped loving you. I'm sure how she received the news is inconsequential. The fact that she has you back with her is all that is important."

"It's what is important to me, too," she heard Damien say, his words sounding so sincere. Even though Olivia knew they weren't.

Rotham reached for her hands. "I just want to wish you the best, Olivia, and tell you how happy I am for you. I didn't get a chance to say it . . . the last time I saw you."

Her cheeks warmed. "Thank you, Rolland," she said, squeezing his fingers. "For everything."

Rolland kissed the back of her fingers, then turned his attention to Prudence.

"If you'll excuse me, I promised the lady this next dance."

"Of course."

Rolland held out his arm. Prudence placed her hand on it, and they turned to walk away.

"Rolland?"

He stopped and looked back at her. "Be happy. Always."

Both he and Prudence smiled. "We will, my lady. And you, as well."

Olivia watched them walk away, then lifted her gaze to Damien's. The look on his face was hard, as if chiseled from stone. She could not read it. A blessing for which she was thankful.

Damien studied the expression on Olivia's face as Rotham and Lady Prudence walked away. She wore a forlorn look that said Olivia had lost her last means of escape.

A knot formed in the pit of his stomach when he realized from what she might want to escape.

Or from whom.

He tried to ignore the ache that ate away at his insides.

"I'd ask you to dance, but I don't trust my legs yet to maneuver the steps."

She quickly looked away. "That's all right. I don't see my uncle here, so there's no use in staying. I prefer to go home. It's been a long day."

"As you wish."

They bid Lord and Lady Maddenly good night and Damien led her to their waiting carriage.

She didn't speak on the way home, and he let her ride in silence. He was more interested in mulling over what she'd said earlier. That the kiss they'd shared had been filled with anger and control and dominance.

He couldn't deny it. It had been—at first anyway. When he was trying to prove how easy it would be to govern her, to steal her self-control and make her do what he wanted. Before lust gave way to a passion that was so fierce he couldn't fight it. Now he realized how much that passion dictated every move he made. Every emotion he felt. And how much of his heart she still possessed. How easy it would be for her to destroy him!

He sat back against the velvet cushions and watched the London townhouses go by in a darkened blur. By the time they arrived at Olivia's townhouse, he knew that the only way he could protect himself was to keep her at arm's length. That was the only way to make sure she never had the power to hurt him again.

When the carriage stopped, he helped her down and gave her his arm. They walked through the door Chivers held open for them and stopped to give him their wraps. Olivia silently gave hers over, then walked toward the stairs.

"Would you care for a glass of wine before you retire?" he asked.

Damien wasn't sure why he wanted to stop her. Wasn't sure why he was loathe to be separated from her.

"No, thank you. I'm quite weary. Do help yourself. You know where Father kept his liquor."

"Yes, I do."

She turned her back and began her ascent up the stairs. She'd only taken a few steps before she was stopped by a loud pounding at the front door.

Chivers reached to open it, and a very distraught Earl of Pellingsworth rushed into the house.

"Olivia!"

"Uncle?" Olivia descended the stairs until she stood in front of him. "Is something wrong?"

Damien stepped forward, but Pellingsworth didn't cast a glance in his direction. His focus was on Olivia, and he stumbled across the room to get closer to her.

The earl's clothing was in disarray, and his face held a frantic expression. He tried to speak twice, but issued breathy, guttural gasps as if he couldn't make the words come into the open. When Pellingsworth finally spoke, there was a desperation in his words that sent a wave of alarm racing through Damien.

"Tell me it isn't so! Tell me!"

"Tell you what isn't so?" Olivia grasped her uncle's hands and held them. "What's wrong, uncle? Has something happened?"

"Where is he? Where?"

"If you're looking for me," Damien said, stepping out from the doorway, "I'm right here."

Lord Pellingsworth spun around, then took a step backward.

"Oh, my God! It's true."

Pellingsworth clutched his hand to his chest and took several huge gulps of air. His face paled and he lifted a trembling hand and pointed to Damien in disbelief.

"You can't be! You're here! You've returned!"

Olivia turned a worried gaze in Damien's direction, then looked again at her uncle. "Please, come into the study, uncle, and sit down."

She reached to lead her uncle to the study, but he swung out his arm. He would have struck her if she hadn't moved back.

Damien closed the distance between them as much as he safely dared. "Come here, Olivia," he said softly. "Now."

Damien tried to keep his voice calm, but it was hard when he saw the fury on Pellingsworth's face.

Damien looked at Olivia and nodded, giving her a sign to step past her uncle and come to him. She did, taking a wide berth around her uncle. When she reached his side, Damien pulled her behind him.

"You've returned," Pellingsworth gasped. "But everyone said you never would."

"Yes, I have. Now, why don't you tell me why my return has upset you so?"

"Because of the ships. She'd have sold them if you hadn't come back," Pellingsworth said, a disjointed tone to his voice. "I could have made her."

Pellingsworth nervously rubbed his hand against the material at his thigh. "Now it's too late," he said, shaking his head. "He knows you have returned, and nothing will stop him now." Pellingsworth paced back and forth like a tiger locked in a cage. "Oh, it's all my fault. All my fault."

"What's your fault?" Damien stepped around the desk and faced Olivia's uncle. "Who are you talking about?"

"Richard. My son, Richard." Pellingsworth turned his attention to Olivia. "Oh, Olivia. If only you had sold me the ships when I offered to buy them."

"You know I couldn't sell you the ships. I could never give them up."

"But you had to. You just needed time to realize it. That's all."

Damien didn't have time to ask what he meant before Chivers knocked, then entered the room with Captain Durham's first mate close behind him.

"You have a visitor, my lord," Chivers said. "He insisted on accompanying me."

"It's fine, Chivers. What wrong, Harrigan?"

"We've got one of the men who's been causing the trouble aboard the ships, sir. Captain Durham said for you to come right away."

Pellingsworth's eyes widened, and he bolted toward the door. Damien stepped in front of him to block his exit.

"Who is he?" Damien asked Harrigan. "Do you know him?"

"No, sir. We have him trapped aboard ship. He was trying to set fire to the *Commodore*. He ran for it when we saw him and is holed up on the upper deck."

"Is he armed?"

"Yes, my lord. Captain Durham wanted you to decide if we should rush him or not. Pinky can get a clean shot off from the crow's nest of the *Wayward Lady* docked alongside the *Commodore*."

"No! Don't kill him!"

Damien rushed to the desk and pulled a pistol from a drawer. He walked around the desk and stopped when he saw Olivia rise to follow.

"You will stay here."

She shook her head. "I need to—"

"No! I don't have time to worry about you. We'll take care of this, Captain Durham and I."

Damien was surprised when her shoulders sagged in resignation. Then he remembered the other times she'd gone where she shouldn't have: the morning of the duel, the night of the fire, the . . . "Promise me, Olivia. I want your word you'll stay here and not follow me to the docks."

"I, um . . ."

"Your promise!"

She opened her mouth, then finally spoke. "I promise."

Damien turned his attention to Pellingsworth. "I'll give you one chance to talk your son into surrendering. The choice will be his. If you can't, we'll go in after him."

Pellingsworth nodded and followed Damien and Harrigan out of the room. Damien let the others go to the waiting carriage first, and when he reached the door he made the mistake of looking back. Olivia was standing in the middle of the entryway, looking terribly alone and frightened.

Damien wanted to go to her and hold her for just one second. He wanted to feel her in his arms once more before he left.

Instead, he said, "You gave me your word, Olivia. I'm holding you to it."

She nodded. He turned, but not before he saw the look of concern on her face.

Damien walked out the door and down the walk to the waiting carriage.

The look of concern on her face caused his heart to soften. And Damien knew Olivia's cousin, cornered and ready to shoot anyone who came near him, was not what he needed to fear most.

⁓

Olivia paced the floor from the study through the foyer and back to the study until she was certain she'd worn a path in the thick Persian carpet. What if this time Damien didn't come back alive? What if Richard wouldn't listen to his father and refused to peaceably surrender? What if Damien were lying hurt right now and needed her help?

Olivia nearly ran to the closet where Chivers kept the cloaks and reached in for her wrap.

"May I be of some assistance, my lady?"

Olivia froze with her hand still on her cloak and turned her head to see Chivers standing just beyond the door. She felt like a child who'd been caught stealing money from her mother's reticule.

"I was just . . . I mean . . ."

"I understand, my lady."

Chivers carried the tray Olivia hadn't noticed he had in his hand to the study.

"Cook sent up a fresh pot of tea and something to eat. She thought perhaps you'd like a bite while you were waiting for Lord Iversley to return."

Olivia closed the door to the cloak closet and followed Chivers into the study.

"It's been hours, Chivers. You don't think—"

Olivia stopped, unable to go on.

"I think Lord Iversley is quite capable, my lady. These things take time."

"Perhaps if I just went down to see for myself. I could stay in the carriage and—"

Olivia stopped when Chivers looked at her from beneath disapproving arched brows.

"I'm sure Lord Iversley expects you to stay here where you promised you'd be."

Olivia wanted to reprimand Chivers for his impertinence, but how could she? He'd been a part of her father's household even before she'd been born. And he was right. She had given her word. Damien would be furious if she went down to the ships. Even more furious if she got in the way.

"But if he's—"

Olivia swallowed the rest of her sentence when the mantel clock struck midnight. He hadn't even been gone an hour.

"Perhaps you'd like to rest for a while. Tilly's waiting upstairs in case you require her."

Olivia knew what they were doing, all of them. Trying to keep her occupied to ease her worrying. She should be grateful.

"Yes, Chivers. I think I'll go up to change. They haven't been gone all that long, have they?"

"No, my lady. Not that long at all."

Olivia went upstairs to her room and changed out of her ball gown. She tried to go slow to occupy more time, but her movements matched the racing of her heart. It was as if she couldn't get downstairs fast enough, in case Damien returned sooner than expected.

But when she reached the study, the room was still empty. Hot tea and small sandwiches were waiting for her.

Olivia drank a cup of the tea, then paced the room. She stopped in front of the window and looked out onto the deserted streets, then she drank another cup of tea and paced the room again. And the clock struck one.

Then two.

And three.

And four.

Olivia stared at the mantel clock, daring it to strike six. She'd already made up her mind that on the last chime she'd call for her carriage and go down to the docks. She was past nervous. Past being so frightened that she'd become ill. Now she was just numb.

It was over. She knew it had to be. Damien could be in pain. He could be dead.

She couldn't stand the wait any longer.

As much as she told herself he was experienced enough and good enough to take care of himself no matter the situation, she knew how easily disaster could strike. How quickly the man she loved could be taken away from her.

. . . the man she loved.

Olivia clutched her hands around her middle and rocked back and forth on the edge of the settee. She didn't want to admit it. She'd fought the truth from the day he'd come back to her, but she couldn't deny it any longer. Not now. Not when there was a chance she had lost him.

She loved him.

She loved Damien as desperately now as she had the night she'd made the decision to save his life. Only it wasn't a love he'd ever reciprocate. Damien didn't love her. He'd never *allow* himself to love her. He'd bluntly told her so. Told her he considered what she'd done an act of betrayal. An act for which he could never forgive her.

The clock on the mantel struck the hour. She rose to look out the window for the thousandth time, expecting to see an empty street as she had each time before. Determined to call for her carriage and go to find Damien. But in the distance she heard the clopping of horses' hooves and the rumble of carriage wheels.

Olivia strained to see if the carriage slowed in front of her townhouse.

It did.

Captain Durham jumped from the carriage and helped Damien to the ground. Damien was hurt.

Olivia raced to the front door as Captain Durham helped him into the house.

"Damien!"

Olivia looked at him, searching for any sign of blood but didn't see any. What she saw was even more frightening.

Damien's features were devoid of color, his face a pasty white. A heavy sheen of perspiration covered his forehead, and rivulets of sweat streamed down his face. He kept his jaw clenched tight, his lips drawn taut, and his eyes were glazed in agony.

Chivers rushed to Damien's other side, and he and Captain Durham slowly helped Damien up the stairs.

"Where's he hurt?" Olivia said.

"It's his legs," Captain Durham answered.

Olivia turned to go back down the stairs. "I'll send someone for Doctor Barkley."

"No!"

Damien's pain-ravaged voice stopped her, and Olivia froze at the bottom of the stairs. Damien's face had gone even paler, and as she turned to Captain Durham, he said, "A doctor won't do his lordship any good. I'll take care of him, my lady."

Olivia sucked in a breath and rushed back upstairs to turn down the bed.

"What do you need, Captain?" Olivia asked when Chivers and Captain Durham had brought Damien into the room and close to the bed.

"I'll need a bucket of hot water—very hot. And plenty of towels."

Olivia rushed for the door. Captain Durham's voice stopped her.

"And send someone up with a full bottle of whiskey."

Olivia looked at the stark pain on Damien's face and raced out of the room. She'd only taken a few steps down the hall before Damien's loud moan of anguished torment stopped her short. With tears blurring her vision, she headed for her father's liquor cabinet while issuing orders for the hot water and towels along the way.

Olivia grabbed the fullest bottles of whiskey on the shelf and raced back into Damien's room just as Chivers and Captain Durham were laying Damien on the bed.

They'd stripped him of his shirt and breeches and were positioning his naked body facedown on the cotton sheets.

Olivia tried not to stare but wasn't strong enough to turn her face away from him. Only it wasn't his nakedness that held her gaze. It was the wide strips of puckered flesh that crisscrossed the backs of his thighs and legs. A raw redness distorted his limbs, and she realized how much pain he must have endured to cause such horrific disfigurement.

Olivia swallowed hard as she watched Chivers and Captain Durham hold Damien's shoulders. She rushed across the room with the bottles clutched tightly to her breast.

With trembling hands, she poured a good amount into a glass and leaned down to hold it to his lips.

"Here, Damien," she said, then fell backward when his arm swung out and made contact with her shoulder.

"Out! Get the hell . . . out of here!"

Olivia scooted back on the floor to move out of Damien's reach.

"Get her out of here," Damien said, his voice a hoarse, raspy whisper filled with pain. "For God's sake, Durham. Get her out."

"Yes, my lord. But first drink this."

He held a bottle to Damien's lips, but Damien pushed it away with a vile oath.

"I want her . . . out!"

Olivia stood on legs that barely held her and staggered back to get out of Damien's line of sight. Several footmen entered the room with buckets of steaming water and tall stacks of towels. Captain Durham reached for a towel and dipped it in the water.

"Perhaps it might be best, my lady . . ." Captain Durham said, leaving the sentence unfinished.

"Out! Get her out!"

"I'm going, Damien," Olivia said, backing toward the door. "I'm going."

Olivia watched Captain Durham lift the bottle to Damien's mouth again, then lay a steaming towel across the backs of his thighs.

Damien bucked on the bed and clutched great wads of the bedsheets in his fists while the captain kneaded his legs like a baker kneaded mounds of unbaked dough.

Olivia closed her eyes at his first agonizing moan.

"Is she gone?" Damien said between gasps of pain.

Captain Durham looked behind him to where Olivia had her back pressed against the wall. She stepped out of the room.

"Yes. She's gone."

Olivia walked a few feet down the hallway and sank down on the nearest chair and buried her face in her hands.

She'd never seen such suffering. Never seen a human being in such agony. Her stomach roiled at the muffled groans coming from inside Damien's room.

"What happened last night?" Olivia whispered to Captain Durham. She kept her voice low enough so she wouldn't wake Damien. Even though there was no way she could. The amount of whiskey he'd consumed, plus the two doses of laudanum Captain Durham had forced down his throat, guaranteed he wouldn't wake for hours.

Captain Durham leaned his head back against the cushion and closed his eyes. "We had your cousin trapped aboard the *Commodore,* but he escaped the barricade we'd set up, and Lord Iversley gave chase. None of us were close enough to help, and his lordship," he said, looking down as Damien tossed restlessly on the bed, "was left to follow the blackguard on his own. I know he hurdled a number of crates your cousin threw in his way as well as raced down blocks of crowded alleys. We got to him as quickly as we could, but there was a fight. Before any of us could reach them, your cousin slammed a board across the back of Lord Iversley's legs."

Olivia swallowed past the lump in her throat.

Captain Durham rose from his chair and walked to the window where the sun rested high in the sky.

"Lord Iversley was forced to exert himself far more than he's physically able to handle right now. By the time we got to him, the damage was already done."

"Will he heal?"

"Yes, he'll heal. But he'll need care for some time now."

Olivia watched Damien sleep for a while, then asked, "Where's Richard?"

"One of my men fired a shot to stop him, but he got away. He no doubt isn't finished. We'll keep an eye out for him." Captain Durham turned to face her. "I saw you watching what I did to Lord Iversley."

Olivia felt her cheeks warm and her stomach churn. "How does he stand it?"

Captain Durham raked his fingers through his hair. "The procedure isn't pleasant for either of us. I don't enjoy inflicting such pain. But it's worse for him," he said, glancing to where Damien lay.

"I can understand the hot, moist towels. I can see where they would soothe the muscles. But is it necessary to knead his legs so? Or lift and pull him the way you do?"

"Yes. You remember the man I told you about?"

"The man from China?"

The captain smiled. "He would have told me I was too gentle tonight. He would have lifted and stretched Iversley's legs until he screamed. He would have scolded me using Chinese words I couldn't understand and made me work the earl's legs even after the earl had fainted from the pain."

Olivia turned her head to hide the tears swimming in her eyes.

"And he'd be furious if he knew how long it had been since someone had done what I did tonight. I told Iversley when he came to stay with you, he needed to teach Chivers or one of the other footmen what to do so when I left his legs wouldn't grow stiff. But he said I wouldn't be gone that long. That he could get by until I returned."

Olivia felt a wave of anger wash over her. "How often does this have to be done?"

"Ideally, every day. Every other at the least."

"Then more than one of us will learn."

"Us?" Captain Durham asked with raised brows.

"Yes. There is no reason I cannot learn the procedure. Perhaps I'm not as strong as you, but I still need to know what to do should the need arise."

"He's not going to like it," Captain Durham said, crossing his arms over his chest. "He doesn't like for anyone to see his legs."

"He'll get used to it. Just as he's gotten used to the world seeing the scar on his face."

"Perhaps. But I'm not sure he'll ever get used to you seeing him as naked as the day he was born."

The air caught in Olivia's throat. "I, uh. I hadn't . . . Oh, my."

Captain Durham smiled and Olivia tried not to look so mortified. "Then I guess that's something we'll both have to get used to."

Chapter 19

Olivia stood outside Damien's door, clutching a bottle of whiskey and a stack of towels to her breast. She forced herself to leave the cork in the bottle, when what she wanted to do was take a drink of it herself. She took several deep breaths, praying they would help her work up the courage she needed to enter Damien's room and face him.

"Did you need assistance, my lady?"

Olivia looked over her shoulder to face Chivers who'd come up behind her.

"No, Chivers. I was just . . ."

"I understand, my lady. Allow me." He reached around her to open the door.

Olivia had no choice but to bolster her courage and march into the room like an invading army. It was all she could do not to run when Damien turned his head and looked at her.

"How are you?" she said, stacking the towels on the end of the bed in a very precise manner, then pouring a small amount of liquor into a glass. He watched her with a questioning look on his face, but she didn't hold his gaze long enough to let him know she'd noticed.

"Olivia. About last night."

She stood still. She knew he was referring to the shove that had sent her sprawling to the floor.

"I'm sorry. I didn't mean to—"

"I know. Pain makes people do things they'd ordinarily never do."

"That doesn't excuse what I did, but yes. The pain hasn't been that bad since—" He stopped and looked away from her. "Well, it was rather severe last night."

She held out the glass. "Do you need some of this?"

"No. I had enough last night."

"You needed it."

He smiled. It wasn't a big smile, but was warm enough to heat her insides.

"But I don't today. Besides, if I start drinking already, I'll get as bad as Baron Haddley."

"No you won't," she answered, as aware as the rest of Society that Haddley hadn't had one sober day in the last twenty years. "You're stronger than he is."

"Am I?"

"Yes."

"It's funny, but some days I don't feel like it."

Olivia pondered his words, words he'd spoken more to himself than to her. Yet words that opened a small window so she could see inside him. Inside to where he harbored his fears. Well, today she had fears of her own.

She took a fortifying breath and placed the glass back on the table. The door opened and a servant carried a basin of steaming water into the room. Olivia cleared off a place for the basin.

"What are you doing?"

There was a hardness in his voice she chose to ignore. "I'm preparing to minister to you the same as Captain Durham did last night."

"No!"

Damien made a move to lift himself up from the bed, and Olivia stepped closer. She shoved her palm against his chest to push him back down.

"Lie back down and turn onto your stomach."

"No!"

"Turn over, Damien."

Their gazes locked, the battle line clearly drawn.

"Bloody hell, woman."

"Please, don't curse, Damien. It doesn't do any good."

"I don't bloody care. I'm not going to let you see—"

"I saw everything last night."

"Well, you're not going to see it in broad daylight."

"I'm afraid you don't have anything to say about it."

"The hell I don't!"

"Don't argue with me. Captain Durham said the exercises should be performed every day. Since I intend to see they are, you'll *bloody well* lie down and let me get this over with."

Damien glared at her with raging fury. Then he shifted his gaze to the door.

"Don't even think about it. You're not strong enough to make it across the room, let alone out of the house to escape me."

His glare darkened, and Olivia tried to show how unaffected she was with his show of temper by continuing to prepare for what she had to do.

"I'm not letting you touch me. Captain Durham will do it."

"He's not here."

"Well, get him," Damien roared.

"No," Olivia roared back just as decidedly. "He was awake all night. He has to oversee the unloading of the cargo on the *Commodore*, and he needs to rest."

"Then I'll wait until he's rested," he said through clenched teeth.

"You can't. That's what put you in this condition. Your stubborn bullheadedness. We're going to do this now."

"You don't know what to do."

"Captain Durham explained what I should do, and I watched most of what he did last night."

"Blast!"

Damien pounded his fist against the bed then hollered, "Chivers!"

"It will do you no good to bellow for anyone to come to your aid. I've instructed everyone to ignore any ranting that comes from this room."

"You can't do this—" he started to say, as Olivia threw the covers off him.

He stiffened when his protection was removed, and Olivia busied herself by wringing out a towel from the hot water. She cringed, whether from the heat that burned her hands or from his discomfort at being so helpless, she wasn't sure. But this couldn't be helped. She refused to let the injuries that she was responsible for causing be a barrier between them for the rest of their lives.

"I won't be as proficient as Captain Durham," she said wringing out another cloth, "but I'll endeavor to improve."

"Olivia, don't—"

"Please, let me get started, Damien. These towels are losing their heat."

His jaw clenched in anger, and his fists tightened as if they wanted to strike out at someone—perhaps her—while his chest heaved with raging fury. And he lay immobile on the bed, refusing to turn.

"I've already seen your legs, Damien. They were not a pleasant sight, and I would give the world if I could turn back the hands of time and prevent what happened to you, but I can't. And I refuse to offer you my pity. It will hardly help you improve. What will, however, is doing what the healer told you to do."

Damien impaled her with his glare.

"Yes, I know about the healer you went to, and what he told you. Therefore, we are left with no option but to follow his instructions to the letter. Captain Durham tells me it is the only way you will regain your strength."

Olivia sighed when he still didn't move. "Please turn over onto your stomach and make this easier for both of us."

"This is the reason you sacrificed a good pair of satin breeches?"

Olivia looked down at the navy satin breeches he wore from which Chivers had cut off the legs.

"I did it as much for you as for myself, my lord. I realize what part I must play to make you well again and am more than willing to help you. But I'm afraid I don't have the courage to touch you so intimately while you're naked. You'll have to give me at least a day or two before—"

"A day or two? It'll be a hell of a lot longer than a day or two before—"

"Damien, turn over. The water's growing cold."

A long, fragile silence separated them while his eyes focused on the ceiling. He was the one to finally break it.

"I don't want you to see me, Olivia. I'm not sure I can let you touch me."

His voice was a whisper that tore at her heart. She swallowed hard before answering.

"How long do you think you can stay hidden from me? Unless your threat for us to marry was a false one?"

"No. We'll marry."

"Then it really matters little whether I see you today or later."

He closed his eyes and breathed a sigh she took as his resignation, then rolled onto his stomach. His whole body stiffened as if he realized how exposed he was to her. She tried to push the humiliation he must be feeling to the back of her mind.

"Do you need anything before I begin?" she said, trying to keep her voice from revealing how the sight of his hideously scarred legs tore at her insides. How the thought of touching him so intimately set her on fire.

"No. I doubt you're strong enough to cause much pain."

"Perhaps not today. But there's always tomorrow. I will be stronger tomorrow."

And Olivia laid the steaming cloths over his thighs and calves. Then she took a deep breath and touched him. Every muscle in his body stiffened when her hands came into contact with his flesh. She fought the urge to pull her hands away from the warm heat of his body. Fought not to show any sign he could mistake as revulsion.

She clamped her lower lip between her teeth and bit down, trying to focus on something other than the intense heat swirling in the pit of her stomach and Damien's nakedness at the tip of her fingers.

Olivia placed one warm towel after another on his legs while thousands of stinging needles pierced her skin, sending shock waves up and down her arms. Her heart pounded in her breast and she suddenly had difficulty breathing. Touching him set her on fire as wave after wave of molten heat seeped through every part of her. How on earth would she survive rubbing her fingers over his flesh, touching him in ways she never thought she'd touch anyone? Not even her husband.

But she had no choice. Not if she wanted Damien to get stronger. Not if she intended to do everything in her power to help him heal.

Olivia lifted the warm cloth from the calf of one leg and pressed down on his knotted muscles. She didn't notice the puckered skin or the raw, red scars, but only how alive and vibrant he was. Even marred, he was more masculine than anyone she'd ever met. She was like a bow stretched tight, ready to spring. And she had no idea how she would endure what she knew was coming.

She took a deep breath and concentrated on the instructions Captain Durham had given her. With trembling fingers and her heart thundering in her breast, she began kneading the knotted muscles in Damien's legs.

Her touch was at first tentative and she knew she didn't have the brute strength it took to work the muscles with the same force as Captain Durham. But more than once she heard Damien gasp when she rubbed an especially tender spot.

She changed the cloths time and again, and when the water cooled, she sent for hotter water. She kneaded his flesh until her arms ached, then lifted his legs, bending them and stretching them until a spot between her shoulder blades burned as if on fire. And when she was finished, she helped Damien onto his back and repeated the process.

Only it was much more difficult with him on his back. There was a chance she'd look up and find him watching her. A chance that he'd look into her eyes and realize the effect he had on her.

Olivia concentrated harder, making sure she kept her focus on what her hands were doing and not lift her gaze to his face. With relentless energy, she worked on one leg then the other, bending and pushing until his knee nearly touched his chin.

"Enough!"

Her gaze darted to his, and she saw the strain on his face. And the sheen of perspiration on his forehead. She suffered a wave of panic. "Have I hurt you?"

"Yes . . . No . . ." He rolled his eyes, then lifted his hands and let them fall against the bed. His hands were balled into fists. "I've endured enough," he said through clenched teeth.

She couldn't stop the smile from her face. She may be damp in a most unladylike fashion, but she knew she'd challenged him more than he'd expected.

"Are you all right?" she asked.

"Just fine."

Olivia smiled. With an inordinate sense of self-satisfaction, she gathered the towels she'd used and put them in a pile. "The captain said you were to stay abed for the rest of the day, and tomorrow you could get up if you thought you could manage."

"I'll manage," Damien answered, his chest heaving as if he'd run a race.

"Do you need something for the pain?"

He laughed, and her heart skipped a beat. "Oh, yes. But I doubt you'd want to oblige me further."

It took her a moment to realize he wasn't talking about the pain in his legs. With burning cheeks, she reached to pull the covers over him.

With lightning speed, his fingers clasped around her wrists. "Or maybe you would."

"No."

He slowly moved her arms until they were spread wide on either side of him, leaving her no choice but to drop down until she was lying on top of him.

Olivia's breaths came in harsh, ragged gasps, and Damien's were no different. He moved his arms out further until her breasts were flat against his chest.

It was a torture of the worst kind, being so close to him, having her body pressed against his, feeling the heat from his naked flesh burning through the material of her gown. Olivia was certain she would go up in flames at any time.

She looked into his eyes. Waited for him to say something. To put a reason to the hunger she saw. To give an excuse to what she knew was about to happen. To pretend for just a moment that what he felt was something more than lust.

Perhaps if he'd just let himself, it might be possible for him to admit he cared for her. She so desperately needed to know there was the slightest chance he could learn to love her again.

But his eyes turned predatory, and she knew he could not. With a heavy sigh that roared with anguish, he ran one hand up the length of her arm and over her shoulder, then cupped the back of her head with long, strong fingers that wouldn't release her.

She knew he was going to kiss her. Knew from the desperation in his gaze that he wanted her. Perhaps even as much as she wanted him. And yet, a small voice deep inside her warned her it wasn't just a kiss they would share. It was the surrender of a part of her heart. A part that, if damaged, she'd never find a way to repair.

The gamble was so great. It was as if they were playing a game, but the odds were vastly uneven. The stakes were so much higher for her than for him. She had so much more to lose, for he was not risking any part of his heart.

Olivia wanted to fight him. She knew the second she gave in to him, all hope would be lost. He would have the advantage and would use it to his benefit. He would use that advantage to dominate her. To rule her.

And then it would be too late.

Damien increased the pressure, bringing her head down until their mouths were a breath apart. Until she felt herself melding with him.

Flames of desire raged inside her, from her tingling breasts to the heat swirling deep in her belly.

She needed to save herself. But she couldn't. She wanted him too badly. Couldn't control the emotions that had lain dormant since she'd thought him dead. And even if he could never love her—and suddenly she was scared to death that that's how it would always be—she could not stop herself from loving him.

Fiery flames licked with unrelenting intensity. With the slightest lift of his head, he ground his lips against hers, and she gave in to him.

Their mating was the violent clashing of two lost souls. Their passion frantic in every sense of the word. Not the slow, languorous sharing of emotion or the gentle giving of one's self, but the needy taking of what would not be denied.

Damien opened his mouth beneath hers, thrusting his tongue inside her as if possessing her with his hands and mouth made him the victor. It was as if she'd awakened a sleeping dragon, and she knew if she gave in to him now she would be the loser.

He deepened his kisses, demanding more than she thought she could give. His hands roamed over her body, touching her with an intimacy that set her ablaze. With each touch, he took her closer to the edge of a precipice, expecting her to leap with him into the unknown where they would spiral downward toward a promise of physical release.

But only one of them would survive the fall. And it would not be her.

With the strength of someone fighting for her life, she pushed away from him and rushed from the bed. Her legs were weak beneath her, and she stumbled once before reaching out for a cushioned armchair near the wall. She leaned against it while gasping for air. His voice hit her with the force of an unexpected blow.

"I will get the special license tomorrow and we'll be married one week from today."

Olivia closed her eyes to block out the burgeoning regrets swarming before her. She knew what it was like to be loved by Damien. She remembered it from before.

There was no love in what they'd just shared, only lust. There was no emotion in the words he'd spoken. Only a demand.

It left an emptiness she knew would never go away.

Olivia sat in the darkness and listened to the familiar creaks and groans of a house long asleep. She couldn't sleep, not when every time she closed her eyes, the feel of Damien's lips against hers brought her instantly awake. Not when every time the thought of how completely she'd given herself to him enveloped her with a sense of loss. She'd give the world to believe she had the power to break down the barrier that guarded his heart and kept her from getting close to him.

Olivia leaned her head back against the cushion of her chair and closed her eyes. She heard another moan from Damien's room and knew he was having a restless night. She would not be so foolish as before and rush to him. Not unless he really needed her. Not after what had happened the last time. And especially after what had happened earlier in the day.

Olivia had no doubt if he kissed her again, she wouldn't have the willpower to stop him. She wouldn't *want* to stop him.

If only she didn't love him so desperately. If only she could remain as detached as Damien. But she couldn't.

Nor could she ignore the growing desperation in the sounds coming from his room. She tried to ignore the hurt she heard, tried to hold herself back from going to him. But as if her feet had a will of their own, they carried her across the room and down the hall.

She opened his door and stood on the other side of the room, her eyes focusing on where he lay in his bed.

"Damien?"

She stepped farther into the room and called his name again.

"Damien. Are you awake?"

She heard him suck in a sharp breath as if she'd startled him.

"What are you doing here?"

"You're having a nightmare. Are you in pain?"

"No, I—"

He suddenly flew forward, clutching his leg. His cry was filled with torment. Olivia raced over to the bed.

"Where does it hurt?"

She threw the covers from him and pushed his hands away from his calf. He flopped back against the mattress and threw his arm over his eyes. Olivia worked the knot in his leg until her fingers ached, and only when she felt him relax did she lighten her touch.

"Is it better?"

"Ah, hell," he growled, lifting his arm from over his eyes. "I haven't had a cramp that bad for a long time."

"You overdid it, and your legs are letting you know."

"Yes, doctor."

Olivia gently rubbed both his legs a little longer then pushed herself off the bed. A thousand firelights of emotion sparked between them, and an instant wash of liquid heat raced through her body, sucking her under, stealing her breath. She needed to get away from him before she was consumed by the need surging through her. "Do you want something for the pain before I leave?"

"No. It's better now. Thank you."

Olivia turned and stepped away from him. "I'll go back to bed then. Call if you need something."

Her legs trembled as she walked away from him. How many times would she have to touch his flesh, then walk away as if such intimacy didn't leave an ache deep inside her? How many times could she lie to herself and pretend she wasn't affected by such closeness? How many times would just being near him set her body on fire with a heat that burned from the inside out? A heat she knew there was only one way to extinguish, and if she ever yielded to the temptation, all that would be left would be an emptiness that would never go away.

"Olivia, don't leave."

She walked a little faster, needing to separate herself from him. Needing to put enough space between them so she wasn't tempted to run back into his arms. She almost ran the last few steps and reached out for the handle to the door with a frantic desperation.

"Liv, please."

She froze with her hand on the knob and shook her head. She couldn't stay. She would only be hurt if she did.

She heard the rustle of the sheets and covers and knew he'd gotten out of bed. She heard his uneven gait as he crossed the room. Her breath caught in her throat when the heat from his body pressed against her.

His breath brushed against her neck and his arms snaked around her waist from behind, and he pulled her against him.

"Stay with me, Liv."

Olivia turned in his arms. "Why, Damien?"

When he didn't answer her, she cupped her palm against his scarred cheek, hoping he'd realize with her actions that his disfigurement didn't matter to her. Then she stood on her tiptoes and kissed his cheek. "Why, Damien?"

"Because I want you."

Olivia squeezed her eyes shut tight. He hadn't said, "Because I *need* you." He hadn't said, "Because I *love* you."

Olivia waited, praying that Damien would amend his words, would show some sign that he cared for her. Because he had feelings for her. She prayed that he'd give some indication that he wanted more than a partner for his physical needs. Needs a common whore could satisfy as well as she.

But he said nothing.

Olivia knew a loneliness unlike anything she'd ever imagined.

With trembling hands, she pushed away and let herself out of the room.

Chapter 20

Damien paced his bedroom with long, agitated steps. It had been hours since she'd left him, and he could barely survive the guilt gnawing away at him. From the second she closed the door behind her, a part of him wanted to go to her. Another part warned him to stay away.

Bloody hell! How could he live with what he was doing to her? How could he survive another night like the one he'd just shared with her without risking his heart? He knew she'd wanted to hear words he couldn't say, declarations of love he wouldn't allow himself to make. But he couldn't. He'd learned long ago what happened when he expected the person to whom he'd given his heart to love him as desperately as he loved her.

He forced himself to remember waking up aboard the *Princess Anne* and struggling to survive the betrayal that had nearly killed him. Well, it wouldn't happen a second time. She'd never hear those words from him again.

He grabbed his navy jacket from the back of the chair and shoved his arms through the sleeves. He'd thought it would be so easy. Thought he'd been ready to take her as his wife without risking his heart in the process. But that was before he'd held her in his arms. Before he'd kissed her.

Damien gave his satin cravat another tug and took a final look in the mirror. His gaze moved to the side of his face where the scar marred his features. He wore it like a trophy to remind him of what she'd done. A shield that would repulse her so she'd shy away from the sight of him.

Instead, she hardly seemed to notice. And last night, with his face mere inches from hers, she'd pressed her palm against his cheek, as if her touch could somehow erase his imperfections. Then she'd kissed him. She'd pressed her lips against his disfigured flesh while begging him with her eyes to tell her that he loved her.

Damien turned away from the mirror and walked out the door.

He raked his fingers through his hair and put the wall around his heart firmly back in place, then walked toward the stairs. He'd only taken the first step down before he stopped short. Olivia was below him, walking to the door.

"It's rather early to be going out, isn't it?"

She stopped, then looked up at him with eyes open wide in surprise. His heart jolted in his chest.

Her face was pale and dark circles rimmed her eyes. He could tell she'd slept as little as he had, but there was no triumph in knowing that. Except, it wasn't the lack of color to her cheeks that bothered him. It was the weary look in her eyes. Eyes that were at first void of all emotion, then sparked with an emotion he wished he hadn't been able to read.

"I'm going out, my lord. Down to Pellingsworth Shipping, if you must know."

"Yes, Olivia. I must know. And I don't think you should—"

She stopped his words with a hostile glare and a quick step closer. "Pellingsworth Shipping is mine! For six more days it is mine! And I will go there when I want!"

Damien noticed how close to the surface her temper seemed to hover. He held up his hands in surrender. There was something very disturbing about the frantic tone in her voice. He stepped closer to her and softened his voice.

"Then at least take someone with you. One of the footmen."

"There's no need. It's broad daylight. My cousin will hardly risk showing his face in the daylight."

"I realize that. I would just—"

He stopped when she scowled at him a final time, then she turned away and walked toward the door.

"Olivia."

She stopped.

"We'll attend the opera tonight. Society expects to see us together."

"I'm not concerned with what—"

Damien held up his hand to stop her refusal. "I would like to go. It's been a long time since I've been, and I'd like you to go with me."

He saw her features soften, then saw her shoulders sag as she capitulated. She didn't answer in words, only nodded, before leaving the house.

Damien walked across the foyer and into the dining room where breakfast was waiting on the sideboard. He filled a plate then sat.

"Did she eat?" he asked when Chivers placed a plate of tea cakes on the table within reach.

"No, my lord. I believe all the lady had was a cup of tea."

Damien sighed heavily. "Have Cook pack a light lunch. And put some of these in with it," Damien said, sliding the plate of cakes over to Chivers.

"Very good, my lord."

Damien had just finished his meal when Chivers came back with a small box containing the food Cook had packed.

"I took the liberty of having a carriage brought round, my lord."

"Thank you, Chivers. I have an appointment with my solicitor, and when I'm finished, I need to stop by my townhouse in Mayfair. It will be some while before I'll be free to go to the shipping office myself. Send one of the footmen to keep an eye on Lady Olivia until I get there."

"Very well, my lord."

"And tell him if he values his life, he won't let her see him."

"Yes, my lord."

Damien pushed his plate away and walked to the door where Chivers was waiting with his cloak and hat. And a cane.

Damien hesitated, then took it. His legs were stronger than yesterday, but he was still a little unsteady. "Thank you, Chivers."

"Have a good day," Chivers said, closing the door behind him.

Damien leaned on the cane as he walked down the path to the waiting carriage. He leaned back against the maroon velvet cushion and remembered the determined expression on Olivia's face when she left.

. . . it is mine. For six more days it is still mine!

Did she really think he would forbid her to go to the shipping office after her father's will became final?

A heavy pressure weighed against his chest. She did. She thought when her father's will took effect she would lose everything: the ships, the land, the estates. Everything she'd taken care of for the last four years. Everything she loved. Because that's the impression he'd given her.

That had been his original intent. Now . . .

Damien knew he was weakening in his resolve to make her pay for what she'd done to him. The more he was with her, the more impossible it was to think of exacting revenge for what she'd done. The love he'd felt for her before she'd betrayed him was surfacing again. His desperation to be with her, to take care of her, to have her in his life, was all that was important. No matter how hard he tried to keep from loving her, he couldn't. His heart wasn't dead like he thought it was. And she still possessed it.

The carriage stopped in front of Cyrus Haywood's office, and it took longer than Damien thought to make sure the shipping concerns as well as the estates were left in Olivia's care should anything happen to him. He knew how unexpectedly disaster could strike and wanted to make sure his papers were in order so she and any heirs they had would always be provided for. He picked up the special marriage license from Cyrus Haywood and rode the short distance to his townhouse.

He hadn't visited with his mother as much as he should have since his return and wanted to stop to see her, as well as make sure his cousin had moved out. He'd also told Henry Lockling that he wanted to see him. This seemed the best place for the meeting.

Burnes, the butler, had the door open before he reached the house.

"Good day, Lord Iversley."

"Good day, Burnes. Is my mother in?"

"Yes, my lord. She's in the morning room."

"Thanks, Burnes. I'll see myself there." Damien walked down the hall to the morning room.

"Very well, my lord. Will you need fresh tea sent up?"

"No, thank you. I won't be staying that long."

When he reached the morning room, he knocked once, then entered.

"Damien," his mother said with a smile on her face. "What a nice surprise. I didn't know you were coming."

Damien walked across the room and kissed his mother on the cheek. "I just wanted to stop by and make sure my cousin has moved out."

"Yes, Damien. I'm not sure what you said to Brian, but he arrived in quite a huff, ordered his belongings packed, and left without even saying goodbye."

Damien sat on the sofa near his mother. "I'm glad I was effective."

"You certainly were."

"Now, tell me about Penelope. Is she in?"

"No. Two friends stopped by earlier, and they went for a stroll through the park."

"What two friends?" Damien asked.

"Two very *acceptable* female friends, Damien," his mother answered with a smile. "They are having their coming-out this year, too."

"I assume you sent a reliable chaperone with her, too?" he said.

"Nanny Graybill," his mother answered.

Damien smiled. "I won't worry, then, Mother."

"Not with Nanny Graybill anywhere near. There's no need."

"No, no need." Damien stretched his cramped legs out in front of him. "Now, what young man has caught Penelope's eye?"

"Viscount Claremont."

Damien tried to place the name. "I don't believe I'm familiar with Claremont. What do you know about him?"

"He's the Earl of Pendent's heir."

The name registered immediately.

His mother's smile broadened. "I thought you'd be pleased."

"Yes. If Claremont is anything like his father, Penelope has made an excellent match."

"He is," his mother assured him. "I couldn't have picked anyone more perfect if the choice had been mine."

"Has Claremont mentioned that his feelings for Penelope are serious?"

"Not in so many words. But he did compliment me on having a wonderful daughter, and mentioned that he thought Penelope would make a perfect Viscountess."

Damien had been sitting long enough and needed to stretch his legs. He rose from the sofa and walked to the window and looked out. "Let me know when he's ready to speak with me."

"Why?" his mother asked. "So you can frighten him off?"

Damien looked over his shoulder and focused on his mother. There was a smile on her face. "I'm glad to see you weren't serious," he said.

"I was, to a certain extent, Damien. You need to learn to smile at least a little. I'm sure Olivia would appreciate seeing a smile on your face."

Damien turned to watch out the window.

"Have the two of you set a date for your wedding?"

Damien braced his hand on the side of the window. "Probably within the week," he said, knowing they didn't have much time. "It will be a private affair. I've acquired a special license."

"And do you intend to invite me to this private affair?"

Damien pushed away from the window. "Yes, Mother. I'll let you know the time and date so you can be there."

"Thank you, Damien. I would appreciate being in attendance when my only son marries."

There was a knock on the door, and Burnes announced that Henry Lockling was here to see him, and that he'd put him in the study. Damien rose and kissed his mother's cheek. "I need to meet with my steward," he said. "Then I'll be on my way. But I'll come again soon."

His mother reached for his hand and held it. "I wish you could come to task with whatever's bothering you, Damien. I hate seeing you so unhappy."

"Who told you I was unhappy?"

"No one had to tell me," his mother answered. "A mother knows when one of her children is troubled. And you are exceedingly troubled."

Damien gave his mother's fingers a gentle squeeze, then walked away from her. "Don't worry, Mother. It's just the newness of being back after being gone so long."

Damien walked to the door, but heard his mother's last words before he left: "I wish that's all it was."

"So do I, Mother," he whispered as he made his way to the study. Henry Lockling rose when he entered.

"Mr. Lockling," Damien greeted, then walked to the chair behind his desk.

"Lord Iversley. I can't tell you how glad I am to see you."

"I can imagine you are. I must apologize for leaving you with so much responsibility for so long. But I'm prepared to assume the running of the estates now so you will not have so much to do."

"Of course I'm relieved that you have returned, my lord, but things have run relatively smoothly in your absence."

Damien was glad to hear Mr. Lockling say things were in good order, but he knew that wasn't entirely true. How could it be with no one to manage the accounts, or give the orders as to what improvements needed to be made? "I'm sure you did as much as you were able without anyone to make the major decisions."

Lockling twisted the old cap he always wore. "I'd like to take credit for the running of Iversley Estate and the rest," he said, not lifting his head enough to meet Damien's gaze, "but I can't."

"And why is that?" Damien asked.

"Because . . ." Lockling hesitated, then lifted his gaze. "You have to understand, my lord. I promised I wouldn't tell anyone, but since you're so close to the lady, I'm sure she'll understand."

"Is the she you're talking about Lady Olivia?"

"Yes, your lordship. It's Lady Olivia, and she's done a remarkable job with the estates. Her improvements have made the estate more profitable than ever, and have allowed the tenants to fix up their homes more often."

Damien paused to let Lockling's words sink in. "Exactly what improvements did Lady Olivia make?"

"Well, there's the drainage ditch she had built on the north corner of Cardonbury estate. That part of your estate has never been too profitable because of its lack of water. But for the past two years we've been able to grow an abundant crop of barley, which we've sold to the Burmham Brewery.

"And three years ago, she purchased a small herd of sheep, mostly Lincoln and Leicester Longwool."

"Sheep?"

"Yes, my lord. This year we'll harvest our second season of wool and take it to market. It's been quite profitable, if I may say so."

Damien tried not to look too shocked. "What else has Lady Olivia done?"

"Not too much, other than taking care of the estate books, and deciding on the crop rotation, and terracing two of the hillier fields. That's made a remarkable difference with runoff. And we've just started construction on a new barn next to William Proctor's. It will mostly be used to store wool from a new breed of sheep she bought two years ago."

"What breed is that?"

"It's called Merino. The wool's in high demand 'cause it's so soft. For babies and such."

"I see," Damien answered.

"You won't tell her I told you what she's done, will you, your lordship? She made me promise to let everyone think I was running the estates in your absence. But I could never have done such a good job."

"No. I won't tell her. I'll give you the credit."

"Thank you, my lord."

Damien rose. "Thank you, Mr. Lockling. I'm sure your help was invaluable to Lady Olivia."

"I tried, your lordship."

Damien stood as if chiseled from marble as Henry Lockling left. Why did it bother him so much to learn how much Olivia had done? She'd taken care of Pellingsworth Shipping, cared for her ailing father, managed his estates as well as her own, taken care of his mother and sisters, and made major improvements to his properties. Why did knowing what she'd done for him make him want to take her in his arms and take care of her, like she'd taken care of everything that was his?

Damien braced his hands atop the desk and dropped his head between his outstretched arms. The more he discovered how much she'd done while he was gone, the more she wended her way in and around his heart. How could he stay angry with her when he was starting to fall in love with her all over again?

Damien pushed himself away from the desk and walked out of the room. As he left the house, he leaned on his cane and strode toward his carriage, which was parked on the other side of the narrow street. He stopped to let a hansom go by, then put his cane down in front of him before he stepped off the low curb. The cane he'd come to rely on slipped on some loose gravel and fell to the cobblestones.

Damien leaned over to pick it up as another carriage rumbled closer. It picked up speed as it approached him. Before he rose, a bullet whizzed past his head and the sound of a gunshot exploded in the air. Damien dove for the ground, falling into a hedge as the carriage sped past.

"Are you all right, my lord?" his driver yelled, racing over to him.

Damien struggled to his feet, then turned to look where the bullet had lodged into the trunk of the tree behind him. "Yes, fine, Johns. Did you happen to recognize the carriage or see who fired at me?"

"No, my lord. I just heard the clap."

"Let's get out of here," Damien said, leaning on his cane a little harder as he crossed the street. He climbed into his carriage and sank back against the cushions.

Someone had just tried to kill him.

The *who* was not terribly hard to narrow to three suspects: Cassandra's brother, his own recently displaced cousin, or Olivia's cousin. The *why* was almost as obvious. But he'd be damned if he'd let any of them get away with it. Damned if he'd let Strathern kill him for something he didn't do. Damned if he'd give his cousin another chance to squander away an inheritance he'd already proved he didn't deserve. And damned if he'd let Olivia's cousin have Pellingsworth Shipping.

Damien fingered the special license he had in his pocket, not sure he could give Olivia her six days.

Chapter 21

Olivia sat in the darkened opera house where only the flicker of shaded lamps on the walls gave any light and listened to the hauntingly beautiful melodies of Verdi's "La Traviata." Damien sat at her side in their private box, his chair so near that more than once his arm brushed against her. The feel of him next to her made concentrating on the opera impossible. Just as having him come to the shipping office to ensure she ate the lunch he'd brought made the food sit in her stomach like a heavy rock.

All day long her thoughts had gone back to last night. To the night she'd waited for her whole life. The night that would have been perfect if only Damien had been able to say that he loved her.

From the time her father had walked through the front door with Damien at his side, she'd known he would be the only man she'd ever love. Even when she thought he was dead, she knew there wouldn't be room in her heart for anyone else. And when he'd walked back into her life after letting her believe he was dead, she tried to hate him. But she couldn't. He was still the man with whom she'd fallen in love. Except now his scars on the inside were as deep as his scars on the outside. And thinking she could make him love her was as impossible as trying to find the stars in the sky while the sun was shining. His silence confirmed it. And yet . . .

She couldn't forget how he'd kissed her. How he'd held her with such gentleness and such passion. Almost as if there were the slightest chance . . .

Damien slid his arm around the back of her chair and leaned close. "Do you know what 'La Traviata' means?" he whispered in her ear while his finger rubbed a small circle on the soft flesh of her upper arm beneath the short sleeve of her gown. "It means 'The Lost One.'"

Olivia turned her head, her face perilously close to his. "And which one of us do you think that more closely represents?"

His finger stopped circling her flesh. "Both, Olivia. We are both lost."

He turned back to watch the stage and moved his fingers from the back of the chair to rest atop her shoulder. It brought him nearer to her and put them in the closest proximity imaginable, perilously close to being scandalous. Olivia was certain the gesture was for show. And yet . . .

Damien looked at her. Oh, the torment in his eyes. As if he knew how close he was to succumbing to his emotions, to yielding to his feelings for her. She was nearly blinded by the first glimmer of hope. He was losing the battle to stay angry with her. She knew he was.

"Have you noticed how intently Society is watching us? I'm not sure if my return after all these years is the cause for their curiosity, or if my scar is the draw, and they can't believe you aren't repulsed by the very sight of me."

Olivia jerked her head and stared at him in disbelief. "Did you think I would respond in such a way?"

His brows arched in a questioning manner. "I've had four years to observe the reaction of people who are not prepared for what they'll see when they glimpse my face. For most, the sight of the scar running down my face is quite shocking. Take Lady Dunning in the box across the way. She's had her opera glasses focused in our direction more often than on the stage. Her obvious pity for you is almost laughable.

"And the Ladies Eileen and Marlys Puttnam. They've both made a point to keep their eyes averted from the moment we arrived so they weren't forced to look at my face. The looks of condolence they continually give you are almost comical. Do you think you'll be able to weather their compassion?"

Olivia smiled. "Are they looking at us now?"

Damien's eyes moved around the room.

"Oh, yes. Conversing with me has drawn their attention."

Olivia turned to face him, then reached up with her hand and cupped his cheek. She placed her palm over his scar and did not take it away.

"Are they duly shocked, my lord?"

"Oh, yes," he answered with a smile. "Duly shocked."

Damien kissed the palm of her hand as the orchestra played the last note. The crowd erupted in a thunderous approval that barely drowned out the pounding of Olivia's heart.

Oh, yes. She'd take down that wall brick by brick. Damien was right. There would be boundaries to their marriage. Only she would not allow him to set them. Just as she wouldn't allow him to remain at such a distance. There would be passion in their lives. So much passion there wouldn't be room for doubt.

Damien stood and helped Olivia to her feet. They took their time leaving the theater, stopping to talk to the scores of people who were curious to get a good look at the two of them together. They made their way through the exit, then down the walk to the curb where the carriages were lined as far as the eye could see. Olivia saw Johns wave when he saw them, then ease the Pellingsworth carriage closer.

"Who are the men standing with Johns, Damien?"

His hesitation made her take pause, and for a moment, Olivia wasn't sure he intended to answer her. Then she noticed two more men who looked conspicuously out of place come up and stand close behind them. They were dressed in dark clothing and wore long, black cloaks that none of them seemed comfortable wearing.

"Damien?"

"The carriage is here, Olivia. Watch your step."

Olivia stepped into the carriage. After Damien climbed in behind her, the carriage swayed again as two men climbed atop with Johns and the other two climbed on the back. Olivia leaned back against the squabs.

"Your jacket was torn when you came to the shipping office this afternoon. What happened to it?"

He looked at her in surprise. "I must have torn it."

"And how did you get the grass stains on your pants?"

"I had a small mishap. That's all."

"I think not, Damien. I think something happened, which is why we have four men, probably armed, riding along with us. What are they protecting us against? Or should I ask *who*?"

The impassive look on Damien's face held its hooded expression as the carriage rumbled down London's cobbled streets. It was strange how hard he fought to keep her in the dark. As if she hadn't had her share of battles over the last year and handled them on her own. As if letting her into one part of his life exposed every part of him.

"I'm waiting, Damien."

She kept her voice steady with a certain amount of command in it, hoping it would put her on equal footing with him. She heard his heavy sigh and knew it had worked.

"Someone shot at me today."

Of all the things she'd envisioned him saying, it hadn't been that someone had tried to kill him.

"Do you know who?"

"There are not *that* many possibilities, I hope."

"Of course not. Who do you think it was?" She hesitated. "Surely not your cousin. You said he left London and is—"

"It's not Brian. I sent someone to the country, and they reported that my cousin had been there all day."

Olivia turned to see the expression on his face. "Do you think it was Richard?"

"Either Richard, or Nathan, Viscount Poore."

"Surely you don't think it was Nathan?"

"Why shouldn't I?"

"Because Lord Strathern is dead. That incident is over. I spoke to Nathan and he assured me—"

In the flickering lamp that faintly lit the interior of the carriage, she saw his expression turn hard. "You spoke with Poore?"

"Yes."

"When?"

"Shortly after his father died."

"Why didn't you tell me?"

"I tried," she answered hotly, "but you weren't interested in listening to anything I had to say."

Olivia saw the chagrin on Damien's face.

"Did you discover anything?" he asked.

"No. Nathan claimed he didn't know who the father of Cassandra's babe was."

"Do you believe him?"

She hesitated. "No. I think he knows but is reluctant to say."

"Then perhaps it's possible he intends to exact revenge for his sister's death?"

"No. Nathan knows you had nothing to do with Cassandra's death."

"Does he?"

"Nathan believes his sister told her father the babe was yours because his father wouldn't give up until she gave him a name. Anyone's name. But none of this comes as a great surprise to you, does it, Damien?"

When he didn't answer, Olivia continued.

"You already knew Cassandra was pregnant and wanted you to marry her. She'd already begged you to marry her. The only part you didn't know was that when you refused, she tried to rid herself of the babe before anyone found out."

"How did you know that?"

"I figured it out from my conversation with Nathan."

"After you thought I was dead."

Olivia twisted the satin edging of her pelisse between her fingers, but kept her gaze lowered. There was anger in Damien's voice and she was glad it was dark in the carriage. She wasn't brave enough to look at him. "Yes, after. I went to him after his father's death. He told me everything. Only it was too late." She took a breath that shuddered in the darkness.

Damien slammed his fist against the cushion. "If Nathan knew the babe wasn't mine, why didn't he say so? Why did he let his father call me out?"

"Guilt, I think. He's the one who found the healer who had a potion that would get rid of the babe. Only something went wrong and Cassandra died."

Olivia pulled her pelisse tighter around her to ward off the chill. "I don't know why she gave him your name, except perhaps because of your past association with her. Or because you'd refused her."

"But that hardly matters, does it, Olivia? You believed Strathern's accusations the minute he spoke them."

Olivia felt each painful word pierce her heart. "And why shouldn't I have? Do you remember how you reacted only moments before to our conversation about Cassandra? Your behavior was odd the minute I mentioned her. Of course I had reason to doubt. Not that I would have ever believed that you were the father of Cassandra's child. But it was obvious that you were keeping something from me.

That you were starting out our lives with secrets you intended to withhold from me."

"That doesn't explain your reaction to Strathern's claim that I only wanted to marry you for the ships."

"And you'll never forgive me for that one moment of doubt, will you Damien?"

Olivia was spared Damien's answer when the carriage stopped in front of her townhouse. Damien stepped to the ground and held out his arm. The minute she placed her hand on him she was startled by the knotted muscles that pulsed beneath her fingers. The wall he was so good at erecting was again firmly in place.

She walked with him to the door. Damien's gait was steady, yet his limp quite pronounced. Olivia knew the muscles in his legs were probably as knotted as the rest of him felt.

She handed her wrap to Chivers, then headed for the stairs. "Chivers, send hot water and towels to his lordship's room."

Damien's voice echoed through the silent house. "Olivia, I don't—"

Olivia ignored Damien's interruption and continued on her way to her room.

"If you'll recall, your legs have not been tended to today. I want to change into something that will allow me to move more freely, and I'll do what has to be done."

"It's too late—"

"It's very late, my lord. Well past midnight. And I'm anxious to get to bed. But not until you've been seen to. I have no intention of having my sleep interrupted by your discomfort again tonight."

And Olivia marched up the stairs, not caring that Damien was glaring holes through her back.

Hell and damnation!

Damien threw another swallow of brandy down his throat and waited for her to come. Why did she have to fight him every step of the way? Why did she continually search for a way to break through the hostility he'd cloaked himself with for the last four years? With every word and action, she tried another tactic to make him forget—and forgive what she'd done.

And now she would torment him even further with her smell and her touch and the feel of her body against him. And his flesh would ache as if she'd thrown him in the fire and left him to burn.

Damien took another swallow of brandy and froze when she walked into the room.

"Is the water still hot?" she asked coming toward him.

"Yes."

"We should begin then, before it cools. Are you ready?"

"I'd prefer it if you'd—"

"I know what you'd prefer, Damien, but I'm not about to let you have it. You'd destroy me if I did."

"I don't know what you're talking about."

"Don't you?"

Damien watched her walk to the basin of steaming water and put a towel in it. Her eyes turned to him and without words, gave the order for him to lie down. He did. He lay on his stomach so he wouldn't have to look in her eyes.

She put the first hot towel across his left thigh. That was the leg that pained him the most. Then repeated the process on the other leg, until Damien could feel the tension ease in his knotted muscles.

"I'm talking about the plan you've perfected over the last four years to make me pay for sending you with Captain Durham. The plan to come back to me, make yourself a part of my life, yet make sure I'm never a part of yours. I'm talking about your determination to show me every day of my life that it's impossible for you to love me ever again."

She removed the towels from one leg with a snap. "Well, it's not going to work. I was young and naïve, and I'd just heard the man I was supposed to marry had fathered another woman's child and was marrying me for my father's shipping company. I reacted exactly as any other nineteen-year-old would have reacted, with shock and disbelief."

Before he could argue, she poured something over his flesh. It was cool and made his flesh tingle.

"What is that?"

"It's an ointment Johns gave me. He said it will soothe your muscles."

Damien jerked his head up to look at her. "Johns works with the horses, Olivia."

"So he does."

She put her hands on his flesh and began the painful kneading of his calves and thighs. Damien let his forehead drop back onto his forearms and sucked in a harsh breath.

"Who do you most suspect of trying to kill you?" she asked without a hesitation in her movements.

"Your cousin."

She paused. "Yes, he's the most obvious candidate."

"Your cousin is buried in debts, and with me back from the dead, he's lost any hope of paying them off."

She continued massaging his legs, bending and stretching them, lifting and pulling each one until he gasped for breath. Damn, but she didn't know what she did to him.

Then she rubbed the muscles high on his thighs and he clenched his teeth. She moved her fingers far to the inside of his leg. He bit down hard and moaned. Ah, hell.

"So what do you intend to do about him?" she asked.

"I have men watching the house, as you already know. And Captain Durham is searching for him. There aren't too many places he can hide."

"Aren't there?"

She stopped rubbing his legs. Thank heavens.

"You can turn over now."

He didn't want to. Knew keeping his distance would be that much harder when he looked her in the eyes.

"Turn over, Damien. I'm tired and want to go to bed."

Damien turned, and he was right. It was harder.

The minute he rolled over on his back he was forced to look up into her face. Her brown eyes were darker than before, her mahogany hair a richer shade of coffee, her creamy complexion flushed from exertion. Ah, hell.

He knew there were two kinds of pain in the world.

Then she touched him and he realized there were three.

She performed each step of the process, laying the steaming towels across his legs, then removing them. Pouring the cool, tingly ointment over his skin and massaging it in. Her touch drove him to distraction and he wasn't brave enough to look into her eyes any longer.

He lowered his gaze from her face and froze at the sight of her breasts moving beneath her loose gown. He could almost feel their heaviness. And knew that with a flick of his fingers, he could unfasten the buttons to her gown and free them.

As if his hands had a will of their own, they reached out, his fingers wrapping firmly around her neck. She clasped her hands around his wrists and held him firm.

"You're not going to win this battle you've waged," she whispered, locking her gaze with his and refusing to let him go.

"Are you sure?"

"Oh, yes," she said, bringing her face closer to his. "Because I can't let you."

Damien pulled her nearer and she came willingly. She lowered her head and kissed him on the mouth, her lips touching his, her breathing melding with his.

His need was a frightening thing and he despised himself for his weakness. He deepened his kisses, delving into her warm, moist mouth until he met the treasure he searched for. A thousand explosions rocked his world, and he kissed her until they were both panting and breathless.

He wanted her. He needed her.

His heart thundered in his chest, his desire to have her was a mind-shattering explosion that rocked the earth from its axis.

He turned his head and ended the kiss.

This wasn't the way he'd intended things to happen. Loving her again wasn't part of the plan. With fierce determination, he concentrated on her betrayal and how it had nearly destroyed him, and he hardened his resolve. He would have what should have been his four years ago without sacrificing his heart.

He took a deep breath and rolled away from her. "Enough. I've had enough."

She pulled away from him and stepped to the door. He stopped her with words he was sure she didn't want to hear. "We'll marry day after tomorrow, Olivia."

She stopped with her hand on the doorknob. Her gaze flew to his face. Her eyes were wide with—

He sucked in a painful breath. He'd seen sailors with less terror on their faces when battling for their lives in the midst of a raging storm.

Her jaw clenched. "I have five days. You can't make me marry you for five more days."

His blood ran cold. "Make you? I'm not forcing you to marry me, Olivia. Your father did that when he wrote that stipulation into his will."

Her face paled and her hands trembled when she clutched the handle on the door.

"But I still have five more days."

Damien tried to keep the niggling anger from building inside him. What miracle did she expect to happen in five days? "I refuse to give you any more time."

With a sigh of frustration, she opened the door, and left him without a glance back.

Chapter 22

One day.

All she had was one day.

Olivia pushed away the stack of shipping papers she'd brought home to work on and rubbed her fingers against her throbbing temples. Heaven help her, but loving Damien hurt.

Every day since he'd returned, she'd hoped things between them would change. Prayed he could bring himself to tell her—

Tell her what? That he loved her?

Olivia dried a traitorous tear that seeped from beneath her lashes. She knew the wall around his heart was thick. Knew the barrier he'd put up to protect his emotions was too firmly in place. With an insight that left her breathless and aching, she knew he would always have the power to hurt her, the power to make her suffer for her doubt. For her decision to send him away where he'd be safe.

And she knew, until he cared for her enough to risk loving her, there was no hope for them. A life together without love was not one worth living.

But if she didn't marry him, she'd lose the ships.

Olivia thought of losing the *Lady's Mist*, the *Conquest*, the *Viking*, and the *Princess Anne,* and the vice clamped around her heart tightened until she couldn't breathe. But what choice did she have? She could spend the rest of her life married to Damien, knowing he would never love her, but at least she'd have her father's ships. Or, she could walk away from Damien and the shipping company.

Either choice was unthinkable, but Damien had left her with no other option.

Olivia slid back her chair and rose when she heard Damien's voice from beyond the door. She didn't want to face him, didn't want to see the impassive expression on his face, as if seeing her meant nothing.

The door opened, then closed with a soft thud.

It was funny how she could feel his presence, how she knew he was in the room without looking at him. How the air was suddenly alive and that place inside her where her heart rested moved like the swell of the tide onto shore. She took a steadying breath and turned.

She didn't quite trust her voice to speak. But he just looked at her like he always did, as if evaluating how she'd changed since he'd been gone. As if trying to come to terms with his dislike for her.

Well, she would let him look. Because she had changed. She was stronger now and didn't see the world through a young girl's eyes. She didn't view him through a young lover's eyes.

"Have you been working on the shipping ledgers all morning?" he said, casting a glance at the papers strewn about on the desk.

"Not all that long."

"Really? When I asked, Chivers said you were working in here when Cook got up. And she's always up well before dawn."

Olivia tried to hold her temper. Arguing would do no good, and with the little sleep she'd gotten last night, she wasn't sharp enough to match wits with Damien this morning.

"There were a few estate matters that needed taking care of. I—"

"You could have left them for me. I assume they concerned estates for which I am now responsible."

Olivia felt as if she'd been hit hard in her middle. "Yes, my lord. They are, of course, now yours again. How remiss of me."

"That's not what I meant, Olivia. I just don't want you going without sleep to take care of concerns I can now handle."

Olivia's smile was tight. She thought her life had changed when her father died, but that was nothing compared to the radical change that would occur when she married Damien and her life consisted of nothing more than teas and balls and planning dinner parties. She couldn't imagine anything worse. Not after the challenges of running several estates as well as Pellingsworth Shipping. She wasn't sure she could return to a life so mundane. She wasn't sure she could stand to be excluded from doing the things she'd done for the last four years.

She tried to shake off the dread that settled over her. But it was hard. "Perhaps you would like me to review the books with you. Or don't you think that is necessary?"

"Yes, of course. But that isn't what I want to talk about right now." He pointed to the sofa. "Please, sit down for a minute."

Olivia walked to the sofa and sat.

"I sent a note to the Reverend Dunlevey informing him our wedding would take place tomorrow afternoon at two o'clock. I hope you don't mind the lateness of the hour, but the *Commodore* is sailing on the morning tide, and Captain Durham wants to be there when she sails."

Olivia's heart raced, its frantic pounding so hard she couldn't think. "Does he anticipate a problem?"

"There's always a possibility. Especially with Richard still out there. The *Commodore* has been heavily guarded, so Captain Durham and I don't anticipate danger, but one never knows. Captain Russell will go to Bordeaux for the last shipment of wine. Captain Durham will be here for our wedding. I know how important it is for him to be with you."

Olivia sat there numbly while Damien outlined the following day's events.

". . . anyone else you'd like to have attend, Olivia?"

"What?"

"Is there anyone else you'd like to have attend our wedding?"

She shook her head.

"Very well. Then—"

Olivia felt a cold shiver of dread race up and down her spine. "Did you ever love me, Damien?"

"Oh, yes, Olivia. Before I learned that love was a weakness. Before I knew what it meant to have the person with whom you wanted to spend the rest of your life choose freedom over you."

"Is that what you thought I did?"

She thought she heard him laugh. Only it wasn't a laugh that held any humor. His next words proved it.

"Nearly dying taught me a very valuable lesson. I'm not strong enough to survive loving you again."

Olivia felt as if she'd been punched in the gut. No matter how hard she tried, she couldn't catch her breath. Damien didn't give her the chance to. "I spent four years preparing for this day, Olivia. Four years dreaming of having everything that was taken away from me. You, the ships, the estates. Everything. And now I will have it all. Especially you."

"But without love," she said, her heart in her throat.

"As I said, I'm not strong enough to survive a love like that again. But," he said, walking to the window and looking out into the flower garden, "there's something else I wanted to talk to you about."

He turned to face her with an expression that brooked no argument. "Until I've dealt with your cousin, I want your promise that you'll stay indoors and not leave the house."

Olivia studied the serious look on his face and knew he made his demand out of concern for her welfare. If she understood anything from what he'd just said, it was that in some way, he did care for her.

"I have no intention of going out today, Damien. You don't have to worry on my account."

"Good. Then perhaps we can spend some time going over what I missed while I was gone."

There was a softness to Damien's features, and she was reminded of how he used to look at her. When he still loved her.

Olivia looked away to keep him from seeing how much those looks still meant to her. A knock on the door saved her from revealing too much of herself. Chivers entered, carrying a small silver tray.

"A messenger just delivered this from Captain Durham, my lord. He said it was important."

Damien reached for the message and opened it. His face turned serious.

"I have to go."

He walked to her father's cabinet against the wall and took a gun from one of the drawers.

Olivia's heart skipped a beat. "What is it, Damien?"

"Captain Durham spotted Richard at the wharf where the *Commodore*'s docked."

"What are you going to do?"

"I'm going to have a little visit with him."

Damien tucked the gun in his jacket and headed for the door. Olivia started to follow.

"Take someone with you."

Damien stopped with his hand on the knob. "Captain Durham's there. I'll be fine."

Olivia fought the niggling fear that consumed her the minute Damien left the room. The same fear she felt the morning Damien went to meet Strathern. She raced across the room and followed him into the foyer.

"Don't leave the house," he said, the warning in his voice unmistakable.

"But—"

"No! I don't want to have to worry about you, too, Olivia. Stay here! I mean it!"

Olivia took a step back and leaned against the table in the center of the room. When the door closed behind him, she returned to her father's study and sat on the sofa. She clasped her hands in her lap and sat there, listening to the steady ticking of the mantel clock. It was quarter past the hour.

"I took the liberty of bringing tea, my lady," Chivers said, placing a tray on the table near her. "I thought perhaps it might help."

Olivia looked at the tea tray and plate of biscuits, then back up to Chivers. "Thank you," she said, knowing she should pour herself a cup before it turned cold, but not able to find the energy. Chivers did it for her.

"Lord Iversley will be fine, my lady. Captain Durham's there. He'll watch out for him."

"I know, Chivers," she answered, taking the cup he held out for her. And the clock on the mantel struck half past.

Olivia tried not to stare at it. She knew a watched clock didn't move, but she couldn't keep her eyes from returning to the mantel again and again. Before the first half hour had gone by, Chivers opened the door and rushed into the room.

"My lady?"

Olivia knew something was wrong the minute she saw his face. "What is it, Chivers?"

"Captain Durham's here, my lady. He asked to see Lord Iversley."

"Captain Durham?"

Olivia stood as Chivers stepped aside to let Captain Durham enter.

"Is something wrong, Olivia? Chivers looked at me like I was the grim reaper himself."

"Where is he?"

"Where's who?"

"Damien. Where is he? What's happened to him?"

Captain Durham looked from her to Chivers, then back to her, and Olivia knew he had no idea what she was talking about.

"Your message," she said, running to the desk where Damien had dropped the captain's message. She rushed back across the room and handed it to Captain Durham. "This. You sent this."

Captain Durham read the message and looked at Olivia, shaking his head. "I didn't send this. I've no idea where your cousin might be. That's what I came to tell his lordship."

"It's a trap. He's walking into a trap."

"How long ago did he leave?" Captain Durham asked, already racing out of the room.

"Half an hour ago. The minute he received the message."

"That's not so long. I'm sure I can get there in time. Did he take a gun?"

"Yes. He's armed."

Olivia raced behind Captain Durham, trying to keep her legs steady beneath her. "My wrap, Chivers."

Olivia's words brought both Chivers and Captain Durham to a halt. "You can't go with me. Damien would kill me if I brought you."

"If we don't hurry, Damien will be dead and it won't matter."

"It's too dangerous, my lady. We don't know what we're going to run into and—"

Olivia ignored Captain Durham's warning and rushed past him, out the door, and into the waiting carriage. Before she'd even situated herself in the seat, he was in the seat opposite her, and the carriage was rumbling down the street.

Thankfully, the captain let them ride in silence, and not until they reached the docks did he issue the order for her to stay inside the carriage, which she ignored.

The minute the carriage stopped, Olivia jumped to the ground and raced to where the *Commodore* was docked. She knew Captain Durham wasn't far behind. He wasn't as fast, and she'd soon widened the distance.

She didn't stop, but looked from the deck of the *Commodore* to the long walkway crowded with crates and barrels and boxes. It was the middle of the morning, and the wharf was packed with sailors and docking crews, loading and unloading ships that were arriving and getting ready to set sail. But Damien was nowhere to be found.

She looked from one end of the wharf surrounding the Pellingsworth Shipping offices to the other, telling herself everything wouldn't seem so normal if something terrible had happened. She wanted to yell his name, but realized she'd give him away if he were hiding, so she kept quiet. She walked farther down the wharf, then stopped and looked around again.

"Do you see them, my lady?" Captain Durham asked, coming up behind her.

"No. What if he's already—"

"Don't even think it. You stay here, and don't move. I'll go this way. Damien shouldn't be too hard to find."

Olivia watched Captain Durham walk down the alley, but she couldn't stay where he'd left her. What if Damien had gone the opposite way? Olivia turned and walked down the boardwalk.

No one seemed to notice her except a few dockhands employed by Pellingsworth Shipping, and when she reached the end of the first wharf, she turned to her right. This wasn't a through alley, but a narrow space between two warehouses that had no exit. She'd only taken a few steps before she saw Damien.

He wasn't that far away, but a large box blocked her from view so he didn't notice she'd come up on him. She started to yell a warning, but before she could make a sound, she saw a man she didn't recognize rise from behind a large wooden crate on Damien's right. The man lifted his arm and pointed the pistol he had in his hand toward Damien's chest.

"Damien!"

Olivia rushed forward with her arms outstretched and pushed Damien to the side. Damien spun around and grabbed her as a gunshot echoed in the air.

"Get down!" he yelled, pulling her with him behind a row of crates.

She landed with a jolt. When she looked at him she could see the fury in his eyes. He pushed her deeper into a corner to get her out of the way.

"What the hell are you doing here?" he bellowed, glancing at her with eyes that brimmed with fire.

"It's a trap, Damien. My cousin sent the message."

Damien uttered a vile oath, then took a gun from his pocket and peeked around the crate. Another gunshot sent him dodging back. "Where's Durham?"

"He went the other way, but I'm sure he'll be here now that he's heard shots."

"Olivia, listen to me," he said. "We're trapped here. I've got to get to the other side where I can get off a clean shot."

"No, Damien!"

"Yes. But you have to promise you'll stay here. Olivia. Promise me!"

Olivia nodded. "Be careful, Damien."

"I will."

Before Damien turned away, he leaned down and pressed his lips to hers. The kiss was quick and hot and filled with a lifetime of desperation. Olivia wanted to pull him back the minute he left her. But it was too late.

"Don't move until I come back to get you. Do you hear?"

"Yes, Damien."

And he was gone.

Olivia pressed her back against the rough wood of the crate she was leaning against and ignored the burning sting at her waist. All she could think about was the sound of gunfire and the debilitating fear that Damien would never come back for her.

Damien raced from one side of the narrow alley to the other. One bullet whizzed past his ear, another lodged in a plank of wood not a foot to his right. But he kept running. He couldn't stay where he was. It would only be a matter of time before Richard angled his way to the left. Only a matter of time before he got off a lucky shot that could hit Olivia.

Damien's blood ran cold. This was the second time she'd risked her life to save him. The second time she'd come to him regardless of the danger. The second time the depth of her love for him had been obvious to even a blind man. And Damien felt like he was that blind man. A man so filled with anger and revenge, he'd missed what was in front of him all along.

He tucked his thoughts away, not ready to face them, and worked his way from one crate to the next. He saw Richard's slim outline moving closer and checked his gun a final time.

"Give it up, Richard," he hollered, staying low behind a crate. "You don't have a chance."

"Go to hell, Iversley," Olivia's cousin yelled back, then leaned out from his hiding place and lifted his gun.

Richard got off a shot, and Damien returned fire, but Richard ducked back behind several barrels.

Damien waited until Richard fired again, then stood. He fired two shots, then darted back behind his protective wall. He heard a muffled cry followed by a heavy thud and knew Richard was down. Damien waited to make sure he didn't get up again, then stepped out into the bright sunlight.

"Are you all right, Damien?" Captain Durham yelled, coming down the alley with a half-dozen armed men following him.

"Yes. Fine. Take care of him, though," he said, looking down at the man who'd wanted him dead.

Damien turned around, eager to get back to where Olivia was hiding. Eager to give her holy hell for following him, even though she'd undoubtedly saved his life by warning him. Eager to get her out of here and take her home.

He walked behind the stack of crates where he'd left her. She was still sitting on the ground. When he came near, she looked him over as if checking to make sure he wasn't injured. The naked worry he saw on her face filled him with a pang of regret.

"Are you all right?" she said, her voice quivering with emotion.

"Yes. I'm fine. Richard's dead."

She nodded and clamped her teeth together as if she needed help to keep them from chattering. Her face seemed unusually pale, and Damien felt another wave of regret.

He leaned against one of the boxes and rubbed his legs. "How did you know I was walking into a trap?"

"Captain Durham came looking for you shortly after you left."

"I see."

"I was afraid we'd be too late."

"Thank heaven, you were just in time."

Olivia lifted a trembling hand and wiped away a tear that trailed down her cheek. Damien wanted to take her in his arms and hold her. Keep her next to him until they got home, then make love to her until this day was just a distant memory.

"Are you ready to go?" he said, losing his battle to the desire welling within him.

She nodded, and Damien held out his hand to help her up. She didn't take it.

Damien looked more closely at her, noticing for the first time the blue tinge to her lips and the way she leaned to the right.

"I'm sure it's nothing, but I've tried, and I don't seem to be able to stand."

A wave of fear nearly took Damien to his knees. "Don't move, Olivia. Let me see what's happened."

"I'm sure it's nothing."

"I'm sure it is, too." He knelt beside her and ran his fingers down her arms. She seemed fine, and he moved his hands around to her back. He eased her away from the crate and slowly moved his hands over her flesh, working his way from her shoulders to her waist. He stopped when his right hand came away wet and sticky, covered in her blood. How could he not have realized she'd been shot?

"Can you put your right arm around my neck, Liv?"

"I think so. But if you'd just help me to my feet, I'm sure I can walk."

"It's all right. I'll carry you. Put your arm around me now."

She did, but her hold on him wasn't very strong.

"Just lean your head against me, Liv. I'll have you home in no time."

"I'm sure it's nothing," she repeated.

"I'm sure it is, too," he answered, praying that was so.

He picked her up in his arms and carried her toward the open street. Captain Durham was waiting there. "Have Johns bring the carriage as close as he can," Damien ordered when his gaze caught Captain Durham's. "And send someone for a doctor."

"Right away, Damien."

There was a worried look on the captain's face, but Damien couldn't do anything to alleviate his concern. He wasn't sure how badly she was hurt. There was just so damn much blood.

"I'm very tired, Damien. I think I'll just sleep for a while."

Damien walked faster, his whole body feeling the need to run. He knew this feeling—the icy, cold feeling of fear. "No, Liv. Stay awake. Please. Talk to me."

"But I'm so very tired."

"I know you are. You didn't get much sleep last night."

She took a shallow breath and Damien almost shouted for joy when she spoke again.

"Do you think there's anyone else who might want to do us harm?" she asked, her voice weak, and a slight hesitation between words.

"No, Liv. I can't imagine who it might be. We haven't alienated *that* many people, I hope." He was struck by another wave of panic. "Are you awake, Liv?"

"Uh-hum."

The carriage pulled up a few feet away and Johns rushed to open the door. Damien picked up his pace.

"Do you know," she said, her arm slipping from around his neck to dangle at her side, "you've started calling me Liv again."

"Have I?"

"Yes. I like it when you call me that."

Damien stepped with her into the carriage and sat with her on his lap while Johns raced through the city streets.

"I'm going to sit you up," Damien said, ripping his cravat from around his neck. "You seem to have hurt yourself. This is going to hurt, Liv, but I have to stop the bleeding."

"It's all right, Damien. It doesn't hurt much at all any more. I'm sure it's just a scratch."

"Of course," he said, knowing it was much more than a scratch.

Damien leaned her forward, and she clasped her hands around his arm and laid her head on his shoulder. He took the cloth and pressed it against her flesh. The minute he touched her, she cried out.

"I think you are getting even with me for all the times I caused you pain," she gasped, and Damien pressed harder.

Although the trip was short, it seemed to take forever to arrive home. The minute the carriage came to a halt, Chivers was there to open the door.

Damien rushed into the house and up the stairs. "Send Tilly up with hot water and bandages."

Damien laid Olivia on the bed and lifted his cravat from her side. Thankfully the bleeding had stopped. Maybe she wasn't hurt too badly.

"There's no need for such a great frown, Damien. It's really not all that bad. I think I just scraped my back against a corner of one of the crates."

"Yes, that's probably what happened. The bleeding's already stopped."

When he cut her gown away and washed the blood to see the damage, he wanted to cry out for joy. Her wound wasn't that severe. Bad enough that it might need to be sewn, but not life-threatening.

And it hadn't been caused by one of the crates. A bullet had grazed her. A bullet that should have gone through his flesh, but that she had taken instead.

Chapter 23

Damien rose from his chair the minute the door opened and Doctor Barkley emerged from Olivia's chambers.

"How is she?"

"She's fine, Lord Iversley. The bullet didn't go deep, just grazed the skin enough to cause Lady Olivia to lose a significant amount of blood. She's very lucky."

Damien felt the weight lift from his shoulders. Captain Durham breathed a sigh of relief from behind him.

"Is she awake?" Damien asked.

"She's asleep right now. She wouldn't take anything for the pain, so she'll more than likely be awake shortly. When she does awaken, try to get some broth down her."

Damien nodded, then gave Chivers orders to have Cook warm some broth.

"Well, if there's nothing else," Doctor Barkley said, putting on his cloak, "I think I'll make myself available to someone who really needs me."

"Thank you, Doctor," Damien said, walking Barkley to the door.

"Just have her rest for the remainder of the day, and keep her activities to a minimum for the next week or so. No balls, no dancing. Nothing strenuous."

"Of course."

Damien closed the door behind the doctor, then reentered the study where Captain Durham was waiting for him.

"The lady's mighty lucky, my lord," the captain said, leaning back against the cushions in the burgundy wingback chair where he'd spent the last hour or so. "I was afraid this time she'd taken one chance too many."

Damien walked over to the side table and poured them each a snifter of brandy. He thought of the two times Olivia had saved him, and his heart jolted with an emotion he seldom let surface. "She does seem to have a habit of stepping in to protect me."

"Three times is quite a lot for one lifetime."

Damien's breath caught. "Three times?"

"Why yes, my lord. He held up one finger. "Today." He held up a second finger. "The day of your duel with Strathern. Strathern's son would have killed you for sure. And . . ."

"When was the third time?"

The captain held up a third finger. "When she put you aboard the *Princess Anne.*"

Damien couldn't contain his laugh. "You consider that saving my life? I nearly died because of what she did."

"You would have died for sure if she had left you here."

Damien's fingers tightened around his glass. "What are you talking about?"

"The contract, of course. The ten thousand pounds Strathern put on your head for whoever killed you."

Damien felt the blood rush from his head and reached out to steady himself against the mantel of the fireplace. "Who said there was a price on my head? How did she—"

Damien couldn't believe it. Surely Strathern wouldn't, but he knew he would. That he had. Strathern was so overcome with grief he would have done anything to avenge his daughter's death.

"How did Olivia know there was a contract?"

"She overheard some men say it didn't matter if Strathern killed you or not. That you were a dead man anyway. The number of men who'd commit murder for ten thousand pounds is endless."

"So she sent me on the *Princess Anne* because she didn't think I was a match for Strathern and his schemes."

Damien pounded his fist on the top of the mantel. "Damn her!" He hit the mantel again in an effort to fight the rage that thundered through him.

"I told her that night you wouldn't thank her for it," Captain Durham said, setting his glass on the nearest table and rising to his feet. "I told her you'd probably hate her for sending you away. But she told me at least you'd be alive to hate her."

Damien gripped the edge of the mantel until his fingers ached. "Didn't she think I might want to stay and fight my own battle? Didn't she think by sending me away it would make me look the coward?"

"Her father knew. He told her not to take you away. He knew you'd never make the choice to leave, but I don't think she thought of anything other than trying to keep you alive. She loved you that much, my lord."

"Loved me! She made it look like I'd run away."

"And I don't doubt she'd do it again."

The air caught in Damien's throat. He knew Captain Durham was right. Olivia would do the same thing again in a heartbeat.

"She loves you, my lord. She always has."

Damien braced one arm against the fireplace and lowered his head. For several long seconds he stared into the lifeless grate. "I nearly died. I was close, more than once."

"I know, my lord. I was afraid if the fever didn't kill you, the gun you had hidden in your bedside drawer would."

Damien looked over his shoulder. "Not without bullets, Captain. And you'd put them where I couldn't reach them."

Captain Durham smiled. "I wasn't sure you'd realized I'd removed them."

Damien smiled at his friend. "Do you know how much courage it takes to end your life?"

"Some would say the opposite—that it takes more courage to live a life rather than end it," Captain Durham answered.

Damien pushed himself away from the fireplace and walked across the room to the window. "But I survived. And that was when I knew what I was going to do. That was when I knew I was going to come back and get everything she'd taken away from me."

"She didn't take it away. She did what she thought she had to do to save you." Captain Durham rose from his chair and stood within a foot of Damien. "A word of warning, my lord."

Damien arched his brows at the serious tone to Durham's voice.

"Don't hurt her more than she's been hurt already. Thinking you were dead nearly killed her. Losing her father almost finished the job. And running the estates and ships alone while her cousin was doing everything in his power to destroy her, took its toll. Her greatest sin was that she loved you. Perhaps too much."

"That will also be her greatest weakness. If I learned one lesson the whole time I was fighting for my life, it was to never risk giving my heart to anyone again. I know what she wants from me. She wants to hear I still love her."

Damien threw what was left in his glass to the back of his throat and set it down on the mantelpiece. "Well, she'll never hear it. Never."

Damien cast Captain Durham a look that screamed with the anger he still felt. "I'll never give my heart to anyone again. Not even her."

"Then why are you marrying her?"

"Because she's mine. Because I need her, and she needs me. Even her father realized it."

"So, she's nothing more to you than a possession?"

"She's the woman I'm going to make my wife."

"No, my lord. You have no intention of making her your wife. Not if you can't give her your heart."

Damien stared at Captain Durham until the captain broke the silence. "What you're doing to the lady isn't what her father intended."

Damien clenched his teeth until his jaw ached. "She won't ever have cause to complain. I'll make sure she never wants for anything," he said, as if he needed to defend himself.

"Except what she'll truly need. Your love."

Damien turned his back on Captain Durham and stared down at the cold ashes lying in the grate.

He heard Captain Durham move behind him but didn't turn around. He was too numb to argue with him further.

"I've got to get back to the wharf. The *Commodore* is set to sail for France at first light and I want to check with Captain Russell and make sure everything is in order. If Lady Olivia needs anything, send for me. Otherwise, I'll see you tomorrow afternoon."

Captain Durham walked through the open doorway, leaving Damien alone with his doubts. He stayed in the darkening room until the shadows lengthened and the silence closed in around him. Then, on legs that moved with an undeniable purpose, he walked up the stairs into Olivia's room.

Olivia was still asleep, her face turned away from him, her long, mahogany-colored hair spread out around her. Heaven help him, but she was a beauty. Even pale from the pain, hers was still the face he'd dreamed of every day and night for the last four years. This was still the woman he loved more than life itself.

He thought of what he'd said to Captain Durham: all lies. He hadn't just come back to get everything she'd taken away from him. He'd come back for her. Because he couldn't live without her.

He'd told the captain that he'd never give his heart to anyone again, but he realized Olivia had always possessed it.

He was being truthful when he told Durham that he was marrying Olivia because she belonged to him. Just as he belonged to her. And always would. Because he would never love anyone but her.

Damien kept his eyes on her, watching the shallow rise and fall of her breasts, and he was filled with an ache that wouldn't go away. She could have died today. If the bullet had struck her more than an inch in either direction, he might be burying her instead of standing here watching her while she slept. Wishing he could lay down beside her and wake up with her in his arms.

Damien sat in the cushioned wingback chair by her bed.

The door opened and Chivers entered with a tray of steaming broth. He put it on the bedside table and turned to walk away. Damien could read the concern on his face.

"She'll be all right, Chivers. The doctor said her wound wasn't so bad, and she should be fine in no time."

"Yes, my lord. I know."

Chivers gave her one more look, then walked across the room and opened the door. "It's not her wound I'm concerned about," he said, then softly closed the door behind him.

Olivia lay in the darkness a few minutes after Damien left. She assured him she was fine and that she wanted to be left alone so she could sleep. He reluctantly bowed to her wishes and ordered Tilly to come for him if Olivia needed him.

Tilly promised she would, but Olivia knew that wouldn't happen. She'd never need Damien again.

She'd heard enough through the open doorway during his conversation with Captain Durham to know that Damien would never love her. That he'd never forgive her for what she'd done. And that he intended to make her pay for what he considered her betrayal every day of their marriage.

That may be the kind of marriage he envisioned for them, but she wanted no part of it.

Chapter 24

Damien stood in the middle of the morning room with his hands clasped behind his back and his mind only half attuned to the somber ticking of the mantel clock. With each steady pulse, it struck down the minutes until he would be married.

1:42.

Eighteen more minutes and Olivia would be his.

Only in his dreams had he dared to believe this day might come. Dreams he'd held onto with such desperation that there were times when they were all that kept him alive. All that gave him the strength to survive. Because even though he'd never say the words, he'd always loved her so much, he'd refused to let death separate them. For four years, he'd dreamed of the day when he would be with her. And that day was finally here.

Damien took in the lavish decorations Olivia had ordered to celebrate their wedding and felt a sense of expectancy. Captain Durham and Reverend Dunlevey stood next to the tall double windows to the east talking casually, and servants still rushed in and out, taking care of several last-minute details.

Huge bouquets of fresh flowers crowded each other for room on the flat surface of every pedestal stand and table scattered throughout the room. Long rows of tables, covered in white linen and laden with enough food to feed a hundred people, lined every wall. Bunched satin of the richest shade of purple Damien had ever seen draped every door and window.

He scanned the room and wanted to smile. At least she considered her wedding day a special occasion.

"I'm glad to see your bride has chosen to observe her wedding in style."

Damien turned and smiled at Captain Durham. "Yes. Thank you for being here."

"I wouldn't miss it. Olivia is like a daughter to me. You, a son."

Damien reached for two glasses of champagne from a passing footman and handed one to the captain. "Did the *Commodore* get off this morning?"

"Yes. It sailed shortly after dawn. Captain Russell anticipates his return in two weeks if all goes well."

Damien nodded.

"Your bride must feel much better," Captain Durham said, casting an approving glance at the lavish decorations that adorned the room.

"Yes, although I have to admit I hadn't realized Olivia was partial to such bold colors. I always thought she preferred softer shades."

"The room does have a conquering feel about it. Do you think she'll be strong enough to come down, or will the ceremony be held upstairs?"

"She sent a note earlier that the ceremony would be held here."

Damien could see the relieved look on Durham's face.

"I won't lie," the captain said, lifting his glass to his mouth. "I was more than a little concerned about her last night. I'm glad she's better today. Did she sleep well?"

"I assume she did. I haven't spoken with her yet today."

Captain Durham looked at him from beneath lowered brows, then smiled. "Well, it's not all that uncommon for the bride not to want to face the man she's about to marry before the vows. I'm sure it's wedding day jitters. Every woman suffers from them, they tell me."

"Yes, perhaps. She sent down a note when I inquired about her, saying she was much improved. I'll be glad when the ceremony is over. I wish her father hadn't forced both our hands. It's making it hard for her to accept the way things have to be."

"The earl made the stipulation for Olivia's own good," Durham said. "As he became more ill, she took on more responsibility, what with running the estates and the shipping ventures. And he wasn't sure you'd come back if he didn't force you."

"Oh, I would have come back," Damien said, taking another small sip of the champagne and looking again at the clock. "Everything I want is right here."

1:55.

The captain stiffened. "And he knew you well enough to fear that when you did finally come back, your pride wouldn't let you marry her unless he gave you no other choice."

"I'm not marrying her for the ships."

"I know you're not. You're marrying because you love her."

Damien clenched his jaw tight, refusing to give Durham's comment credence. But Captain Durham didn't give up.

"You're marrying her because you love her, and you could never give her up to another man. Her father knew if he gave you the ships, you wouldn't let the deadline pass because you know how much Olivia loves them. He gambled you wouldn't deliberately take them away from her."

Damien took another sip of the champagne, then let his gaze travel over the opulent decorations adorning the room. He ran his fingers down the side of his face. The scars were still there and would be until the day he died. "But how could he be sure she'd marry me? I'm hardly the same man I was four years ago."

Captain Durham didn't hide the look of censure on his face, nor did he hesitate to speak bluntly. "I say this in Olivia's father's place, because I know he would give you the same advice. It will do neither you nor Olivia any good if you can't come to terms with the choice she made to save you. She put you aboard the *Princess Anne* because she loved you and didn't want to lose you. But as long as you see it as an act of betrayal, your blindness will kill the love the two of you need to make yourselves happy."

"There's no need for you to worry, Captain. Olivia and I both understand perfectly how our marriage will be. We are both older and wiser, and are not walking into this with starry eyes and unattainable expectations. Perhaps," he said, setting his glass of champagne down on the table, "we are more content with each other than ever before."

"I hope so," the captain said. "But there is still something very special about the newness of love. The depth of first-discovered passion."

"And something dangerous about it, too."

Damien heard the first chime of the clock.

Two o'clock.

"Now, if you will excuse me. It's time for us to start. I'll go upstairs and bring down my bride."

Damien walked across the room and down the narrow hall that led to the open foyer. With his back straight and his uneven gait as steady as possible, he walked across the entryway to the winding staircase. He took the first step upward and stopped when Chivers's voice spoke from behind him.

"If you are going to get Lady Olivia, she isn't there."

Damien spun around, then gripped his fingers around the polished oak banister. "Where is she?" he asked, but his chest was already weighed down with dread.

"Gone, my lord. She sailed at dawn on the *Commodore*. She left you this."

Chivers took a step forward and held out a piece of folded paper.

Damien knew he should take the paper bearing his name, but deep inside he was certain that nothing would be the same if he did. So he stared at Chivers' outstretched hand until he had no choice but to take Olivia's message.

He didn't open it immediately, but let it dangle from his fingers as he slowly walked down the hallway to the study.

He stopped to look around the room. Olivia's presence was as powerful here as anywhere in the house. Maybe more so.

He could almost see her sitting behind her father's desk. Almost hear her voice and smell the familiar lilac water she bathed in. Almost feel her hands wrapped around his neck and her lips pressed against his.

Damien wasn't sure how long he sat behind the massive oak desk and stared at the folded paper in his hands. When he finally worked up the courage to open her message, he noticed that his hands were shaking.

That revelation caused a pain to settle in his chest because he realized it wasn't anger that caused his body to tremble or fury that stole the air he needed to breathe. It was fear. Raw terror because he knew without looking at her words that his life would never be the same. He knew he'd gained everything he thought she'd taken away from him: the Pellingsworth ships, the estates, everything that should have been his when they married. But he also now understood that he'd lost the only thing that was truly important.

With trembling fingers, he read the words that confirmed his greatest fear.

I concede.

Chapter 25

Damien paced up and down the dock while the *Commodore* dropped anchor and the crewmen rushed about securing the ropes and lowering the gangplank. It had been two weeks and three days since the *Commodore* had set sail with Olivia aboard. Seventeen days of torture unlike anything he'd ever survived.

He wasn't sure he would be able to survive one more day without her.

He kept his eyes focused on the deck of the *Commodore*, scanning above him from one end of the long ship to the other, searching for any sign of her. He needed to make sure she was all right. That she was safe.

Then he saw her and his breath caught in his chest.

She stood on the upper deck, her thick dark hair pulled back from her face, hidden beneath the wide brim of her bonnet. She wore a dark-burgundy gown and carried a matching parasol she didn't open. She stood alone on the starboard side of the deck, her gloved hand resting on the wood railing, her eyes focused out to sea, as if longing to return from where she'd come and not step foot on English soil.

Not step foot near him.

A painful ache knotted deep in his gut when he thought of how small and fragile she seemed. How alone.

She hadn't seen him yet, but he studied her, taking in every inch of her. How he wanted to run to her and take her in his arms and hold her. He wanted to pull her against him and never let her go. Instead, he took advantage of the fact that she didn't know he was there and just watched her.

"If it's any consolation, she doesn't look any happier than you do," Captain Durham said, walking up behind him.

"That hardly makes me feel better."

Damien didn't turn around to look at his friend, the man who'd spent that first week after Olivia had left rescuing him from more drunken brawls than Damien could remember, putting him to bed when he couldn't find his way home, and staying with him when the nightmares and the pain had such a strong hold he couldn't escape them.

Damien prayed she wouldn't force him to live the rest of his life in the hell he'd been in since he realized he'd lost her.

Damien watched Captain Russell step across the deck and speak with her. She dropped her hand and slowly turned, then made her way to the lowered gangplank. She took one step and stopped when she saw him.

Damien wasn't sure if her face registered shock or disappointment, but she grabbed the makeshift railing as if she needed to steady herself. Then, with a slight lift of her chin, she took another step, with Tilly following behind.

"Be careful, lad," Durham said softly. "You've nothing more to bargain with. She has nothing more to lose."

Damien cast him an angry look. "You think I only intended to take everything away from her?"

"Didn't you? What does she have now that she didn't have before you returned?"

Damien clenched his hands at his sides and watched Olivia walk slowly toward them. Even though she cast a look in his direction, Damien had the feeling she had to force herself to stay focused on him and not look away.

He held his breath, then walked as if to meet her halfway. It was as if they were two opposing armies closing the distance between them.

There was a proud lift to her chin and a regal bearing to her carriage. She stopped in front of him and faced him as confidently as the general of a victorious army.

And Damien suddenly realized she was the victor. That even though she'd lost everything she held dear, he'd lost far more.

"Olivia."

"Lord Iversley."

She held his gaze only a moment, then walked past him to greet Captain Durham.

"Captain," she said, kissing his cheek and giving him a hug. "It's nice to see you."

"You, too, my lady. Did you have a good trip?"

Damien noticed the small hesitation before she answered. "Yes. The weather was perfect."

She looked past him down the walk to the street where wagons were lined up to haul the freight from the incoming ships. "Is Johns here?"

"Yes. He's waiting for you."

"Good. I hope to see you later, then," she said, giving him another squeeze. "Come, Tilly."

"Wait, Olivia."

Damien saw her stiffen as she came to a halt. "Did you need something, my lord?" She didn't turn to face him.

"Yes."

An uncomfortable silence stretched between them.

"Could we please go somewhere private?"

"Lord Iversley, I'm not sure there's any need. I think we've both said everything we need to say."

Damien felt a cold breeze wash over him. "No. I don't think we have."

"Then perhaps later. In a day or two."

"No. I think now would be best."

Her head dropped forward and he heard her sigh. "Very well."

"Would you mind if we went back aboard the *Commodore*?"

She shrugged her shoulders and looked back toward the ship as if where they went was inconsequential. "If that is where you prefer. The *Commodore* is now yours, my lord."

Damien ignored her sarcasm and held out his hand for her to take. She didn't touch him, but turned to where Tilly stood a little ways off.

"Wait for me in the carriage, Tilly. I won't be long."

Without looking at him, Olivia walked back to the *Commodore*, leaving him to follow.

When they reached the deck, he held out his arm to escort her, but she twisted past him and walked to the hatch and down the stairs that led to the captain's cabin. Once there, she opened the door herself and went in. He followed, and when they were both in the room, he softly closed the door behind him. An action that wasn't lost on her.

A small frown deepened on her forehead and she walked to the opposite side of the cabin, putting as much distance between them as possible. "I didn't expect you to be here."

"Really? Why not?"

"Why would you? I can't imagine why you'd care when I returned. Unless I didn't make myself clear when I left?"

"No. You made yourself very clear."

"Then is there something else I have you intend to take from me?"

Damien felt her words as the barb they were intended. "No. It was never my intent to take *anything* from you. Once we married, the ships as well as everything else would have been *ours*. *You* are the one who forfeited everything."

"Only because the price was too high."

"What price? I demanded nothing of you."

She spun around to face him in a flash of fury. "Oh, but you did."

"What?"

"Would an admission of my guilt and betrayal every morning upon rising have been satisfactory enough for you? Or would it also have been necessary for me to play the part of the adored wife in public and live the life of the scorned wife in private? No, my lord. At least in this I can choose the form of misery I will have to endure the rest of my life."

"Bloody hell, Olivia. What kind of man do you think I am? Or have you likened me to a monster?"

She took a step toward him. "Not a monster. Just the kind of man who is not able to forgive or forget."

"Why, Olivia? Why did you send me away?"

"Because I didn't want to lose you."

"You thought if you sent me away you wouldn't lose me?"

For a fraction of a second, she kept her gaze locked with his, then she closed her eyes and turned away from him. The soft leather of her boots made a muffled sound as she walked away from him. All that broke the silence was the gentle lapping of the waves against the sides of the ship as Olivia stared out the octagonal window that was open enough to let in a gentle breeze.

"It doesn't matter any longer, Damien."

"Yes, it does. I need to know."

She shook her head. "It's too late, Damien. You now have what you want. I wish you much happiness."

She reached out to lift the latch and Damien stepped up behind her and braced his hand against the door to stop her. "You know I never wanted just the ships."

"I know. But we can't all have everything we want."

She tried again to open the door and he held it closed. "I can't let you leave."

"You can't make me stay, either. It's too late."

"No."

"I made a terrible mistake when I sent you away. A mistake I can never rectify. I admit it and accept the consequences for my actions. I concede, Lord Iversley. The ships are yours. The estates are yours. Everything is yours."

"I don't want the bloody ships! I want you!"

"I'm sure you do, Damien. Because I'm part and parcel of what you had been promised by my father. To you I am nothing more than an item included in our marriage contract. I am no more valuable than the *Commodore*. Only, you can't have me."

Damien was suddenly overcome by a fear so debilitating he didn't know how to manage. He was going to lose her.

Damien clasped his fingers around her upper arms and forced her to face him. "What do you want from me?!"

She slowly lifted her chin, and when she looked at him, Damien saw a real sadness in her eyes. "Only what you're unwilling to give."

Damien stared at her as his heart thundered in his chest, and the blood roared through his head. Let her ask for anything else—the ships, the estates, his wealth. He'd give them to her gladly. Only not his heart. Not the one thing that could destroy him.

He stepped back from her. "Marry me, Liv. Spend your life with me. I need you. Want you. I—"

She stared at him, her face containing a wealth of hope and expectation as she waited for him to say the only words she would accept from him. The only words he couldn't say.

He watched the emotion drain from her face. She lowered her gaze, then reached out to lift the latch on the cabin door. Her fingers shook, but she didn't look at him again. Just opened the door and stepped out into the hallway.

He heard the swish of her satin gown as she walked away from him and he knew an emptiness more painful than he could bear. She was leaving him, and he would never get her back.

A cry started somewhere deep inside him, building and growing until it became a keening wail of unrelenting agony. He pounded his fist against the side of the door and cried out her name.

"Liv! No!"

He couldn't lose her. Couldn't.

Couldn't.

He rushed through the open doorway and looked down the narrow hallway. She was almost to the stairs. Three more steps, and she would be gone from him. And he would be worse than dead.

"I love you, Liv. Oh, God, I love you. Don't leave me."

She froze with her hand gripping the railing and her toe poised on the first step. But she didn't turn around.

"I love you," he repeated. "I won't survive if you're not with me. I almost didn't before."

Her hands dropped to her sides, and her foot fell back to the floor. Damien heard a soft cry before she slowly turned around to face him.

Tears streamed down her cheeks.

"Please, don't leave me," he said as he opened his arms to her.

Another muffled sob escaped her before she ran to him, and they were in each other's arms.

"I love you, Liv," he said again just before he lowered his mouth and kissed her.

She wrapped her arms around his neck and kissed him back.

"I was so afraid," she said when he lifted his mouth from hers. "I thought you were going to let me go."

"It would have been the biggest mistake of my life."

She reached up and kissed him again on the lips, then buried her face in his chest. "I love you, Damien. More today than ever."

"You're getting no great bargain, Liv. There are those who will always wonder how you can wake up every morning and bear to look at this face on the pillow next to you."

She smiled then cupped her palm to his scarred cheek. "Then I will have to tell them how impossible it would be to go to sleep each night without being able to look at your face on the pillow next to me."

"Do you think they will believe you?" he said, kissing her again.

"Beauty is in the eye of the beholder, and when I'm in your arms, I behold perfection."

"Oh, I love you, Liv."

Damien kissed her again and sighed with relief. He could have lost her. Instead he gave her his heart to cherish for the rest of his life.

And he knew a peace he hadn't felt for a very long time.

Acknowledgments

A special "thank you" to the talented Melody Guy, who took *Betrayed by Your Kiss* and made it the best book it could be. Thank you, Melody!

About the Author

Laura Landon enjoyed ten years as a high school teacher and nine years making sundaes and malts in her very own ice cream shop, but once she penned her first novel, she closed up shop to spend every free minute writing. Now she enjoys creating her very own heroes and heroines, and making sure they find their happily ever after.

Laura lives in the Midwest, surrounded by her family and friends. She has written more than a dozen Victorian historicals, six of which have been published by Montlake Romance, and eight of which have been published by Prairie Muse Publishing and are selling worldwide.

You can keep up with Laura's latest releases by following her on www.lauralandon.com.